"Here we go again."

Guthrie sighed and laid down his spoon. "Say it. I was stifling you. I was jealous and possessive and all I wanted was for you to be barefoot, pregnant and in the kitchen."

Jessie flushed. "That's all true."

Guthrie pushed aside his bowl...sat very still for a few moments, as if gauging her outburst. He stood. "I was hoping things might've changed between us, but I guess they haven't. I'm sorry you feel the way you do. I'm sorry you believe I ever meant to stand in your way." And he moved to leave. "I'll be back to help in the morning."

"I don't need your help," Jessie said. "You ran off to Alaska at the first sign of trouble, didn't you?"

"You were the one who told me to go, Jess. Remember?" He strode out the door, closing it quietly behind him.

She wanted to cry, but she couldn't. The cataclysmic events of the past year had hollowed her out, emptied her of the ability to feel anything remotely soft or vulnerable.

Anger. Of late, it w~~ ~~ ~~uld feel. Terrible pe~~ ~~hat her father had ~~ ~~lls had skyrocketed. ~~ ~~ raked him over the ~~ ~~d save the land she s~~ ~~give it to someone else.

Worst of all, she felt a terrible anger at Guthrie Sloane for abandoning her when she needed him most....

Dear Reader,

On a recent business trip to Montana I snuck away from the structured activities and spent a memorable afternoon riding into the high country with a surly old wrangler who was searching for some stray horses. Once he got used to being saddled with a greenhorn from Maine, he filled the afternoon with wonderful stories about the land and its history. On the ride back to the ranch (driving eight horses ahead of us at a dead gallop—over rough country for the last mile!) the threads of all those stories wove themselves firmly into my imagination.

By the time we reached the corrals, several strong characters and the different dreams they shared in this last great place were already coming to life. This is their story.

Nadia Nichols

Montana Dreaming
Nadia Nichols

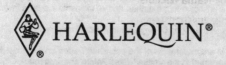

HARLEQUIN®

TORONTO • NEW YORK • LONDON
AMSTERDAM • PARIS • SYDNEY • HAMBURG
STOCKHOLM • ATHENS • TOKYO • MILAN • MADRID
PRAGUE • WARSAW • BUDAPEST • AUCKLAND

ISBN 0-373-71085-2

MONTANA DREAMING

This edition published by arrangement with Harlequin Books S.A.

® and TM are trademarks of the publisher. Trademarks indicated with
® are registered in the United States Patent and Trademark Office, the
Canadian Trade Marks Office and in other countries.

Visit us at www.eHarlequin.com

Printed in U.S.A.

For my mother and father,
for encouraging me to follow my dreams

CHAPTER ONE

What is life?
It is the flash of a firefly in the night,
the breath of the buffalo in the wintertime.
It is the little shadow which runs across the grass
and loses itself in the Sunset.

—Crowfoot

IT WAS TEN MILES to town, eight of them on the old dirt track that ran alongside the creek—the same road that her father's grandfather had ridden back when the Crow Indians still lived in and hunted this valley. Ten miles of gentle descent that curved with the lay of the land and the bend of the creek. Ten miles that traced the path of her childhood and were as familiar to her after twenty-six years of traveling them as were the worn porch steps of the weather-beaten ranch house that sat at the end of that road.

Ten miles on horseback in a late-October rain. A cold rain, too, that might've been snow had the wind quartered out of the north. She couldn't begrudge the rain. The only rain they'd had all summer hadn't amounted to two kicks, as her old friend Badger was so fond of saying: "Two kicks and you're down to dust."

She rode a bay gelding called Billy Budd, which she'd raised herself and ridden for the past fourteen years. He was a good cow horse, not fast or flashy, but Billy could always be counted on when the chips were down.

Today, the chips were down. Her truck wouldn't start— a chronic fuel-pump problem she'd put off fixing—and she was late for the signing at the real estate office. Her phone had been disconnected months ago due to nonpayment of bills. But it was no matter that she couldn't call. She knew they'd be waiting for her when she finally arrived. They'd wait all night for her if need be.

Ten miles by truck took a mere twenty minutes. Ten miles on horseback took a good deal longer. By the time the small cluster of buildings came into view through the sheets of cold rain she was nearly an hour late.

Katy Junction sat at a crossroads that connected five outlying ranches with the main road to Emmigrant. It had four buildings: a garage with gas pumps, a general store, a feed store and a tall narrow building that shouldered between the general store and the feed store, and housed the Longhorn Café downstairs and a combination real estate–lawyer's office up. There were still hitch rails in place fronting the boardwalk, recalling an era when horsepower had nothing to do with a mechanical engine. In fact, not much had changed in Katy Junction for a very long time, but Jessie Weaver was about to alter all that.

She tied Billy off to the hitch rail, parking him between a battered pickup and a sleek silver Mercedes. On the far side of the Mercedes she spotted the familiar dark-green Jeep Wagoneer and felt an irrational surge of relief that its owner would be at the meeting. She loosened the saddle cinch, removed her oilskin slicker and draped it over the gelding's flanks. He was hot, and she didn't like leaving him standing in the cold rain.

"I won't be long, Billy," she said. "This won't take but two shakes."

The stairs to the office ran up the outside of the building. When she burst into the room she was slightly out of breath. "Sorry I'm late," she said as she entered. "My truck's broke and I had to come a'horseback. My fault. I should've fixed the truck when I got the new fuel pump, but I kept putting it off."

Three people stood in the cramped room, grouped around a small round table. The real estate agent, who was also her lawyer, Allen Arden, nodded to her. "That isn't all that's broken, by the looks of you. What happened to your arm?"

"Tangled myself in a lasso two days ago," she said, giving the cast, which stretched left wrist to elbow, a scowl.

"That's hard luck, Jessie," Arden said.

"Could've been worse. Could've been my signing hand. At any rate, it won't slow me up. I'll still round up my mares in time to be off the ranch when we agreed."

Arden nodded again, hearing the bite in her words and shifting his eyes. "Jessie, you already know Caleb Mc-Cutcheon and his attorney, Steven Brown."

Jessie stepped toward McCutcheon. She was so rattled that she felt this was the first time she'd laid eyes on the man, though she'd met him several months earlier. His handshake was firm, his eyes keen and blue and framed with crow's-feet, his body long and lean, his features as rugged and tanned as if he'd spent his entire life out-of-doors. There was hardly a hint of gray in his sandy hair. She had come to like him more than she expected she would in the brief time they had known each other.

"Hi," she said shortly. She turned and acknowledged Steven Brown but didn't offer her hand. She didn't want him to feel how it trembled, yet she was enormously grateful for his calm, solid presence. Although he was Mc-

Cutcheon's lawyer, he had helped her tremendously through all these proceedings. He looked somber and handsome in his dark three-piece suit, his shoulder-length glossy black hair pulled neatly back. He nodded to her in return, predictably stoic.

Arden motioned them to sit. Jessie glanced down at the papers on the table. Land maps. She snagged the nearest chair with her booted foot and drew it toward her, then dropped into it and studied the maps. When she bent her head, water streamed from the brim of her felt Stetson and spilled onto the table. She removed her hat as the others sat, and rested it in her lap, staring down at her paper dynasty. She was cold and wet and had never felt quite like this before, so disoriented and distraught. It was all she could do to keep her features from betraying her turmoil.

I'm doing the right thing, she told herself for the thousandth time as her fingers worked around and around the brim of her wet hat. *I'm doing the right thing, and no harm shall come!*

Arden had a stack of papers in front of him. He began shuffling through them in his usual ponderous way and Jessie's fingers tightened on her Stetson. "My horse is standing in the rain and he's all hotted up. I'd appreciate it if we could make this quick." Her voice was taut, her words clipped. Arden glanced up and nodded anew. She avoided looking at the other two men and picked up one of the pens scattered on the table. "If you'll just show me where I need to sign."

Papers rustled and were pushed toward her; Arden's stubby finger pointed to this spot and that. She scrawled her signature again, and again, hoping no one noticed how her pen shook. Out of the corner of her eye she saw that McCutcheon was signing the papers, too, at his lawyer's direction. There was little to say. The negotiating had been done in the months prior to this meeting. Everything had been written up as agreed upon. All was in order, and the only thing required to make the agreement legal and binding was the signatures.

It was over in a matter of minutes. Chairs scraped back. Jessie stood so abruptly she nearly toppled hers. She bolted for the door and was nearly out of the room, when Arden's voice stopped her. ''A moment, Jessie,'' he said. She turned around, unaware how pale her face was and how tightly drawn she appeared to the three men who watched her. Arden held something in his hand. ''You're forgetting the bank check,'' he said.

Her eyes dropped to the piece of paper he extended toward her and quite suddenly she felt she was suffocating. She fled the room. Clattering down the rickety staircase, she struggled awkwardly into her oilcloth slicker. She jammed her hat back on her head, tightened the cinch using her good hand and her teeth and reached for the wet strip of rein that tethered Billy to the hitch rail. A wave of nausea swept over her and her knees weakened. She slumped against the saddle, forehead pressed against the cold wet leather, fingers clutching the horn. She drew several deep slow breaths and swallowed the bitter taste of bile.

It's okay, she reassured herself. But it didn't feel the least bit okay. It felt awful, worse than she had expected— and she had fully expected to die on the spot the moment she signed her name, struck down by the wrath of her betrayed ancestors, white and Indian both. What she was feeling now was far more painful than anything death could have handed out. She racked herself up and was stabbing her foot in the stirrup, when she heard a man call out behind her.

"Jessie!" Steven Brown's deep, familiar voice arrested her as she swung into the saddle. She was glad for the icy rain that streamed down her cheeks and hid her tears. He stood bareheaded in the storm, an island of calm. His dark eyes steadied her. "Take my Jeep back to the ranch. I'll ride Billy."

"No," she said. "It's only right that my last journey home should be a long one, and hard. Thank you, Steven. I couldn't have gotten through all this without your help." She reined Billy around, shrugging more deeply into her slicker as he stepped past the fancy silver Mercedes and the battered pickup. They had a wet, cold, ten-mile ride ahead of them and an early darkness was already beginning to gather in the foothills.

She rode out of Katy Junction and didn't look back.

The darkness thickened around her on the long ride home and she welcomed the gloom. The rain lashed down and she gave herself to it, letting it wash the very thoughts from her head. Billy plodded on. When he finally stopped she raised her eyes and was looking at the side of the pole barn just below the ranch house. She slid out of the saddle, landing on legs that were stiff and numb from the cold, and led Billy inside the pole barn. There, she stripped the gear from him, rubbed him down as best she could, draped a light wool blanket over him after and fed him a good bait of sweet feed and a flake of hay.

She left the barn but didn't go to the house. Instead, she walked up the hill behind it to a grove of tall pine. It was a sacred place. Here they were buried. Here in the wet gloaming, she could see the solid roof of the ranch house, the pole barns and corrals and, tucked close to the curve in the creek, the roof of the original homestead, with its massive fieldstone chimney. She could listen to the wind blow a blue lonesome through the trees and hear faintly the rush of the creek. Here on a clear day she could see pretty much forever, and on an overcast one still could see the Beartooth Mountains, rearing their imposing bulk over the valley below.

It was a good place to spend eternity.

She knelt and unfolded her pocketknife, and with it cut the lower third of her braid, then laid it upon the ground. She drew the same keen blade across the palm of her left hand and felt warm blood flow in the darkness. She pressed her palm against the cool wet earth. There were no tears, no laments. She was beyond all that now. She knelt among the graves of those she had loved the most and spoke in a voice that was low and quiet.

"This I promise all of you. No harm shall ever come to this place."

SHORTLY AFTER the signing in the second story of the old building, tongues were wagging in the Longhorn Café directly below.

"If you ask me, she's just plain damn crazy," Badger said, stirring the third heaping teaspoon of sugar into his black coffee and leaning his elbows on the cracked linoleum bar. "I mean, that developer from Denver offered her a fortune." He lowered his voice a few notches. "I heard it was well over three million dollars. Three *million* samolians! And she turned him down so's she could sell the whole shebang to that wannabe cowboy from someplace back East for a whole lot less money. Crazy! Guthrie tried to argue her out of it, tried to get her to keep the ranch buildings and sell the land."

"Didn't work, obviously," his friend observed.

"Nope. If I told that boy once, I told him half a hundred times. There's two theories to arguin' with Jessie Weaver, and neither one of 'em works." Badger lifted his cup and took a slurp, then smoothed his mustache with his knuckle. "Where'd you say that rich city slicker was from?"

"Can't remember," Charlie replied. "But someone said he made his money playing baseball. Probably one of them sorry souls that was signed on for a trillion some–odd dollars over ten years."

"No! Baseball?" Badger shook his head in disgust. "By God, that cracks it! Well, at least he ain't another one of them smarmy movie stars. We've got way too many of them as it is. But I betcha he eats quiche just the same as them. Anyway, he can't be whacking balls with a bat anymore, not if he's plannin' to live here. He must be retired."

"He didn't whack the balls with a bat. He was a pitcher. A pitcher throws the balls, in case you didn't know. And he's too young to be retired. Hell, Badger, you retired when you were seventy-three and I still say you hung your spurs up too soon. Speaking of quiche, you know how to cook one?"

"Certain I do!" Badger racked himself up on his bar stool and narrowed his eyes while he recalled the recipe. "First, you scramble a bunch of eggs into a piecrust, then you put it in the oven. Meantime, grill up a nice thick steak, and when it's medium raw, eat it. As for the quiche, leave it in the oven and forget about it. Say, Bernie, got any more of that lemon pie?"

Bernie was two tables behind them, taking someone's order. She pointedly ignored his question until she had finished her task and given the slip to the cook, then she scooped a piece of homemade pie onto an ironstone plate. "There you go," she said, sliding it in front of him. "You don't need another piece, but that won't stop you." Her voice was stern, but her expression was cheerful. She was petite, thirty, the mother of three, wife of the best Ford mechanic in the state and highly thought of by everyone who patronized the Longhorn—which was everyone who lived within thirty miles of Katy Junction. Badger hunkered over the pie and eyed it with relish.

"Say, Bern, how about that Jessie? Guess she won't be waitressing here now that she's gone and got herself that big chunk of money."

"I'm glad for her," Bernie said. "I know she didn't want to sell the ranch, but she's been working way too hard for too many years."

"She busted her arm two days ago," Badger said in an aside to Charlie. "Was reelin' in one of them wild horses of hers and got caught up in the rope somehow. Jerked her right out of the saddle. She drove herself to Bozeman to get it fixed. Too stubborn to ask anyone for help."

"That don't surprise me much," Charlie said with a shake of his head. "Knowing Jessie, I'm surprised she didn't just fix it herself."

"Say, Bern," Badger mumbled around a mouthful of pie, "what's she gonna do now? She tell you her plans?"

"She's been pretty quiet. I hope she stays around here. I wish she and Guthrie would hurry up and get back together. They've been miserable ever since they parted ways. They need each other, but they're both too stubborn and prideful to admit it."

"Stubborn and prideful just about sums the two of 'em up. But I'm with you, Bern. Seems foolish of them to throw all them years of friendship over this ranch sale. Still and all, so long as Guthrie stays away nursing his wounds, there ain't no chance in hell of us hearin' any wedding bells. Didn't he take a job up near the North Pole somewheres?"

"Valdez, Badger." Bernie sighed with exasperation. "That's in Alaska. And the job was just seasonal. My guess is he'll be hauling back into town any day now."

Bernie topped off his coffee, did the same for Charlie and went briskly about her business.

"Well now," Badger said. "Seems to me Guthrie's probably going to have a lot of competition when he gets back."

"How's that?" Charlie emptied two sugar packets into his mug. "Jessie hasn't looked at another man since she was twelve, unless you count that Indian lawyer, but I didn't see no sparks flyin' there."

"That don't mean much. Injuns keep their sparks hid pretty good, and lower your voice, you old fool—he just walked in the door! Anyhow, sparks or no, every available gonad-packin' money-grubbing bundle of testosterone in the county's going to be courtin' that gal, now that she's a wealthy woman. Don't hurt none that she's prettier'n a speckled pup, either."

Badger finished the last of his pie and pushed his plate away, carefully smoothing his white mustache. "Jessie can separate the wheat from the chaff, but if I was Guthrie Sloane, I don't guess as I'd have pulled foot and run off to Alaska after that big fight they had. A woman's heart is kind of like a campfire. If you don't tend it regular, you'll lose it, sure enough."

STEVEN BROWN DID NOT return directly to Bozeman. After reading over the final papers with McCutcheon, he went to the little diner that Katy Junction supported in a big way and ordered an early dinner, keeping to himself and ignoring the gossip circulating in the small room. When he had finished his meal, he requested a large container of soup to go. Bernie raised her eyebrows questioningly. "Don't you even want to know what kind of soup you're ordering?"

"Whatever it is, I'm sure it will be good." He nodded politely.

Bernie smiled, in spite of her resolve to remain aloof. After all, Jessie's friendship with the Indian lawyer was one of the reasons she and Guthrie had parted company. "Today was the closing on the ranch, wasn't it?" she inquired. "I was hoping she might stop in afterward. Is she all right?"

He said nothing, his stoic demeanor a wordless reprimand.

Bernie's shoulders drooped and she shook her head. "No, of course she isn't. Stupid question. Poor girl, my heart goes out to her. You wait right here and I'll get the soup. I have some fresh sourdough bread, too. How about a loaf of that and a big wedge of apple pie? It's still warm from the oven."

She gathered the components of a good, home-cooked meal and packaged them in a small cardboard box, not deluding herself that the lawyer was taking the meal back to Bozeman with him. No; he'd be delivering it to Jessie, to make sure she had something to eat after the traumatic event she had just endured. It was kind of him, but Bernie wished he wasn't doing it. She ladled the hearty soup into the two-quart container and silently but heatedly summoned her absent brother: *Why aren't you here, Guthrie? Didn't you get my letter? Jessie needs you right now! Why aren't you here!*

STEVEN DROVE to the Weaver ranch wondering how he would find Jessie, and if she would resent his presence.

Jessie drew him in a way that no other woman ever had. It seemed as if all his life he had been unconsciously waiting for her, and on that fateful day when she had walked into his Bozeman office, he had sat back in his ergonomic padded executive chair, struck speechless by the sight of her. She was possessed of the same strength and beauty of spirit as the wild, mountainous expanse she loved and had fought so hard to protect. She swept through the door and brought into his cluttered space all the freshness and freedom of the wind that blew across the lonely mountain valleys and the high, snow-crowned peaks.

"I need your help," she had said, standing before his desk with her hat in hand, dressed in faded denim jeans and a white cotton shirt open at the throat, sleeves rolled back, her long black hair drawn into a thick plait that hung clear to her waist, her dark eyes lustrous with turbulent emotion and her lithe figure vibrant with life.

He had risen from his chair, compelled by her very presence to leave off the frittering details that comprised his logically structured and suddenly stifling lifestyle. The urge to tear off his silk tie, suit jacket and vest, to take her hand and flee the office he had worked so hard to get, flee the tangled city streets, the noise and the chaos of the white man's world and return with her to the place of his ancestors, became really overwhelming. She had reawakened in him the mystery and wonder he had felt as a young boy on the Crow Indian reservation when counting all the colors of a Rocky Mountain sunset.

"*I need your help,*" she had said, and with those four powerful words she had altered the very fabric of his carefully constructed life.

The ranch house was dark. He parked where he usually did and walked up the porch steps, bearing the small box of food in his arms. Knocked on the door and heard her little cow dog moving about, but nothing else. He looked toward the pole barn. Had she gotten back all right? He was about to set the food down and go check for her horse, when the door opened.

"Jessie?" he said. "It's Steven. I brought you some food."

The silence stretched while he waited patiently and then she said in a low, weary voice, "Thanks, but I'm not hungry."

"Hunger will come. This isn't the end."

"It feels like the end."

Steven stepped past her then, not waiting for her to invite him inside. The room was cold and dark. He fumbled for the table he knew was there and set the cardboard box down. "Light the lamps," he said.

She did so reluctantly as he went about the business of kindling a fire in the kitchen's woodstove. While it caught he found a pan and poured the soup into it, then laid the sourdough loaf atop the cast-iron stove to warm. "I'll come back Sunday morning. Early. I'll bring help. Pete Two Shirts manages the Crow Indian buffalo herd. It's the largest herd in the country—over fifteen hundred head. Remember? You said you'd like to see the buffalo someday. Our *bi'shee*, grazing over the land, like the old times.

"Pete's a good man with horses. We'll ride up and find your mares for you," he said, reaching down a bowl from a shelf and setting it on the table. "I'd come tomorrow, but Pete works at the agency. I'd come alone, but I'm not good with horses. Anyway, there's no rush. McCutcheon says to take all the time you need. We'll get your truck fixed, too."

Eyes grave, he took her ice-cold signing hand in his. He turned it over and saw the shallow cut she had drawn across her palm. "When I go, you eat something. Tend to yourself. Get some sleep. This isn't the end. It is a beginning."

He left her then, because he knew she needed solitude in which to grieve for what she'd lost.

CALEB MCCUTCHEON couldn't sleep. He lay in his bed, fingers laced behind his head, and listened to the rain. The luminous dials on the bedside clock read 2:00 a.m. No traffic passed the little motel some twenty miles northwest of Katy Junction. He had chosen to stay close to the ranch rather than return to Bozeman, and had brought a bottle of champagne with him from the city, planning to celebrate after the signing, but he felt no desire to celebrate now. All he could think about was that girl.

He hadn't expected to meet Jessica Weaver and be completely swept up in her turmoil. Steven Brown had told him bits and pieces about her—that she'd lost her mother when she was seven years old, that she'd inherited the ranch when her father died a year ago, that he'd left her with insurmountable debts and that she'd struggled to make ends meet, waitressing at the local diner nights, working the ranch by day. She'd raised fine bloodstock—Spanish horses—and sold the foals before they hit the ground, but it hadn't been enough. Too big a ranch, too much work, way too much debt. Too much for one woman alone.

He'd waited several months to sign, and now the historic Weaver ranch belonged to him...and he didn't feel the least bit good about it. Could he have done things differently? Would anything have made it easier for her? The money certainly hadn't eased her pain. That much was obvious when she fled the lawyer's office without the bank check.

McCutcheon sighed. Jesus, he was getting soft, pitying a woman he'd just made wealthy even after all her enormous debts had been settled. "She chose to sell the ranch to me," he'd said to those gathered for the signing. "She could've kept it by selling off parts to developers—they've been after it for years. She could've kept the house, the outbuildings, enough land to run a small herd of horses. But she didn't. She chose to sell.''

The words had echoed in the room and sounded false even to his ears, for he was fully aware that Jessica Weaver had made the greatest of sacrifices. Rather than see the land divvied up in lots, she had ensured that it would remain whole for eternity. She had done this the only way she'd known how: by writing numerous conservation restrictions into the deed, thereby taking a tremendous loss in land value.

On her own, in a last-ditch move of sheer desperation, she had approached a local chapter of the Rocky Mountain Conservancy with her plight, and there she had found Steven Brown, a full-blooded Crow Indian and an environmental advocate, whose legal knowledge had made him a perfect choice for the Conservancy's chairman. Brown had phoned him to ask if he might be interested in looking at the property, since the Conservancy did not have the funds to purchase it outright. Through previous contacts, Brown had known of his interest in buying a big ranch. He explained that the land holding was a watershed of great ecological value embracing critical plants and wildlife. As well, it provided an important buffer to the Greater Yellowstone system.

Were there any buildings on the property? he had inquired of Brown. Oh, yes, he was told. Some of them dating back to the 1800s. Brown's description of the ranch had intrigued him enough to schedule a flight within the week to view the property. One look and he was sold on both the ranch and the girl, Jessie Weaver. That she loved the land was apparent to anyone who watched her gaze out upon it. That she would give it up in the manner she had only proved the depth of that love. It must have been a terribly difficult thing for her to do.

As if that weren't enough, just before the signing she had broken her arm. How would she fix her truck, load her things, round up her little band of broodmares all by herself? She'd ridden ten miles in that rainstorm to make it to the property closing. She was tough, but she needed help. Maybe he could arrange for some for her. Or maybe... Maybe he could provide it himself. Hell, why not? He'd fixed his share of beaters in his teen years. He could repair her truck easily enough. He could do a lot for her. Maybe then he'd feel the joy he thought he'd be feeling right now.

In the morning. He'd go in the morning, first thing. Somehow, he'd make things right with Jessie Weaver.

CHAPTER TWO

THE RAIN BROKE at dawn and a stiff wind blew out of the west, driving the wet with it and bringing a chill out of the mountains that crisped the grass and glazed the water buckets with ice. Jessie poked up the fire in the kitchen stove and put the coffeepot on to boil. She didn't bother to light a lamp. The murky darkness suited her mood. The little cow dog, Blue, sulked at her heels, sensing her disquiet and misery, and tried to dispel it with frequent displays of affection that went unnoticed, unreturned. Her arm ached, but she welcomed the pain. It was a distraction she needed.

This place had always been her home. This place was her mother and father, her grandparents, her great-grandparents and a handful of loyal hands long dead now and buried with the family in the plot up on the hill. All of them would remain on the land they had so fiercely loved and slaved over and fought for and defended. All except her. In a few short days she would walk out the door, never to return.

This was McCutcheon's place now. Perhaps he would bring in grid power from the main road. He might even pave the dirt track that paralleled the creek. He most certainly would throw parties here, grand parties, and he and his wealthy friends would drink and laugh and look out at the valley and the mountains for a day or two before returning to their rich and sophisticated lives in the city.

They would never know of the immense struggle that had shaped this land. They would never know of a man with a dream who had driven a herd of longhorns up from Texas in another century and made a life for himself here, back when the West still had enough snap and snarl in it to give a body pause.

Jessie fed a few sticks into the woodstove and pumped water into the sink. Everything her family had fought so hard for was for nothing. Over one hundred and forty years of mighty struggle upon the land was gone, signed away forever with the sweep of a pen.

She didn't eat breakfast. Wasn't hungry. Hadn't been hungry for weeks. Hadn't slept well for months. For the past year a part of her had been dying, and now it was time for the funeral, time to bury the past and get on with life.

But how could she bury the very best part of herself? How could she possibly leave all this behind? This beloved room, this warm homey kitchen. Damn that Guthrie Sloane! Damn him for running out on her when she needed him the most!

She sat down at the table and dropped her head into the cradle of her arm, her body rigid with pain. She was so absorbed in her wretchedness that she didn't hear the dog bark. Didn't hear the rattle of the diesel engine until it was right outside the ranch house. A car door slammed and she jumped to her feet, smoothing her hair back from her face. Who?

She opened the kitchen door—and visibly recoiled at the sight of the Mercedes and the man mounting the steps. Caleb McCutcheon, and he was carrying a toolbox.

"Hello," he said, apologetic. "I hope I'm not too much of an intrusion. I know it's early, but I figured you for an early riser."

Jessie was completely taken aback. "I had until Tuesday. That was the agreement!"

"Yes, ma'am, it was." He nodded. "Though you can have ten years if you want. I thought I'd give you a hand with your truck. I was a pretty fair mechanic way back when."

"When what?"

He paused, looking very much like a chastened little boy. "When I was a lot younger than I am now," he said.

"I don't need your help, Mr. McCutcheon. I can fix my own truck."

"Well, with that broken arm, I just—"

"Come to think of it," she interrupted, "if I can't fix that old junker I guess now I can buy myself a new one."

He nodded again. "I guess you could, though I didn't figure you were that type."

"What type might that be?"

"Extravagant."

"Have you seen my truck?"

"I passed it on the way in. Ford, 1986-ish? Flatbed, supercab, four-wheel drive. Sweet old girl. The fuel pump's gone—isn't that what you said?"

Now Jessie nodded. "I've had the part for weeks. It's out in the barn."

"Right. Okay, then." He stood there for a few moments, uncertainty flickering in his eyes, then shrugged in a what-the-hell manner. "Well, I suppose if I search long enough I'll find it." He made to go.

"Mr. McCutcheon, I surely wish you wouldn't."

He stopped, half turned and considered what he wanted to say. "I didn't sleep at all last night, thinking about things. After what you did to save this ranch, to keep it whole…" He raised the toolbox. "Fixing your truck is the least I can do."

"You don't owe me anything. All I ever ask is that you respect the land. I would have done anything to keep it, anything at all...except sell it off piecemeal to pay off debts until nothing of it was left."

McCutcheon lifted his gaze to the glaciated summits of the mountain range that towered to the east. "I understand that, and I respect you for what you've done. But to tell you the truth, the way I'm feeling right now I almost wish I hadn't bought it.

"When Steven Brown called me out of the blue, I had pretty much decided that maybe my wife was right—buying a ranch was a foolish dream. Then he started describing the place to me, and suddenly I wanted to see it. See if it was the way I'd imagined it in my dreams. If the mountains looked big enough, the cabins looked honest-to-God real, the creek had just the right bend in it.

"I cut out a picture once when I was a kid living in the middle of a Chicago slum," he said. "Cut it out of a magazine. I've kept it all these years. It was a picture of a ranch, a real working ranch. The house was like this, all weather-beaten and silvery, with a long porch fronting it and facing the river. There were log cabins in the background, a bunkhouse, a pole barn, corrals. Big mountains. Just like this. This is the place I've imagined all these years, right down to the bend in the creek that passes by the old homestead cabin."

The smell of boiling coffee permeated the cold morning air. "I should shift the pot," Jessie said, glancing behind her into the kitchen. She paused, then ducked him a shy glance. "Whyn't you come inside and have a cup."

McCutcheon's face brightened. "Gladly. Maybe you could tell me a little more about the history of this place. We didn't have a whole lot of time for that when I was last here."

She ushered him into the kitchen, poured two chipped ironstone mugs full of hot black brew, and they sat down at the table together. She put her hand on the table, felt the smooth irregularities of it. "My great-grandfather made this," she said. "Hewed it from one thick plank of a big old cedar felled up in the mountains. He made it for my great-grandmother. She was the daughter of a Crow medicine man and she was given to my great-grandfather in thanks for the cattle that kept them alive through a very bad winter. He was also gifted some of the tribe's finest horses. Those horses became the founding bloodlines of one of the purest registries of Spanish Barbs in the West.

"He kept a journal, which my father donated to the Montana Historical Society. In it he wrote often of his wife. When I was young I read that journal a whole passel of times, but it wasn't until I was in my early teens that my father told me my great-grandmother had been a full-blooded Crow Indian. My great-grandfather never made mention of that except for one brief passage in the journal, where he regretted that they couldn't communicate better.

"Which was probably quite an understatement, considering she probably didn't speak one word of English, nor he of Crow. From the way he wrote about her, it was plain that he loved her a great deal, so they somehow managed to overcome the language barrier. She bore him two sons. One died when he was fifteen, thrown from a rough bronc. The other was my grandfather." Jessie glanced at McCutcheon and then let her eyes drop to her mug of coffee.

"My grandfather was a half-breed destined to inherit one of the largest ranches in Montana at a time when people looked darkly on all things Indian, and particularly despised half-breeds. He married another half-breed, a girl from the Blackfeet tribe, whose mother had married a Scottish trapper. She was very beautiful and kind. Her name was Elsa, and she was my father's mother. She is one of my earliest memories. A good memory." Jessie glanced again at McCutcheon, mortified at her unnatural wordiness. "Sorry. I guess I'm giving you the lowdown on the Weaver women."

"Please, continue," McCutcheon urged. "I want to hear it. All of it. Everything that made this place what it is. Tell me about your earliest memory. Tell me about your grandmother."

Jessie held his gaze for a few moments and then nodded slowly. "It was a horseback ride. I was young, maybe four years old, and the horse was as tall as the mountains and as swift as the wind that blew down the valley. The horse was running hard, but I wasn't afraid. I was in my grandmother's strong arms and she held me safe upon that horse as it flew homeward. Over the thundering wind I heard her singing a song in her native tongue. It was joyous and full of life. She sang into the wind as we galloped home from someplace away. That was a good memory!

"I remember that when we got back home my mother was very angry. She was afraid I might have been hurt. She took me from Grandmother and told me I was never to go with her again." Jessie paused and smiled a faint, bitter smile. "That was a bad memory. My mother was white. She loved my father but never understood his heritage, and she feared what she didn't understand. Life out here was hard for her. She came from Denver and she was never happy. My grandparents frightened her. The land frightened her. She hated the sound of the wind, the size of the mountains, the stillness at dawn.

"My father tried to make her happy. He built her this place of boards so she could have the house painted any color she wanted. But the wind and the weather stripped the paint away, and in one bad winter all her rosebushes froze. If she hadn't died of the bad pneumonia, I think she would have left us." Jessie ran her palm over the table. "She died because I brought home a bad flu from school when I was in the second grade and she caught it. I got sick and should have died too, but I didn't. I was seven years old when she died."

McCutcheon sat in silence for a long moment. "I'm sorry," he said. "That must have been a hard time."

"Harder on my father. He loved her so. He never got over her death. My grandparents died not many years after that, just months apart. And then it was just my father and me."

"Any hired hands?"

Jessie nodded. "At first. In the good times we kept three full-timers down at the old cabin and a handful of part-timers during branding and roundup. Then, one by one, we had to let them go. Cattle prices kept falling. Land taxes and living costs kept rising. My father wanted me to go to college, so he took a second mortgage on the ranch to pay my tuition. I finished my four years of college and was in my third year of vet school, when he got sick. The medical bills were staggering, debts piled up, the bank sent notices. I quit school two years ago, Dad died last year...and here we are."

McCutcheon drew a deep breath and released it slowly. "I'm sorry."

She shrugged. "Not your fault. Nobody's fault, really. I'm just glad you came along when you did. Otherwise the bulldozers would already be at work carving out a golf course along the creek."

"I guess we have Steven Brown to thank for that." McCutcheon hesitated. "I have a question about the brand your horses and cattle wear. It looks like a D with a long bar through the middle. Is that what you call this place?

The Bar D? Everyone just refers to it as the Weaver ranch, but don't most ranches have names?''

''Most ranches aren't owned by half-breed Indians,'' Jessie replied. ''The brand you're referring to symbolizes a bow and arrow. If you look sharp, you'll see there's an arrowhead on one end of that bar. It was a pretty radical brand one hundred years ago, so we always just called it the Weaver ranch and let people scratch their heads and wonder.''

McCutcheon sat back in his chair. ''I'll be damned,'' he said. ''The Bow and Arrow.''

Jessie nodded. ''Yessir. Big secret. Might get you scalped if you let it out. What about your wife? You're married, aren't you?''

''Twenty-odd years, no children. She didn't want them. Wanted to be free to travel. She's in Paris right now. Spends six months a year there. She'd never come out here, not in a million years. Not her kind of place. She likes bright lights and big cities. It's not her fault that her husband's a throwback to a different time and place. I can't blame that on her. She's smart, funny, beautiful, well educated. She should've been a politician. Maybe then we'd have a decent president someday.''

''Her?''

He laughed. ''That wouldn't surprise me in the least. She'd be right at home in the Oval Office, and she'd do a damn fine job of running this country, too.'' He finished his coffee, pushed to his feet. ''That was good, thanks. Now, if you'll tell me where to find that fuel pump, I'll get down to business.''

Jessie rose. ''Mr. McCutcheon, really, I can fix the truck myself or hire someone to fix it. I have a little money now, in case you forgot.''

''I realize that,'' he said. ''But I'm going to fix it for

you and you're going to let me. And there's something else." He paused while he phrased his next announcement and shored himself up with a slow deep breath. "I need a caretaker for this place." She shook her head fiercely and he raised a hand. "Yes, you have enough money to buy yourself a moderate spread and continue breeding your Spanish horses, but listen to what I have to say, because I've thought about this a long time.

"Nobody loves this place the way you do. Nobody would ever care about it as much or look after it as well. I'm asking you to stay on as my caretaker. Right here. In this house. I won't be around much for a while, and when I come I'll stay in the old cabin. I'll pay you a good salary and all I ask is that you keep the place in good repair. You'd do that anyhow, without being asked, without being told. You know how to do what needs to be done."

"No."

"You don't have to give me an answer right now. Think on it. And think on this. If you don't stay I'll have to hire someone else to do what you were born to do. I'd hate to do that. This place belongs to you in a way that all the money in the world and countless legal documents can't change, and even more than that, you belong to this place. So please, I'm asking you to seriously consider my offer."

Jessie shook her head before he had even finished speaking. "No," she repeated. "This isn't my home anymore. I have to move on. There's no other way for me."

"I wish you'd at least consider it."

"I already have," she said. "The answer is no, Mr. McCutcheon."

STEVEN TOOK the call in his office. It was Caleb McCutcheon, speaking on his car phone as he drove from the Weaver ranch back to Katy Junction.

"Listen," he began without preamble. "I need your advice...."

Steven sat at his desk while McCutcheon told him about the job offer he had made Jessie Weaver. "She refused me flat out," McCutcheon finished. "I was hoping maybe you could talk to her. Get her to change her mind and stay on. She has to stay. Somehow we have to convince her!"

Steven closed his eyes and kneaded the band of tension between his eyes. He was silent for several long moments. "I'll try," he said. "But she has to walk her own path."

After he hung up he sat in stillness and reflected that, in hindsight, they should have stipulated in deed that Jessie Weaver stay on at least another five years to manage the ranch and make the transition an easier one. Too late now. He stared out the window at the city below, but he was seeing Jessie's mountains.

They were everywhere, those mountains. Rearing up in every direction, walling off the horizon in hues of blue and purple and slate gray, except at dawn or dusk, when they glowed as if lit from within. There was snow on some of the higher peaks—snow that remained nearly year-round, a constant reminder of the harsher life in mountain country. Yet, for all their violent moods, the mountains were heartbreakingly beautiful.

Seemingly rugged and yet so fragile. So vulnerable to the predation of mankind. He understood why Jessie had done as she had. He had seen the ugly urban sprawl, the housing developments, the new roads, the encroachment of a wealthy and burgeoning population into sacred areas that one once thought would never be sullied.

Thanks to Jessie Weaver's sacrifice some of the land was safe. But how was he going to convince her to remain? McCutcheon's plea had aggravated an anguish of his own: the prospect of Jessie leaving this place and the incomprehensible reality that he might never see her again. In their times together Jessie had never led him to believe that anything other than friendship existed between them; still, he felt closer to her than he had to any other woman.

McCutcheon could hire other caretakers, men or women with environmental acumen, who had the good sense to manage the land largely by diplomatic non-interference with Mother Nature. Yet clearly the best of them wouldn't be enough.

So Jessie Weaver had to stay. The fact was as elemental as the sun rising in the east. Without her presence, the very spirit and soul of the land she loved would wither and die; he was as convinced of this as McCutcheon was. Somehow, they had to convince her of the same thing.

But how?

CALEB MCCUTCHEON HAD her truck fixed by midmorning and departed for Katy Junction, but it seemed as though the better part of the day was gone. The best part was early morning, because then the whole of the day stretched before her, as long and golden as the sun's early rays slanting across the valley. There were always half a million tasks to complete before the sun disappeared behind the westward mountain range. So many things to do, and only so many hours of daylight. These had been her days for as long as she could remember, an earthy ferment of timeless cycles, and it was hard to imagine that only three more remained. Time, which had always been immeasurable here, was quickly running out.

She had to bring the broodmares down from the high country. She'd gotten four of them into the home corral already, including the one that had broken her arm, but seven still ranged up in the foothills where the graze was good, although hard frosts had already yellowed the grass.

She sorely missed old Gray, that big handsome stallion that had kept the mares under close guard and brought them down each fall to the safety of the valley. Lightning had killed him in an early-summer thunderstorm—just one more blow to send her reeling, one more wrenching pain to twist an already broken heart.

One of the mares would be hard to root out, a wily mare called Fox, who had lived up to her name on more than one occasion. She was with foal, and impending mother-hood made her even cannier. Fox just plain didn't like being fenced in. She was wild at heart, wild to the core, and to run free in the high country was all she asked of life. Jessie would gladly have gifted her that freedom, but those days had ended for Fox. No more the high lonesome for that tough Spanish mare. It was time for both of them to adjust to a new life. Jessie didn't know which of them would take it the harder—her or Fox.

She saddled Billy, and with the little cow dog trotting at heel, she set out along the river, keeping to the river trail until she intersected the old Indian trace that led up into the foothills. Centuries ago the Crow Indians had worn this trail from the river up over the shoulder of Montana Mountain, through Dead Woman Pass and down to their winter encampment on the eastern flanks of the Beartooth. Some said their ghosts still haunted this trail, though Jessie had never chanced upon one. Nonetheless, she felt a deep connection to the storied mysteries of the historic trace, and rarely followed it without remembering a distant and very different time.

A crash in the brush nearby caused her heart to leap. The dog dashed in pursuit and she caught a blur of ma-hogany, a flash of horn, before dog and steer disappeared into the thicket. She gave a short, sharp whistle. "Blue! Come heel!" She wasn't for chasing after longhorn steers.

They were as wild as the deer, and she held them in the same esteem as the other wild creatures of the land. They had come up from Texas and remnants of her great-great-grandfather's herd still roamed, shy and reclusive, as tough and enduring as the harsh wilds in which they lived. Over the past century they'd interbred with the eastern breeds, but there was no mistaking a cow with longhorn blood running in its veins.

"Come on, Blue. Never mind them wild steers. Find Fox. Find that wily old mustang!" The dog looked up at her bright eyed, ears cocked and head tipped to one side. Fox. She knew the name. That little cow dog was smarter than most humans. "Find Fox, Blue! The rest of 'em'll be real close."

The dog spun around and dashed off. Jessie reined Billy to follow. Two hours later they had climbed nearly one thousand feet up into the pass, and still no sign of the broodmares. Worse, more clouds were building over the mountain range to the west and the air had a keen edge. It tasted of snow and promised an early winter. "Damn that mare!" she muttered, reining Billy around an outcrop of rock as the trail climbed higher. "She knows! Somehow she knows I'm after her, and she's on the run!"

Past noon and Jessie was wishing she'd had the forethought to pack a thermos of hot coffee and a sandwich. Normally she would have, but nothing had been normal of late, including the fact that the ranch's larder was bare. If Steven hadn't brought that food by last night, she'd have gone to bed on an empty stomach. He was such a sweet and thoughtful man.

She paused to rest Billy in a sheltered hollow, swinging down out of the saddle and loosening the cinch. Lord, but it was getting chilly! The wind had picked up and the sun had long disappeared. She shrugged more deeply into her coat and led Billy, keening her eyes for any movement as they climbed, scanning for tracks and wondering where Blue had gotten to. They'd have to turn back soon if they were going to make it to the ranch by dark. She hated to give up the search, but she hated worse the idea of spending a night out unprepared with another storm blowing in.

Another mile passed, another chilly hour. Jessie tightened the saddle cinch and again swung aboard Billy. "Blue!" she shouted. She put two fingers in her mouth and let loose a piercing whistle that was whipped away on the strong wind. "C'mon, Blue! Time to head home!"

Blue knew better than to range too far afield, but something had lured her astray. Still and all, that dog could find her way home in a blizzard. Jessie wasn't overly worried. She was reining Billy around, when she heard the dog's faint barking. She stood in the stirrups, craning to place the sound so shredded by the wind. There—down in that draw!

Billy was as surefooted as a mountain goat, and when Jessie pointed him down the slope he sat back on his haunches like a giant dog and slid in a scatter of loose gravel until the slope flattened out into a thick coniferous forest that darkened the ravine. Blue's barking became much clearer once they were out of the wind. It had a frightened, desperate pitch, and Jessie kept Billy moving as quickly as she dared as apprehension tightened her stomach. "Blue? Hang on, girl! I'm coming!"

Suddenly, Billy shied and blew like a deer. "Easy, easy now... Whoa now..." Jessie soothed, swinging out of the saddle before he could jump again. "It's all right." She tried to lead him forward, but he threw his head back and balked. This was unusual behavior for an old pro like Billy, and Jessie didn't force him. She knew that a horse could hear and smell far better than a human. She ground-tied him and continued toward Blue's bark. Not too far beyond where she'd left the horse, she spotted the dog. Blue was lying in a small gravelly clearing fringed with dense growth. She was lying very still, with her front paws stretched out in front of her. Behind her the ground was scuffed. At the sight of Jessie the dog struggled to rise but failed.

"Blue!" Jessie crossed to her quickly and dropped to her knees. "Oh Blue! What's happened to you!" But even as she spoke, she intuitively knew. Blue had tangled with something—mountain lion, bear?—and had come out the poorer. Why had she attacked it, and more to the point, where was the creature now? Even as she rapidly assessed the dog's injuries, Jessie was taking in her immediate surroundings, the hair on her nape prickling with fear.

Blue was badly hurt. She had half a dozen deep wounds to her side and flank where claws had raked her. The span of the claw marks was far bigger than what a mountain lion would have inflicted. It had to have been a bear. The dog had lost a great deal of blood and was too injured to move any farther—it looked to Jessie as if Blue had dragged herself quite a ways before finally collapsing. "It's okay, Blue. Easy, old girl. I'll take care of you. You'll be all right. We'll get you back home safe."

She needed the supplies in Billy's saddlebags. There was a good first-aid kit, and her rifle was in the saddle scabbard, where it always rode snugly, just in case. She rose to her feet, scooping the cow dog into her arms as she did. "Hold on, Blue. We'll get you home. You'll be okay!" Then she walked swiftly back to Billy.

The bay gelding was standing right where she'd left him, but he was trembling, sweated up, rolling his eyes and obviously in a state of near panic. "Whoa, now. Easy, Billy... Whoa now." She laid Blue down and eased toward the horse. Speaking softly, she took up the trailing rein and pressed her palm between his wide and frightened eyes. Slid that same hand over the crest of his neck and smoothed his long dark mane. "Easy, Billy. I know you're smelling that bear and I know it scares the dickens out of you, but Blue's hurt bad. We have to help her...."

Even as she spoke she was reaching for the saddlebag that held the first-aid kit. She had the buckle undone and her fingers were pushing the top flap back, groping for the cordura bag secured within. "Easy now—"

Without warning, Billy let out a scream of fear, a horrible sound that only a horse in sheer terror can make, and at the same moment he reared on his hindquarters and bolted for home. One second the gelding was a big solid presence right beside her; the next he was the sound of hooves drumming hard in a gravel-scattering uphill run and she was lying flat on her back where she'd landed when his shoulder had knocked her down.

The bear was close. Very close. A grizzly, the same bear that had hurt Blue.

Jessie scrambled to her feet, cradling her broken arm. The cast protected it from the constant insults she heaped upon it, but getting knocked down by Billy had hurt. Considering all the other problems she faced, she barely noticed the pain. She moved quickly to where she had left Blue, who was staring with bared fangs and throaty growls at the thick wall of brush behind her. She wasted no time hoisting the little cow dog into her arms again, and then, cradling her as best she could, she turned tail and ran. Oh, she'd read all the Yellowstone advisories that running from a bear was the very worst thing a person could do, but run she did, as fast as she could while carrying Blue.

She chose the same path Billy had taken and she didn't look back. Adrenaline gave her a speed, power and endurance she would not ordinarily have possessed. She ran with the dog in her arms until every fiber of her body protested and she could run no farther. She was back on the ridge trail and heading for home, and the wind was demonic, screaming out of the west at gale force. It was beginning to snow, and darkness was no longer a distant threat but a near reality.

She gasped for breath, sinking to her knees with Blue in her arms. She had to get below the tree line, out of this killing wind! She wasn't going to make it home, not by a long shot, but they couldn't spend the night up here in the pass. They'd freeze to death, and then historians would have to rename it Dead *Women* Pass. Morbid thought. She weighed her options and pushed to her feet. Her injured arm ached unbearably beneath Blue's weight. "It's okay," she soothed the hurt and frightened dog. "It's all right. I've got you, Blue. You'll be okay...."

She staggered along, her body bent into the wind. Down and down they went, until finally the brunt of the wind was turned by the thickly forested slope. It was nearly full dark now, but she kept moving for as long as she dared, and then finally she knelt and laid Blue down. She had chosen a good spot to hole up. A blowdown had upended its great tangle of roots and earth, making a fine windbreak. She broke the dead branches from it in the last of the fading light and kindled a tiny fire at its base, more out of a need for light than for the little warmth such a small fire would cast. Blue was sluggish, shocky. She was in pain. Who knows what sort of internal injuries she might have sustained from the bear's blows?

The little cow dog had shared a working partnership and a special friendship with Jessie for eight years, and was irreplaceable. Blue mustn't die. She couldn't die. Jessie used her bandanna to bind the deepest wounds on the cow dog's thigh, unzipped her coat and drew the shivering dog against her. Then she zipped the coat back up with the dog inside it. She fed the last of the firewood onto the small fire and sat back, cradling the trembling dog in her warmth.

It was going to be a long, cold night.

CHAPTER THREE

GUTHRIE SLOANE HAD BEEN driving since well before dawn, but he was too close to home to stop now, in spite of the darkness and the near-whiteout conditions. He had a good four-wheel-drive truck and the big plow rigs were out, keeping the drifts pushed back. He'd make Bozeman inside of an hour, and with any luck would be hauling into Katy Junction just shy of midnight.

He felt as if he'd been gone forever. When he'd left this past spring he'd wanted to go. Couldn't wait to put as many miles as possible between Jessie Weaver and him. But over the summer his hurt and anger had faded, to be replaced by a kind of chronic depression. He'd worked hard, putting in sixteen-hour days, seven days a week, at the fish processing plant. The job was inglorious, but it paid very well and kept him busy, kept him from dwelling on his miseries.

That is, until he got the letter from his sister, Bernie, back in Katy Junction. "Jessie needs you," she'd written. "She'd never admit to it, but it's true. Please come home!"

The day the processing plant shut down for the winter Guthrie stood on the wharf smelling the salt tang of the harbor, admiring the mountainous coastline, the rugged beauty that was Alaska, and suddenly he wanted nothing more than to go back to Katy Junction. That very day he'd closed his account at the bank, thrown his collection of moldering camping gear into his truck and headed south.

He had no illusions about returning home to Jessie's welcoming arms, no matter what Bernie had written. Jess had made her position clear and was not the sort of woman to say anything she didn't mean. "We don't share the same dreams, Guthrie," she'd told him at their parting. "Lately all we do is fight. I think it's best we don't see each other anymore."

Or something to that devastating effect.

Jessie's dreams were her wild Spanish mustangs and somehow preserving some small part of the rapidly shrinking range for them to roam free. Her dreams were grand. His were far more humble and modest. He dreamed of marrying Jess and proving up that little claim he'd staked for himself along Bear Creek. He wanted to run a few head of cattle, put some acres to good alfalfa hay, tinker with farm machinery and work for his sister's husband. He wanted to raise a few towheaded, chubby-cheeked, milk-toothed babies, love his woman, have a good dog, a good horse and a dependable truck.

His dreams fell far short of Jessie's aspirations. She wanted to save Montana, and was driven by a desperate passion that intimidated Guthrie. Sure, he saw where she was coming from. Who wouldn't? Didn't they all love the vast rolling plains and towering mountains that boldly defied distance and description?

Guthrie downshifted to slow his truck as he came up behind a small foreign car. Visibility was poor, snow was building up on the road surfaces and his drive south would be arduous, but it would be worth it, because when he arrived, no matter what time it was, he would be home. Finally, he would be back where he belonged.

McCUTCHEON HAD BEEN standing on the ranch house porch for twenty minutes. It was the third time this day that he had made the long drive from town to talk to Jessie, ask her if she'd thought about his offer, tell her that she couldn't pass it up because where else would her horses have as much running room and feel so much at home as right here on their own range?

It was snowing hard, and had been since midafternoon. Jessie had ridden up in the high country that morning to look for her wild mares and she wasn't back yet. And it was dark. Full dark. On a stormy night when an unexpected blue norther was piling down wind-driven snow at the rate of an inch an hour. He checked his watch again, its dials luminescent, and swore softly. This wasn't how he'd imagined this day to be...standing on her porch—*his* porch, dammit—his stomach tied in knots.

Over the sound of the wind came another sound out of the darkness—that of horse's hooves muffled in six inches of fresh snow. "Jessie!" he shouted. He switched on his flashlight and shone it into the whirling snow. "Jessie Weaver!"

There was no answer to his call, but the footfalls came on steadily. A horse, plastered in wet snow, plodded up to the porch rail as if he'd walked up to it hundreds of times before. The animal was exhausted. McCutcheon panned the horse with his flashlight. His initial relief plummeted at the sight of the empty saddle.

"Oh, no," he said. He stepped down the stairs and brushed the snow from the saddle. One of the bridle reins was broken. One of the saddlebags was unbuckled, but still full of gear. He picked up the trailing rein and led the exhausted gelding into the pole barn, where he stripped off bridle and saddle it, rubbed the horse down with a burlap sack, pitched him some hay and water and a bait of sweet feed before making for his car and town to tell the authorities that something very bad had happened to Jessie Weaver on this wild and stormy night.

"DON'T YOU DIE on me, Blue," Jessie said, her voice inaudible to her own ears over the moan of the wind. "Don't you die on me! You've been with me too long to leave me, and I need you now more than ever. You stay right here with me and we'll keep each other warm and safe."

She wasn't frightened by the dark, but the cold scared her. It had the teeth of winter and its bite was painfully sharp. She had dressed as she always did for a high-country ride in fall, and could not lay blame on her choice of clothing. But an empty stomach didn't help. A mug of hot chocolate and a big bowl of spiced beef and beans would see her through this night.

Guthrie!

Jessie jerked at the image that came so suddenly out of the darkness. The unexpected memory flooded through her and galvanized her into wakefulness. She tightened her grip on Blue and fought to quell the butterflies that fluttered through her stomach and made it hard to draw breath. Why on earth was she thinking about him now, of all times? Why was his face so clear to her—its strong, lean planes, the way it felt beneath her fingertips, the sensual roughness of his twelve-hour stubble, and his mouth, so firm and masculine...

Those images usually only came to her at night in her sleep. During the day she could keep them at bay, overshadow them with the anger she felt at his abandoning her in the midst of such difficult times.

"Baloney!" Jessie said, startling the dog. Blue raised her head and whined. "It's all right, honey," she soothed. "It's okay. We'll be okay...."

Guthrie was gone. He'd run off and headed north. Alaska, she'd heard. One bad argument between them and he'd turned tail and bolted, and he'd been gone nearly five months. If that was the sort of man he was, soft and full of butter, she was better off without him. Sooner or later her heart would realize that, then those dreams of Guthrie that tormented her nights would quit.

Jessie shivered with the cold, her trembling matching that of the injured dog she cradled beneath her coat. "I have to stay awake," she said to Blue. "Can't fall asleep. Don't want to dream those dreams anymore...."

"WHAT IN HELL is taking them so long to get here!"

Caleb McCutcheon was mad. He paced the floor of the Longhorn between the counter and the door—a space too small for his big strides, which irritated him even further.

"It's the storm," Bernie said, refilling his coffee cup then those of the others sitting at the counter. Eight locals waited there for the warden, the state police and Park County Search and Rescue to arrive.

The phone rang and Bernie picked it up, listened for a few moments, said, "All right," and hung up. She looked at the questioning faces. "That was the warden. Comstock says the state police are tied up with accidents. Search and rescue are mobilizing, but they won't be here till dawn. He's arranged for Joe Nash to take him up in his chopper at first light. He suggested that someone go out to the Weaver ranch, just in case Jessie makes it back on her own."

"First light? They're going to wait until morning? But that's ridiculous! She could be hurt! Freezing to death!" McCutcheon said.

"What can they do in the middle of a blizzard in pitch-darkness?" Badger reasoned. "No tracks, no scent for the dogs, no direction to start in or head for. Sometimes it's better to set your horse and do nothin' than wear him out chasin' shadows.''

"You can set your horse if you like. I'm driving out to the ranch," McCutcheon said, reaching for his coat.

"Snow's gettin' pretty deep," Badger said. "Your fancy car won't make it. Might even be too deep for my truck, though I doubt it. She'll go through just about anything." He stroked his mustache, considering for a moment, then levered his arthritic body off the stool and reached for his Stetson. "Let's get goin'. This waitin' ain't easy on me, either."

Badger was right about the snow. Where the wind had piled it up, the drifts pushed up against the undercarriage of the truck as they crept down the unplowed ranch road. But they made it.

No one else was there. They entered the dark ranch house and Badger lit an oil lamp in the kitchen after reaching it down from an open shelf with easy familiarity. "I used to work here," he explained, setting the lamp on the kitchen table. "Back when Drew and Ramalda lived in the old cabin that stood behind the corrals. Gone now. Fire took it after they left. Lord, that woman could cook! I'm going to get the woodstove going, put on a pot of coffee. This place is colder'n a dead lamb's tongue."

McCutcheon prowled restlessly, stepping out onto the porch periodically to listen and holler Jessie's name into the stormy darkness before retreating into the warmth and light of the kitchen. The two men shared few words. Badger seemed content to feed chunks of split wood into the firebox and poke at the coffeepot from time to time, waiting for the water to boil. McCutcheon, on the other hand, paced like a caged lion. He couldn't understand how the people of Katy Junction could be so calm. That girl was out there all by herself, certainly very cold, probably hurt, maybe even dead, yet they all acted as though it was just another sleepy Sunday.

"It's got to be nearly zero with that windchill!" he burst out to Badger, as if it were the old man's fault.

"Yessir, I expect it is," Badger replied calmly.

"We have to do something! We can't just sit around and wait! She'll freeze to death!"

"Well now, mister, I highly doubt it. Knowing Jessie, she's holed up somewhere's safe, waiting the storm. And right now there ain't a whole lot we can do, except go out into it and get ourselves good and lost. That don't sound like a very good plan to me. Haul on up to a cup of coffee and cool your jets. We'll head out at first light."

GUTHRIE WAS SURPRISED to see all the trucks parked in front of the Longhorn so late of an evening. Bernie usually closed the café up at 8:00 p.m. sharp to go home and kiss her babies good-night. He parked at the end of the line, relieved that his long drive was over and pleased as all get out at the thought of a cup of hot coffee and the prospect of seeing his sister.

He climbed out of the truck into over a foot of heavy snow and clumped up the boardwalk, knocking the snow off his boots as he pushed open the Longhorn's door. The place was crowded with familiar faces. They all turned toward him and half raised up out of their seats as if they'd been expecting him for hours.

"Guthrie!" Bernie came out of the kitchen holding a platter stacked high with sandwiches. She dropped the platter on the counter and ran across the room to hug him fiercely. "Oh, Guthrie, how on earth did you know? Thank God you're here!"

Guthrie felt a peculiar tightening in his stomach as he

gently pried himself out of her desperate embrace and held her at arm's length. "How did I know *what?* What's the matter, Bernie? *What's wrong?*"

IN SPITE OF THE COLD she slept, and in her dream the snow-laden moan of the wind became the somber voice of her father. He was sitting at his desk, working on the books the way he often did in the evening, his pen scratching spidery figures in the columns, his eyebrows drawn together in a perpetual frown of concentration. He laid his pen down and glanced up at her with a weary sigh.

"Looks like we took another big loss this year, Jessie. Maybe Harlan Toombs was right. Maybe we should've held the prime steers over another year rather than sell them at that ridiculously low price. I don't know." He sighed again and ran his fingers through his thin, close-cropped hair. "I don't know much of anything anymore. Times are changing so fast I can't keep up. Cattle prices keep dropping, taxes keep climbing. You should've stayed in school, Jessie. By now you'd be well on your way to being a veterinarian. You'd be a good one. Hell, you were almost there. There's still time. Go back to school and finish up your degree!"

And then Guthrie was in the room with them, his face lean and handsome, his expression intense in the glow of the lamplight. "Marry me, Jess! We could have a good life together. You don't have to be a veterinarian to have a good career. You have one now, raising those fine Spanish horses of yours. And the most important career you could ever have would be raising our babies."

Another figure moved out of the shadows, a man nearly as tall and lithe as Guthrie in spite of being a good twenty years older. Caleb McCutcheon held out the bank check. "Take it. It's your money now, Jessie. It'll buy you a fresh stake someplace else if you feel you have to leave, but give some thought to my job offer. It still stands. This place needs you, and you'll always need this place.''

Steven Brown was a silent presence in the background, his dark eyes somber. He was watching her, but he said nothing. He gave no opinions, made no requests or demands. He was simply there, the way the rocks and the trees and the mountains were there. She felt herself being drawn to his quiet solid strength.

Fox was running at a dead gallop along the creek where the west fork fed into it. Ears pinned back, nostrils flaring, her mane and tail streaming behind her, she looked as if she were flying just above the earth. The other mares followed at her heels. They were heading for the old Indian trace that led up Montana Mountain. Jessie knew Billy could never catch them up. She reined him in as they raced past, running hard for a place where the wind blew free and the land stretched out as far as the eye could see, a place with no fence lines, no roads, no boundaries. A place that no longer existed except in their memories.

The grizzly was huge and angry. It rose up on its hind legs and stared in her direction, swinging its massive head as it tasted the air for some scent of her. She felt herself cowering, paralyzed with fear. Mouth dry, heart pounding, she was unable to move when it suddenly dropped back onto all fours and began to charge toward her. She opened her mouth to scream, but no sound came forth. Her legs felt mired in quicksand. The bear lunged and grabbed her arm in its powerful jaws, and pain shot through her—

''No!'' She came awake in midcry, gasping for breath in blind panic, until reality reasserted itself and chased the nightmare away. Blue was tense and whining in her arms. Oh, her arm hurt! It ached unbearably. She shifted her position and sat in the inky darkness until her heartbeat steadied.

Where was the bear? What time was it? Surely morning was near. It was so dark. And cold… It was so very, very cold….

STEVEN SET ASIDE the paperwork he'd been reading, or at least pretending to read, and glanced up at the clock. Midnight. He'd called the Longhorn ten minutes ago. Would it be rude to call again so soon? He pushed out of his easy chair, carried his cup of coffee with him to the door and opened it. The windblown snow whirled past. Jessie Weaver was out in the brunt of it tonight. Alone. Perhaps hurt. Maybe dead. And he was here, his back to the warm room, a cup of hot coffee in his hand.

He slammed the door and stood in the foyer of his little cedar-clad post-and-beam house in Gallatin Gateway, hating the fact that he was safe while she was in trouble. Hating the helplessness that had overwhelmed him since he'd gotten McCutcheon's message on his answering machine earlier that evening. He'd spoken with Bernie four times since, and each time had brought the same information.

No news.

He walked into the kitchen, slatted the remains of his coffee into the sink and rinsed the mug. Without even thinking of what he would do when he got there, he dressed himself for a winter storm, and less than ten minutes later he was in his Jeep Wagoneer, heading for Katy Junction.

CHAPTER FOUR

GUTHRIE WAS TAKEN ABACK by the stranger who opened the door of the Weaver ranch when he banged on it just past midnight. "Who the hell are you?" he said.

"Caleb McCutcheon. Are you the warden?"

"No! I'm here to look for—" He spotted someone else in the lamp-lit room. "Badger! Where's Jess!" Guthrie pushed past the stranger and into the kitchen, relieved to see the bewhiskered and familiar face.

"Oh, I expect she's up on the mountain somewheres, hunkered down and waiting for dawn. Same as we are. Only, I don't doubt as we're a whole lot more comfortable. Good to see you, Guthrie. You been gone awhile. Too long. A lot's happened since you left. This here gent's bought the whole Weaver ranch, lock, stock and barrel."

Guthrie rounded on the stranger as if drawing a sword. "You're a developer?"

"No. Like I said, I'm Caleb McCutcheon. And if you have any ideas on how to find Jessica Weaver, I'm listening. We've been sitting around doing nothing for way too long."

The two men measured each other for a brief moment, and then Guthrie nodded curtly. "I brought snowshoes from my place. You're welcome to a pair. She's up on Montana Mountain—like Badger says. Probably went looking for Fox. That mare always heads up there this time of year, trying for North Dakota. Damn mustang thinks they don't have such things as fences there, though that gray stallion of Jessie's usually manages to convince Fox to stick around.''

"Old Gray's dead," Badger said bluntly. "Got struck by lightning this summer.''

Guthrie was taken aback for the second time in as many minutes. "She thought highly of that horse.'' He could hardly conceive of what Jessie had been through in the past year, but if he had thought himself to be suffering this past summer, it was nothing compared with the hell that she had endured. "C'mon, let's go. I have a backpack full of emergency supplies and spare headlamp batteries. I don't guess I'm waiting for daylight. And by the way,'' he said to McCutcheon, thrusting out his hand, "I'm Guthrie Sloane. From what Badger says, we're neighbors."

IT WAS DARK YET, but nearing the dawn. The snow had stopped. Her muscles were stiff and sore and she was cold and hungry, but both the night and the storm had lost their grip, and with the coming of daylight she would be able to walk down out of this high place. It would be slow going, carrying Blue. She could keep to the trail, or cut off it just below the big lightning-struck pine, climb over the ridge and head down for the main road. That would be quicker, and there was bound to be some traffic—a rancher heading for Katy Junction for his morning coffee, newspaper and goodly dose of gossip at the Longhorn; a plow truck sweeping back the drifts.

She could catch a ride, and maybe even get hauled over to Doc Cooper so's she could have Blue seen to. Some of the dog's wounds needed stitching up. Jessie could have done it herself if she'd had two good hands—and made a better job of it, too. Half the women in the county could lay in a neater row of stitches than Doc Cooper. Still and all, he knew his stuff and had helped the Weavers through many a livestock crisis. Never nagged about payment, either—eventually he always got his due and then some. Folks out here just naturally stood by one another in tough times, and lately it seemed that the times had always been tough.

In the gloaming Jessie struggled to her feet, stomping them to restore circulation. She had thought to let Blue free for a bit, but as she started to unzip her coat the zipper had stuck and she gave up. When she moved out from beneath the sheltering overhang of the blowdown, the depth of the snow surprised her. She made up her mind without really thinking about it. She would take the short-cut out to the main road. It would shave five miles off her journey, though still leave her with another ten to cover if no traffic happened by. Ten miles in nearly a foot of wet October snow, carrying an injured dog, ought to be a good workout. And to think that some folks paid good money to join a health club to exercise!

Jessie pointed her feet in the right direction and started walking.

GUTHRIE SLOANE DIDN'T give much thought to the man struggling along behind him, except to note that he was doing all right for a person his age. Jess was in trouble, and he had no intention of holding back. Nossir. If McCutcheon signed up for the trip, he was in for the long haul, and it was proving up to be a long rough haul. The trail up into the pass was steep, and there were a lot of places that a man could run afoul on a dark and stormy night like this.

He was going on pure hunch, figuring what route she'd have taken, where the mares might've been headed until this unexpected storm had caught them out. Of course he could be wrong. Maybe Jess had started up into the pass while at the same time the mares had angled down out of it, sensing the storm. Maybe she'd caught their sign and trailed after them. Maybe she was already out of the high country, encamped in some sheltered draw, with a cheerful fire keeping the darkness at bay, Blue tucked beside her and a billy can of hot coffee boiling.

Such thoughts did little to ease his torment. If anything happened to Jessie he'd blame himself for ever leaving her. He should've stuck it out and helped her through this awful time. True, she'd told him it was over between them and she'd meant it, but could they erase all those years of friendship just because as lovers they had failed?

No! She was his best friend and nothing would ever change that. It was suddenly the most important thing on earth to him that she realize he would be there for her, no matter what. Always.

Guthrie was unaware that the snow had stopped until McCutcheon mentioned it the first time they paused to take a breather. The older man had pulled up beside him and slumped over himself. Hands braced on his knees, he'd drawn deep gasping breaths until his lungs had caught up with the rest of him, at which point he'd raised his head and said, "It's stopped."

"What?"

"The snow."

"Huh." He only rested for three, four minutes at most, and then started out again. The trail was steep and the snow was heavy and wet, sticking to the snowshoes. The next time he halted for a breather McCutcheon bent over himself once more in a prolonged coughing fit and then raised his head and looked around.

"It's getting light," he said.

Guthrie stared out across the valley. He could see the

ranch buildings along the river, a grouping of black rectangular shapes against the brightness of the snow, toylike in the distance. "So you own it now," he said softly. "The whole of it."

"Yes."

"But you're not a developer?"

"No," McCutcheon explained, again struggling to catch his breath. "The land can never be divided up or developed. It's written right into the deed."

"Conservation easements?"

McCutcheon nodded. "Lots of 'em. But that's fine with me. I like it just the way it is."

Twenty minutes later the two men had snowshoed into the dawn, and by the time the sun had lifted over the jagged shoulders of the Beartooth Range they had intersected Jessie's trail in the snow where it left Dead Woman Pass and headed down toward the road.

"Dammit!" Guthrie said, at once wildly relieved that she was okay and bitterly disappointed that she had chosen to take the shortcut and had missed them. "She can't be too far ahead. She's aiming for the road. It's closer than the ranch, and she might be able to flag down a vehicle...if one should happen to pass her by."

McCutcheon nodded in response, too winded to speak. The rising sun was rapidly warming the air and softening the snow. By the time they reached the valley floor they would be slogging through a foot of slush and stripping off their heavy parkas.

Hopefully by then they would have caught up with Jessie Weaver, because McCutcheon wasn't sure how much longer he could keep pace with the younger man.

JOE NASH HAD FLOWN for Yellowstone HeloTours for nearly ten years, but he still felt that peculiar churn of

excitement in his stomach when he got a call from the
state police or the warden service to ask if he'd volunteer
for a search-and-rescue flight. If the chopper wasn't carrying clients he always agreed, and sometimes he did even
with clients on board. Let his boss fire him if he wanted;
seat-of-the-pants search-and-rescue missions sure beat
hauling around a bunch of rich tourists or egotistical chest-
beating hunters, pointing out Old Faithful or a herd of elk
from one thousand feet up.

This time it was Ben Comstock who radioed him with
the request. Joe liked the warden, though they had their
differences of opinion regarding certain game laws. From
what Comstock had told him, this mission would be particularly challenging, for it involved mountain flying, and
mountain flying was always tricky. Sudden updrafts and
downdrafts could toss the chopper around like a toy. Comstock climbed into the passenger seat and strapped himself
in, then studied the map he'd laid out on his lap.

"We'll head straight to Katy Junction and then up into
Dead Woman Pass from this direction here, and fly a routine grid over Montana Mountain," he said over the noise
of the rotor chop, tracing his forefinger along the proposed
route. "It's rough country. The last person who got himself
lost in that wilderness was never found."

"Yeah, well, you should've called me," Joe said lacon-
ically.

"She's been missing since yesterday afternoon, but
she's probably okay. She didn't come by that reputation
of hers by lying down and quitting."

"She? Who'd you say we're looking for?"

"Didn't. It's Jessie Weaver."

"No foolin'? Jessie Weaver. I'll be damned. I read
about her latest scrap in the papers last summer, how that
ornery longhorn bull just up and charged out of the brush,

shouldered into her horse and put him down. How she jumped clear but her rifle was pinned under the horse, so she took off her hat and whipped the bull in the face with it to drive him away. One hundred pounds of Montana cowgirl facing down a pissed-off longhorn bull, and her with a broken collarbone to boot. By damn, but that took nerve! Met her once or twice, but it's been awhile. Hope it won't be too much longer till we see her again.''

Joe fed a stick of gum into his mouth and tried not to look too eager. Weaver, huh? As he recalled, she was kind of a good-looking girl. Must be some kind of rich, too. Maybe there'd be a big reward!

He'd find her, all right. He had no doubts about that. None at all. Joe Nash always found who he was looking for. He had the keenest eyes in the sky. That was why Comstock consistantly tried to engage his help when anyone needed finding. That was why big-game hunters paid him big bucks to fly them to some remote camp in the fall. He not only took them where they wanted to go, but he pointed out all the enticing possibilities along the way. Hell, he could spot a porcupine in a spruce tree from five thousand feet up and count the quills in its tail. Finding lost persons was a lark compared with that.

Which was why Comstock never raised an eyebrow when, less than an hour later, Joe spotted the bear. He was making a low-level run up into the pass, and as he delicately maneuvered the big chopper at an altitude that would have spooked most pilots and caused the FAA to ground him for life, he spied the grizzly, a good half mile beyond where the snowshoe tracks intercepted, then overlaid, the deeper track left by Jessica Weaver. He nosed the chopper toward the spot where the bear had disappeared into the heavily timbered draw.

"See it?" he said, sunglasses reflecting the rugged gandeur of the mountain slopes. Comstock shook his head, and Joe angled the nose a bit more. "There. To the left of that dead snag, near the base of the slope. That's a horse. I'll eat my hat if it isn't. That bear killed a horse yesterday. We spooked it just now as it was feeding. See how the bear dragged all those branches over the horse? Snow's melting pretty good now. That's how I spotted the legs."

Comstock shook his head again. He saw the dead snag at the base of the slope but still couldn't find the horse, let alone the branches or the horse's legs. Truth was, he hadn't even seen the bear.

"Yessir," Joe Nash said as he pivoted the chopper to follow the human tracks back down the mountain. "That big old grizzly killed himself a horse! I bet Jessie Weaver had a run-in with the bear, too. From where she spent the night to where that dead horse lay is less than half a mile. Oh, yes, I bet she's got a scary tale or two to tell." He got on the radio to let his boss know that he might be a little late bringing the big metal bucket home to roost.

SHE RESTED FREQUENTLY on the long hike out to the road. Walking downhill was hard on her knees, and the wet snow was slippery. It was warm out, too, though the warmth was more than welcome after the frigid night. Blue was getting heavier by the moment, though in truth she was a small dog, the runt of her litter, and weighed scarcely more than thirty-five pounds. When Jessie stopped she sank onto her knees and took the weight of the dog on her upper thighs to give her arm a rest. Her pace was much slower than she had estimated. By the time she made it to the road the morning traffic—what little there was of it—would already have come and gone; but there might yet be a plow truck, and there was always the mail carrier.

Even if no one happened along, the hard, even surface of the road would make for an easier trek.

She walked for ten minutes, rested for five. Thought about all the things left to do before leaving the ranch. Wondered how she'd ever get Fox and those mares back. Wanted not to have to think about any of that. Wished there were nothing left to do but eat a hot meal, drink a gallon of coffee and sleep until all her mental and physical aches and pains had disappeared.

Yet so much was unresolved within her. She still had no idea where she was going to go, what she was going to do. Sure, she could bring the mares down, load them into the big stock trailer, throw her personal gear into the truck. But then what? Sit there with the engine idling until inspiration struck? She had some money now, and the bulk of it would go toward finding a new home for herself. But just where would that be? She couldn't stay in Katy Junction. She couldn't bear the thought of living near the ranch, knowing it was no longer her home. It would be better just to pull up stakes completely and find someplace far away.

Canada, maybe. British Columbia. Big tracts of land were for sale up there, some of them pretty reasonable. She'd looked at real estate ads the past few months, but a part of her hadn't accepted that she would have to leave home. A part of her had clung to the foolish hope that some miracle would save the ranch and save her. And a miracle *had* saved the ranch.

But not her, because the ranch wasn't her home anymore.

Guthrie's sister, Bernie, had begged her to stay in Katy Junction. "Dan Robb's place is for sale," she'd said. "It doesn't have any creek frontage, but it has good deep wells and a great big ark of a barn. It's been on the market forever and you could probably pick it up for a song."

Jessie liked Bernie a lot. She missed working for her at the Longhorn. She missed the friendly faces, the banter, the feeling of community she had found there. Once her father had died, she discovered that living out on the edge of nowhere was at times lonely and daunting. Mostly, she was too busy to dwell on it much; nevertheless, the hours she spent working at the café had been as much for social as for financial reasons.

Still, as much as she liked the folks of Katy Junction, staying would be too painful, especially once Guthrie got back. Because as sure as the Canada geese left Alaska in the fall, Guthrie Sloane would be hard on their heels, and she really didn't feel up to facing him. The pain was still there; the raw wounds their failed relationship left had hardly even begun to heal. No, it was time to move on.

Jessie heard a sound and knelt to listen and to rest. The wind was blowing through the pines, but she heard it again. A voice. Way out in the middle of nowhere, a human voice. Familiar.

Very familiar!

And it was calling her name!

McCUTCHEON HAD SPENT far more enjoyable times than this, but as his mother once told him a long time ago, "Son, sometimes you just have to keep dancing even when the music's bad."

He followed Guthrie Sloane as he double-timed it up and down and over and around, never stopping to rest, never pausing to regroup, just shuffling along tirelessly, a young man on an urgent mission. McCutcheon followed until his lungs screamed for air and the muscles in his legs burned in protest and the muscle in his chest warned him to slow down.

"I see her!"

Guthrie's words jerked McCutcheon from the misery of his exhaustion. He stopped, his legs immediately cramping, and gazed down the wooded slope. Guthrie was forging on toward the dark shape that moved far below them. "Jess!" Guthrie belted out, as strong and deep as if he hadn't just covered ten miles in the mountains on snowshoes. "Jess!"

McCutcheon rubbed his burning thighs and watched as Guthrie charged down the slope, kicking up spumes of wet snow. The girl turned to look behind her. She was carrying something in her arms, something heavy enough to make her kneel when she stopped. But it was Jessie Weaver, and she was all right. McCutcheon felt the tightness in his stomach ease. Everything would be okay.

JESSIE COULDN'T BELIEVE her eyes. Blue cradled in her arms as she knelt, she watched as a man plunged recklessly down the slope toward her. She recognized him even from this great distance. Hard not to. She'd known him for more than half her life. Knew the way he moved, the sound of his voice, and if that wasn't enough, she recognized his tall, broad shouldered build, and that hat. His broad-brimmed brown felt Stetson. The same hat she'd snatched from his head and flung into the creek the day they'd had the argument about her working for a veterinarian the summer of her sophomore year at college.

"Arizona!" he'd said, rounding on her in disbelief. "Jess, do you have any idea how far away that is?"

"It's a good opportunity for me. I'm lucky to have been chosen. The practice specializes in horses."

"Why can't you work with Doc Cooper? He does horses. He does cows, pigs, sheep. Hell, he does it all. And he'd love to have your help."

"I want to learn everything I can, Guthrie. I need to.

This lady doc's real smart, real good at what she does. I'm going. I've already accepted the offer. I'm sorry if you don't approve and I realize it'll be hard being so far apart.''

"Hard?'' he'd said. "I don't know how I'll ever survive without you.''

She'd lost her temper at him then. She'd reached up and snatched that hat from his head and flung it into the creek. "Dammit, Guthrie Sloane, all you ever think about is yourself!'' Not exactly true, of course, but she'd been angry.

He'd had to jump into the water to fetch his hat. It'd been cold, too. Early spring, the ice barely out. He'd retrieved it, though, and he'd never said another word about her summer job in Arizona.

As he came down the slope Jessie spotted another man far above, nearly hidden in the trees, but it was Guthrie she watched. And then he was close enough to touch her. He sank to his knees, braced his palms against his thighs and struggled to catch his breath.

They stared at each other, his shoulders heaving, a pandemonium of emotions churning in her.

"You all right?'' he asked, as soon as he could speak.

She nodded. "I'm fine, but Blue's hurt,'' she said.

"How bad?''

"Bad.'' And then, to her absolute mortification, her eyes filled with tears. She turned away, blinking back their sharp sting.

"It's okay, Jess,'' he said. "We'll get her to Cooper. He'll fix her up. What about you? Badger told me you busted your arm a few days ago.'' She gazed down at Blue, unable to speak past the ache in her throat. Tears spilled down her cheeks, and silently she damned herself for being weak. "You're all wet,'' he said. "We need to get you home and into some dry things,'' he said. He touched her shoulder. She stiffened and shook her head.

"Don't."

He pulled his hand away. "Let's have a look at Blue," he said. Jessie tried to unzip her parka but couldn't with just one hand. She dropped her eyes while Guthrie did it for her, then gently extricated the little cow dog from her warm cocoon. "Hey, Blue," he said as he drew out the dog gently and cradled her in his arms. "Hey, old girl. Easy… It's all right, I've got you." He glanced at Jessie. "What happened?"

"Bear," Jessie said.

"She sure enough looks clawed," he said as he stroked Blue's head. "Lost a lot of blood?"

She nodded. "She's pretty weak. I tried to bind up the worst wounds."

"You did just fine. She's tough. She'll be all right."

Jessie raised her brimming eyes to his and shook her head. "She can't die on me. Not now."

"She won't. We'll get her home, take her to Doc Cooper's…"

They heard the sound at the same time and turned their heads simultaneously toward it. It was faint but growing louder, a rumble that sharpened and defined itself as it approached. A helicopter snaked out of the ravine from which she'd just walked. It came into view barely above tree height, skimming right over the top of McCutcheon, so close and looming so large that both she and Guthrie, though already on their knees, ducked. Instead of passing straight overhead, it circled and hovered for a few moments, long enough for her to see an arm wave out the passenger-side window and for her to read the big letters on the side.

Yellowstone HeloTours.

Jessie lifted her own arm in startled response, wondering what the devil Joe Nash would be doing flying his sight-seeing clients way out here. He seemed to be looking for a place to land. The big machine thumped its way down-slope about five hundred feet from where she stood and then, in a clearing scarcely big enough for the spinning helicopter's blades, it set down. The passenger jumped out and raced toward her in a crouch. He was dressed in a green wool Filson jacket that sported a prominent and familiar shoulder patch.

Jessie rose to her feet and stared with disbelief at the entire spectacle. As Comstock drew near, she turned to Guthrie, who was still on his knees, holding Blue, and asked in a rush of remembered anger, "What are you doing here, anyway? I thought you ran off to Alaska!"

CHAPTER FIVE

BEN COMSTOCK HAD BEEN a warden for nearly twenty years. He'd passed through all the standard phases a warden goes through, from the idealism of youth to the disillusionment of experience. He'd seen it all, and he'd long since stopped believing he could single-handedly protect and defend the wilderness and wildlife of Montana. Even though he was aware that Joe Nash had broken just about every game law in existence, slyly eluding all the traps Comstock had set for him, he never hesitated to call on Joe when he needed his services. And right now, he was glad he had. He had both considerable affection and tremendous respect for Jessie Weaver. He'd known her since she was a little girl, having spent many a pleasurable evening at the Weaver ranch, playing poker at the kitchen table and sharing good sipping whiskey with her father.

He'd heard from Bernie that she'd just sold the ranch. For her to do it had taken a lot of guts. He hadn't really believed she'd have deliberately ridden out in the midst of a freak autumn snowstorm, hoping she'd freeze to death up on that mountain she loved, but the doubts had nagged at him ever since he'd gotten the call that she was missing. She had to be pretty depressed after losing her father, breaking up with Guthrie Sloane and now losing the ranch, as well.

No doubt his relief at finding her alive and well showed

plainly on his face as he approached. "Good to see you, Jessie," he said. "Can you make it to the chopper?"

"I'm fine, but my cow dog's hurt."

Guthrie struggled to his feet, holding the injured dog, and Comstock eyed him keenly. He was looking a mite winded, Guthrie was. Hell, that was to be expected. The boy had run more than ten miles of rough mountain trail on snowshoes, searching for his girl. Guess he had a right to appear wrung out. But that wasn't the whole of what was ailing him, either. He felt a strong twinge of paternal pity for Guthrie Sloane. "Sorry to have taken so long getting our tails up here," he said. "The storm pretty much shut everything down. You all right, son?"

A curt nod. "McCutcheon's up on the hill. He's tuckered out. Maybe you could give him a ride back to the ranch."

"The chopper carries four, but I'm sure we can fit you in, too. Jessie doesn't weigh much more than that dog of hers."

"No, thanks. It's not that far to the main road, and you'll make better time with a lighter load. You'll take care of Jess?"

"You know I will." Comstock nodded, gently lifting the injured dog out of Guthrie's arms. "I'll get them loaded while you fetch McCutcheon down." Squinting against the glare of the sun on the snow, both men glanced to where McCutcheon had last been seen. "Oh, jiminy," Comstock said. "You see what I see?"

Guthrie's eyes narrowed. "Damn! You suppose he's had a heart attack?"

"Well, he's definitely down, and the way he's lying doesn't look quite natural, does it?"

Without another word Guthrie started slogging, head down, back up the slope.

Badger had seen a lot of things in his seventy-eight years, but he'd never seen a helicopter land up close. He heard the big machine appraoch long before it set down in front of the Weaver ranch, causing a stampeding panic among the horses corralled next to the pole barn. He stood on the porch, hands shoved deep in the pockets of his old sheepskin coat, and watched as Ben Comstock jumped out of the helicopter's side door. He reached up and handed down none other than Jessie Weaver.

Badger nodded a greeting to Comstock. He'd known darn well that Jessie would be okay. She probably would've walked out herself in another hour or so. The chopper had passed overhead not ten minutes ago, so she had to have been close to home when they found her. 'Course, a fast machine like Joe Nash's could cover some ground in ten minutes.

"Badger!" Jessie said as she climbed the porch steps. She stopped in front of him and stared, then glanced past him to where Steven stood in the kitchen doorway, watching silently. "If the both of you are here, I guess maybe the whole town's in the kitchen."

"No...no, they're not. The state police and Park County Search and Rescue are at the Longhorn, waitin' on Comstock's call." Badger shifted under the burn of her eyes. Jessie didn't like an audience. He understood that better than anyone. Still, she hadn't rounded on that Indian lawyer. In fact, unless he'd gotten too old to read sign, Jessie and that lawyer were real glad to see each other.

"Badger, I need you to drive out and meet Guthrie," she said. "He'll be coming onto the road about three miles shy of Katy Junction near the Bear Creek crossing. You know the place." She was unbuckling her chaps one-handed as she spoke. That done, she flung them, dark and heavy with meltwater, over the porch railing. Badger stood back, fidgeting. He knew better than to offer to help.

"I'll get right out there," he said.

"I expect he'll be pretty tired by the time he gets to the road," she said, straightening. "How're the horses? Did Billy make it back?"

Dang, but she looked wrung out! Her eyes were as intense as ever, but they were shadowed with pain and fatigue, and improbable as it seemed, it appeared as though she'd been crying. This upset Badger more than anything else. Jessie Weaver never cried. Never. "Billy's here and the horses are all fine. Fed and watered," he said. "C'mon inside and get out of them wet clothes—warm yourself up. You've had a time of it. That's plain enough to see."

She shook her head, chin lifting, shoulders squaring. "Blue's been hurt. Got all clawed up by a grizzly. Joe's going to drop us at Cooper's on his way to flying McCutcheon to the hospital in Bozeman. He fell and hurt his ankle. Looks broke to me."

"I could drive you to the veterinarian," Steven said, speaking for the first time. He stepped out onto the porch, thumbs hooked in his rear pockets and head canted slightly to one side, but again Badger wasn't fooled. There was nothing casual about the way that Indian lawyer felt about Jessie.

"Thanks, but it'll be quicker in the chopper, and Joe's offered." She looked at him and the faintest of smiles traced her lips. "Thanks," she said once more. She turned and almost as an afterthought as she descended the porch steps, she said over her shoulder, "I never did find my mares."

DOC COOPER WAS DRUNK. It was nearly 11:00 a.m. and he'd already downed nearly a fifth of good Kentucky bourbon, the kind his daddy had drunk way back when times were easy and the land was bountiful and ranchers could pay their vet bills and people still ate red meat and family farms were the mainstay of an honest and hardworking nation. He was drunk and singing a religious ballad his daddy had sung a long time ago about a wheel way up in the middle of the sky.

"Ezekiel saw the wheel, way up in the middle of the sky.
Ezekiel saw the wheel, way in the middle of the sky!"

Those were the only words that he could remember, because he wasn't an overly religious man himself, but that was okay. He didn't know what the wheel was about, either, but that was all right, too. There was snow on the ground, October was nearly played out and the winter would be long and dark and cold. There was nothing else it could be. All the winters out here were the same. The wind blew, the temperature dropped, the snow fell, animals died. Animals were always dying. In fact, anything at all that was alive was always getting hurt or sick or old, and in the end they always died.

And now he'd lost his best friend. A phone call in the middle of the night from Drew's wife, Ramalda, who could barely speak English, but she'd found just enough words to tell him that Drew wouldn't be makin' it to the Halloween Stomp this year. Dammit all, it was enough to drive a man to drink! He raised the bottle for another sip, then sang some more.

"Ezekiel saw the wheel, way up in the middle of the sky.
Ezekiel saw the wheel, way in the middle of the sky!"

And then he heard the sound. A strange deep rhythmic sound that grew louder and louder. He got up, went outside and stood with his eyes upturned. Great God in heaven! Could that be Ezekiel's wheel? Could such a miracle ever happen to him? He raised the bottle in mute salute as the apparition descended from the heavens and a man who resembled the local game warden came forth from it and moved toward him.

"Ezekiel?" Dr. Cooper said. And then he lost his balance and sat down hard on the wooden bench outside the door of his modest house, spilling a generous splash of good Kentucky bourbon onto the weathered porch boards at his feet. He raised the bottle again, reverently. "Welcome to Katy Junction. Welcome!"

JOE NASH GLANCED to look behind him to where Jessie sat next to McCutcheon, cradling the wounded dog in her arms. "Well, Jessie Weaver, offhand I'd say you got yourself a little problem. What's plan B?"

Jessie had never seen Dr. Cooper in this state before. There was no denying that he was severely incapacitated. He wouldn't be able to stitch Blue up or take X rays to check for internal injuries. He wouldn't be able to reassure her that her longtime friend, companion and working partner would be all right. Dr. Cooper couldn't even stand up. She shook her head. "I don't have a plan B," she said, despair curdling her blood. "Blue needs help and she needs it now."

Joe nodded. "Hey, Comstock! C'mon, crawl your official carcass back in here." He shouted out the door. "We're heading for Bozeman. I know a doctor there who owes me a big favor."

Jessie leaned forward. "Blue needs a *veterinarian*."

"Anything Cooper can do, any competent physician can."

"A people doctor doesn't know anything about dogs."

"No offense," Joe said, "but Cooper doesn't know all that much about dogs, either, though I'm told he's a genius with cattle and pigs. C'mon, Comstock! Hurry it up. We got a man here with a busted ankle, and a dog that needs surgery. And if I don't get this chopper back to home base by 5:00 p.m. my posterior is going to be a sling."

"Let me out, Joe," Jessie said, edging toward the door. "I can tend my dog right here, and when Doc sobers up he can help me."

"Not a good plan, little lady," Joe said, powering up the Bell JetRanger as Comstock climbed aboard. "By the looks of him, that old man won't be sober for a week. Pray all the cows and pigs in Katy Junction stay healthy, and just relax and enjoy the ride."

KATY JUNCTION HADN'T known this much excitement since the day the outlaw Billy Bowden shot Lieutenant John Gatlin right in front of his entire regiment back in 1878. The whole town and half the regiment had chased after Bowden, but they'd never caught him. It took a U.S. marshal by the name of Joe Belle down in Arizona Territory to bring that outlaw to justice. Wouldn't that just figure. An Arizona lawman! Probably shot him out of pocket, too. Them damn Arizonians were famous for hiding pistols in their pockets. But no matter. Bowden had deserved what he got.

Badger shook his head and cut himself a plug of tobacco, shifting on the cracked vinyl of the old truck seat and staring at the place where Bear Creek twisted and tumbled out of the foothills.

Yessir, this'd be a topic of conversation for months to come. What were the odds that Guthrie Sloane would come back to roost on the very night Jessie Weaver disappeared? And then he'd taken off after her in the middle of the night; didn't matter that it was snowing like the blue blazes. Found her, too! Lord a'mighty. Surely this would soften her. Couldn't she see that the boy was crazy about her? Always had been; always would be. Maybe he wasn't perfect. Maybe he didn't have a lot of money. Maybe he didn't think exactly the way she did about everything. But hell, Guthrie Sloane was all wool and a yard wide. He'd do to ride the river with.

Badger caught a flash of movement through the pines that flanked the creek. Yep, there he was. Snowshoes over his shoulder, striding along in what was left of the rotting snow. Paying careful attention where he put his feet because the going was slick. Not noticing Badger's truck until he nearly stumbled over it. Badger bumped the horn with the palm of his hand, leaned out the window and spat a stream of tobacco juice. "Hey, mister, wanna ride?"

Guthrie stopped and stood flat-footed, weaving slightly. He stared at Badger for a long blank moment and then recognition glimmered and he said, "She's okay. Jessie's okay. We found her."

"I know that, son. She's bringing the dog to Doc Cooper's place. She sent me here to pick you up."

Guthrie nodded. He looked worse than Jessie had. Hollow-eyed from lack of sleep and reeling with exhaustion. He and Jessie made a pair, that's for certain. "I better go there, then," he said. "Her arm needs tending, but she won't see to herself until she's seen to Blue. And even then she might just let it go."

He explained this very slowly and carefully, as if Badger hadn't known Jessie Weaver all her life.

"Son," Badger said, "you might as well have something to eat first, before you pitch onto your face. You ain't slept in a couple of days, nor eaten in that long, either, by the looks of you. C'mon. Crawl in the truck. Your sister cooks a mean breakfast, and she's expectin' you."

Didn't matter that it was well past noon. Nossir, it didn't. Badger was right. Steak, eggs, home fries and lots of strong black coffee would go down real fine. Real fine. Guthrie nodded. Rubbed his burning eyes. Rubbed the stubble over his jaw. Hadn't shaved since leaving Valdez. Must look like a rough-cut lumberjack. Didn't care one damn bit. Nodded again. "Okay," he said.

GUILT. Jessie crept into the sterile, high-tech room in the surgical wing and sat gingerly on the edge of a plastic chair drawn up beside McCutcheon's hospital bed, completely overwhelmed by guilt. "I'm sorry about your ankle, Mr. McCutcheon," she said. "This is all my fault, you lying here all stove up and Blue being hurt. It's because I didn't bring the mares down earlier. I should've known they'd sneak off that way when they saw me corralling the others. I should've brought them in first. Without Old Gray to help me...I should've known."

"You can't take the credit for breaking my ankle," Mc-Cutcheon said in a gruff voice. "I did that all by myself, with a little help from my snowshoes and a low-flying helicopter that scared the bejesus out of me. And by the way, there's nothing worse than listening to a Catholic at confession."

"I'm not Catholic," Jessie said, taken aback.

"No? Well, you should've been. Anyhow, no one forced me to tramp off looking for you—I did that voluntarily. I'm just glad you're okay."

"Mr. McCutcheon..."

"Caleb. Call me Caleb. Please."

Jessie rose to her feet. "I can't stay. Joe Nash, the helicopter pilot, is waiting for me. Blue's all right. She's been tended to and he's keeping watch on her until I get back. I just wanted to make sure you were all right."

"What time is it?"

"Suppertime. I can smell the food in the hallways." She smiled faintly. She had gone past the point of hunger a long, long while ago. She was light-headed, giddy; she felt as if she could float away. The pain in her arm was the only thing that kept her grounded. That, and the enormous guilt that burdened her conscience. "Are you sure you don't want me to call your wife?"

"In Paris? No, thank you. My condition is hardly life threatening. I just have to get the ankle fixed. She doesn't need to be wringing her hands at my bedside. Anyway, by the time she got here, I'd be gone. They're releasing me as soon as the surgeon can put the bones back together. The doctor I require happens to be missing at the moment, but they're searching for him now."

"I hope they find him soon," Jessie said. "Mr. McCutcheon..."

"Caleb."

"I just want you to know that I'll be off the ranch by the date we agreed on, but I may have to come back to look for my mares. It shouldn't take long for me to find them."

McCutcheon propped himself up on an elbow. "Listen to me. I want you to stay on. I want you to hire some good people to help you. I want you to manage that ranch the way you've always done. I want you to feel the way you've always felt—that it's home. That it's *your* home."

"Nossir, I can't do that. I appreciate the job offer, but I can't stay." She turned to go.

"Wait a minute."

"Goodbye, Mr. McCutcheon."

"Caleb!" he bellowed in protest.

She shook her head and left him then; walked down the gleaming corridor, past the big food carts, past the nurses station, toward the bank of elevators at the far end of the hall. She got into an elevator and pushed the button. Down and down. The doors opened. Basement. Second door on the right off the elevator. She tapped. The door swung inward and Joe grinned at her. "Your little dog's doing just fine. She's awake and wagging her tail and she just told me she wants to go home. So what do you say?"

Jessie entered the room, which was really nothing more than a large linen closet into which Blue had been wheeled on a gurney. The doctor who had owed Joe the big favor had come and gone, and had done an admirable job tending the injured dog. Blue was indeed awake, though very groggy. She thumped her tail at the sight of Jessie and tried to lick Jessie's hand. "Hey, Blue," Jessie said, her eyes stinging.

"Thirty stitches, one pint of IV fluids and no broken bones. The doc called it a textbook case of a grizzly bear attack on a little cow dog."

"Thank you for arranging this, Joe."

"My pleasure. Now, if we can sneak her out of here without getting caught, I'll fly you back to your ranch."

"It's past five o'clock. You're going to get in trouble."

Joe shrugged. "If I'm not in some kind of trouble, then I figure I'm doing something wrong. But don't worry. Comstock called my boss and made things right."

Jessie didn't have to think about the offer for long. She

was rapidly losing her grip on everything. All she wanted was to get back home. Home? She sighed wearily, pushing away her bitter thoughts. "All right," she said. "Thank you."

GUTHRIE SLOANE HAD SPENT a lot of time at the hospital in the weeks prior to the death of Jessie's father. He stepped through the hospital doors and all the awful memories of watching that good man die flooded back. He would have turned tail and run, except that he had to find Jess and he figured she'd be here, right here, in the waiting room on the main floor.

There were lots of people. But this afternoon there was no Jessie Weaver waiting anxiously for his arrival. It had taken him nearly two hours to get here after going to Cooper's place, then making a bunch of phone calls, trying to figure out where she'd gone. When he learned that McCutcheon had just been admitted to the hospital he'd left a message there for Jess. Had she given up on him and left? Had she taken Blue somewhere to get treatment? Was she getting the cast on her arm seen to? Who would know?

He approached the admitting desk, where a kindly woman told him that no, no one had left a message for him. Yes, she did have a message for a Jessie Weaver about meeting a Guthrie Sloane for a ride home, but no, a Jessie Weaver had not responded to the pages. And yes, a Caleb McCutcheon had been admitted that afternoon. Was Guthrie a family member?

Guthrie nodded without hesitating. "My uncle."

The woman checked her computer screen. "He's in room 210. Take the elevator just down the hall..." She leaned over her desk to point.

"I know where it is," Guthrie said, and thanked her.

The surgical wing was quiet. "You say Caleb McCutcheon is your uncle?" The nurse at the desk tipped her head to one side and gazed quizzically up at him. "Why, Guthrie Sloane, I do believe you're trying to pull the wool over me."

Guthrie felt his face heat up. "Well, he…"

"You don't remember me, do you? I went to school with you! Norma Campbell."

"Oh, sure! How are you, Norma?"

"So what do you want with Caleb McCutcheon? Let me guess. It must have something to do with Jessie Weaver. She left here not twenty minutes ago. It seems that he was *her* uncle, too! Why, my goodness. Isn't that a coincidence."

"Well, you see…"

"Yes, I see," Norma said. "Believe me, I see. I got the whole scoop from Jessie. C'mon. I'll let him know you're here. He was asleep a little while ago. I think he was trying to avoid eating his supper and I can't say as I blame him."

"How is he?"

"Oh, he'll be fine. His ankle's pretty badly broken. He broke it in the same place it was broken before by a baseball. My dad was a big White Sox fan and he was watching on TV when it happened! Imagine that. Caleb McCutcheon was the star pitcher for the White Sox, and that busted ankle pretty much ended his career. My dad still swears that the batter hit him on purpose. We've scheduled him for surgery first thing in the morning. He'll be out of here by early afternoon tomorrow once we get everything straightened out." She poked her head into McCutcheon's room. "Mr. McCutcheon? You have another visitor, if you feel up to it," she said cheerfully. "Guthrie Sloane."

"Good," Guthrie heard him say. "Send him in."

McCutcheon was sitting up in the hospital bed, looking

thoroughly disgruntled, his injured leg immobilized in a traction sling. He grinned up at Guthrie. "This is a hell of a note!" he said. "Come on in. Feel like some supper? I haven't touched mine and they only just delivered it. It's some kind of green-and-yellow pasta explosion with a side of canned peas."

Guthrie shook his head. "I'll pass. I just stopped in to check on you."

"Yeah. They gave me some pills for the pain. I feel great, but I'd rather be anyplace except here. You're looking for Jessie, aren't you?"

Guthrie felt the heat come into his face. Was he so transparent?

"She left about half an hour ago. Joe Nash was waiting for her. He arranged medical treatment for her dog—I'm not sure where—but I have a sneaking suspicion that the doctor who was supposed to be fixing my ankle this afternoon was taking care of a cow dog named Blue who'd been clawed up by a grizzly. Anyhow, she said the dog was fine."

"That's good," Guthrie said, relieved. "Blue's a great dog and Jessie's real fond of her." He shoved his hands in his jeans pockets and studied the toes of his boots.

"I offered her a job," McCutcheon said.

"Sir?" Guthrie glanced up questioningly.

"Managing the ranch. Told her she could stay right where she was and hire the people she needed to help run it right."

"She wouldn't do that," Guthrie said. "She's too damn proud."

McCutcheon nodded thoughtfully. "I had hoped she'd change her mind and take me up on the offer. She loves the place and she'd take good care of it. All I want is for the ranch to stay the way it is. I've got no big plans. I'd like to set up housekeeping in that old cabin, hang some paintings on the walls, roll out that Navajo rug I've been holding on to all these years and maybe get myself a bombproof horse to ride. That's all.'' He sighed in frustration. ''I never thought buying a piece of land would be such an ordeal, but it seems I've also acquired her entire past—generations of family history—and all her dreams for the future, as well. I've been lying here thinking that maybe I ought to donate the whole shebang to the Conservancy just so I can quit feeling guilty.''

Guthrie regarded the older man with a grudging smile. ''Or maybe you ought to set up housekeeping in that old cabin by the river. Sounds to me like she sold the place to the right man. She'll always have her family history and her memories, and if I know Jess, she'll find new dreams. She's a survivor.'' He pulled his hands out of his pockets and extended one toward the man on the bed. ''Anyways, it was a pleasure to meet you, Mr. McCutcheon,'' he said, shaking the older man's hand. ''I'm glad everything's going to be okay. I'd best be heading back. Maybe I'll find Jess walking along the highway, carrying that dog in her arms. Knowing Jessie, that wouldn't surprise me a bit.''

He was nearly out the door when McCutcheon called his name. He stopped and turned. ''What about you? Would you be interested in the job if she doesn't want it?''

Guthrie stared. ''You mean, running the ranch?''

''You have your own place, I realize, but I'd pay you a good salary.''

''Well, I...''

''And who knows? Maybe you could convince her to hire on and help you out.''

''Jess?'' Guthrie shook his head. ''Mister, you got a lot to learn about that girl.''

WITH THE BELL JETRANGER flying at 132 miles an hour, it took Joe thirty minutes to drop off Comstock at his vehicle on the outskirts of Katy Junction and return Jessie Weaver to the historic Weaver ranch. He carried the groggy dog into the ranch house for her and laid it gently on a blanket behind the woodstove. "There," he said, straightening. "Home safe."

"I don't know how to thank you, Joe," Jessie said, trailing him wearily into the kitchen. "Could I fix you a cup of coffee?"

Joe glanced around at the sparsely furnished room. "Got to get that chopper back before my luck runs out. Another time, maybe." He paused at the door and looked back over his shoulder. "That bear I saw," he said. "I bet it's the same one that's been pestering this area for the past five years. Biggest damn grizzly I've ever seen."

"I guess it could be," Jessie said.

"Bears that kill livestock can be taken care of," he suggested diplomatically.

"That bear was just being a bear. He belongs to this land more than you or I. Anyway, we don't even know that it killed the horse. That mare could have died of half a hundred other causes. Leave it be, Joe. I'm not for holding a grudge against a grizzly."

Joe shrugged. "It's your horse and your dog."

Strange woman, he thought, walking back out to the chopper. Every now and then he'd think about seducing her—not only was she beautiful, but she was an heiress, as well. But he was juggling too many other warm and willing women as it was.

Then, too, there was always Guthrie Sloane to consider. He'd hate to get into a tangle with him, and while it was rumored that Jessie and Guthrie had parted ways a while back, Guthrie plainly wore his heart on his sleeve. He probably wouldn't take kindly to anyone who paid too much attention to Jessie Weaver.

Joe climbed back into the chopper and strapped himself in. She came out onto the porch to wave him off, and he gave her a little salute as he lifted the chopper off the ground. Jessie Weaver might not be his type, but she had grit, and he admired that a great deal, especially in a beautiful woman.

JESSIE WATCHED the chopper disappear and then went back inside and lit the lamp against the gathering darkness. She set it on the kitchen table and lowered herself slowly into a chair. The room was still warm, thanks to the fire Badger had made in the cookstove. The few handfuls of tinder and kindling had ignited quickly, and she'd put on the coffeepot to heat. Her legs ached from all the walking, her arm throbbed unbearably and she was completely exhausted. But it was enough that the room was warm and her beloved dog was all right.

For now she just needed to sit here, lean forward, lay her head on her arm, close her eyes... Lord, it felt so good just to close her eyes....

DARK AGAIN. Guthrie felt as though he'd driven down enough dark highways to last him a lifetime. That final mile of muddy ranch road was the longest and darkest mile of all, and he was relieved to see lamplight glowing through the kitchen window as he pulled to a stop and cut the truck's ignition. He climbed the porch steps on legs that ached with weariness and knocked on the kitchen door. Knocked again. After the third knock, he turned the knob and pushed the door open. He saw her immediately, asleep at the kitchen table.

The stove was going and steam plumed from the coffeepot, but there was no coffee in it yet. The can was on the counter. He picked it up, opened it and shook enough Colombian roast into the coffeepot to make a respectable cowboy brew. Fed a few more sticks into the firebox. Took two mugs out of the cupboard and set them on the table. Bent over Blue and stroked the top of her head very, very gently. "Hey, old girl, how're you making it?" he said to the dog, who thumped her tail in groggy recognition.

He sat down across from Jessie at the kitchen table, leaned his weight on his elbows and studied her. In sleep she looked as innocent as a child, and in many ways she still was. How could she possibly look so beautiful after what she'd been through? So angelic, so delicate, so fragile, so vulnerable, when she was without a doubt one of the toughest people on the face of the planet? How would he get over being in love with her? All summer long he'd battled with his feelings and was no closer to a cure. The pain of losing her still twisted him up inside. Just being this close…

The smell of boiling coffee permeated the room. Her long dark eyelashes fluttered on her cheek. She drew a deep breath and her eyes opened. She stared blankly at the glowing oil lamp. Then she shifted her gaze and spotted him sitting there, watching her. Sleep abruptly abandoned her. She lifted her head up off her arm and regarded him as warily as a startled deer.

"I went to Doc Cooper's place to pick you up," he said. She didn't reply, just sat up slowly and raised her hand to brush her hair back from her forehead. "When you weren't there, I drove to the hospital, and when you weren't *there,* I came back here to make sure you'd gotten home okay," Guthrie said. He pushed out of his chair and poured two cups of strong coffee, then placed one in front of her. "I saw McCutcheon at the hospital," he said, returning to his chair. "They're operating on his ankle tomorrow morning." Guthrie raised his cup, blew across the surface of the strong black brew, lowered it again. Too hot yet. "Your cast is falling apart," he said. "I expect you got it wet last night. Don't know why they didn't fix it for you while you were at the hospital. Are they all blind?"

She watched him, not touching her coffee, not speaking. When at length he rose from his chair her eyes followed him. He lit a second lamp, adjusted the wick and replaced the chimney, then left the room carrying the lamp down the hall off the kitchen to her bedroom and returning almost immediately, empty handed. "I'm putting you to bed," he said, as without further ceremony he pulled her chair back from the table, raised her to her feet and lifted her effortlessly into his arms.

She didn't have the strength to protest, the energy to speak. Was barely conscious enough to be aware that he was tugging off her boots, stripping the wet wool socks from her blistered feet, drawing the waist of her damp denim jeans over her hips, her ankles, and peeling the long johns off after. He rubbed her feet with his rough warm hands, pulled the blankets up over her, wool blankets and the down comforter, thick and warm. He was saying something to her, but she couldn't quite make it out. So tired. She was so very, very tired.

She slept.

CHAPTER SIX

IN THE NIGHT it came to him. The Idea. Guthrie lay on the hard lumpy sofa in the living room of the Weaver ranch house, hands laced behind his head, and stared up into the darkness. It was a good idea, about how to keep Jessie here at the ranch, on the land she loved. It came to him like a dream; or perhaps it was a dream—he didn't know anymore. His dreams got all tangled up with reality sometimes. So many of his dreams had been about Jessie.

The seeds of this idea had been planted years ago. Years and years. He was eighteen, just barely. He remembered the day. It was hot. Lord, it was hot! Summertime. No wind. The midday sun was burning down and he'd stripped his shirt off, tossed it aside, baring his upper body to the scorch. He kept the leather gloves on his hands so as not to be blistered by the posthole digger. Seemed he spent most of his time on the Weaver ranch digging postholes and mending barbed-wire fence. He and Jessie, working together, riding the fence lines. It was a big job, a steady job, and it was never done. Cows were always pushing fences down. Fence posts were always rotting off. The wire was always drooping somewhere in a slack twist that needed tightening.

Jess was sweating right alongside him, working hard the way she always did. She used a crowbar to loosen the flinty soil, driving it down over and over with all her might until her strength ran out and she slumped onto her heels, and then he used the posthole digger to excavate what she'd loosened.

Damn, but it was brutal work. He loved it, though. Loved being with her, no matter what they were doing. Loved being near her. Loved the smell of her skin and hair, the sound of her voice; loved the way she moved, and the way she would sometimes pause in the midst of the most mundane of tasks and look around her as if seeing the beauty of it all for the very first time.

"I hate these fences!" she said vehemently when she paused for breath. She'd lost her hat somehow; it'd come off in all the struggle between her, the crowbar and the unyielding earth. She stood bareheaded, her long dark braid over her shoulder, her eyes young and disillusioned, deeply and intensely angry. "I *hate* barbed-wire fences!" she repeated, driving the crowbar into the earth between her booted feet. "Someday, when this place is mine, really mine, I'm going to tear all these damn fences down and then I'm going to rip out all the fence posts and make a big bonfire out of them!"

Guthrie had looked upon her with a kind of awe. Those were fighting words, rebellious words, the words of an environmental visionary, not a cattle rancher. Hell, words like that in a place like this could get a man tarred and feathered and a woman outcast for life. This was cattle country, through and through.

"Really?" he said, leaning on the posthole digger.

"Picture it without the fences, Guthrie. Picture it. No telephone poles, no electric lines, no houses. Just the plains and the mountains going on and on, reaching out forever, and the wind blowing across the entire of it and the bison and wild horses running free. We'll never see it like that.

We missed out by a century or better. But there's enough of it here to make a bit of it right again. The Weaver ranch is big enough to bring a little of it back!''

He'd been in love with Jess almost since the moment he'd first laid eyes on her, but until that day he hadn't known the true depth and the awful power of that love. He'd tried so desperately to share her dream of how the West should be, and to ease the pain she felt at how it really was. "Okay," he said. "When the time comes, I'll help you tear these fences down."

Her eyes had flashed with righteous anger. "You think I'm joking, Guthrie Sloane, but I'm not!''

"Hell, I know that." Guthrie threw down the posthole digger, wiped the sweat from his brow and eyed her with a faint grin. "Let's quit this job," he said.

"Now? We aren't done."

"I know that, too, but what difference does it make if we're going to be ripping all this out in a few short years? The hell with it! Let's go swimming. It's hotter'n Hades and there's this bend in the creek where the water runs deep and cold and sweet grass grows along the banks..."

Guthrie's dream was the reality of another time. His Idea involved the barbed-wire fences that Jess hated, but his dream was of Jessie herself. He lay in the stillness of the night and listened to the beating of his heart, remembering how he and Jessie had gone to the creek that hot afternoon and swum in the shade of the overhanging trees that lined the banks. Remembering how they'd kissed afterward, and how her lithe, sensuous body had moved passionately beneath his.

How had things turned so bad between them? How could something that had once been so beautiful ever have turned so ugly? He lay for a long time wondering, but could find no answers to their failed relationship in the darkness.

JESSIE OPENED her eyes to the familiar sight of the old cabbage rose wallpaper bathed in early light. Morning, and one of her very last to awake in this bedroom. Last night… Had Guthrie really been here? She barely remembered any of it. She hurt all over and wanted nothing more than to slide back into a deep and dreamless sleep, but there was so much to be done. There was always so much to be done—

Coffee. She smelled the sharp rich fragrance of it. Her bedroom door was ajar to let in the heat from the kitchen. She heard small domestic noises and movements. The scrape of a chair pushing back. A man's voice speaking gently. Guthrie, talking to Blue. "All right, old girl," she heard him say. "I'll help you down the porch steps. C'mon, that's it. Easy does it. Good girl." The sound of the kitchen door opening, closing. Then a long and peaceful quiet.

She sat up, pushing the blankets down around her waist. The pain in her arm had become so constant it seemed almost normal. Funny that she hadn't noticed it yesterday, but the cast almost looked as if it had come unglued, and there was a definite crook to it that hadn't been there when they'd put it on, a bend where there shouldn't be one. Damn! As if she needed another problem right now.

She was wearing nothing but a pair of cotton briefs and a camisole, though she couldn't recall undressing. Her stomach growled and the intense hunger she felt became yet another pain to deal with. Ravenous! She could eat a horse. Oh, God. Fox! Could that grizzly have killed Fox? Could such a fate befall such a wily mustang?

And what about Guthrie? When had he gotten back from Alaska? How did he come to find her up on Montana Mountain? Had he spent the night here at the ranch? And what was she going to say to him when she walked out that bedroom door after five months of angry silence?

Well, the first thing to do was get dressed. She stood beside the bed and cast a questioning look around the bedroom. Where had she laid her clothes? Everything she owned was packed up in boxes and stacked in the shed, including all her clothes. So where...?

Okay. Her clothes were gone. Right now it hardly mattered. She pulled a blanket off the bed, wrapped it around herself and padded barefoot into the warm kitchen, where atop the woodstove a pot of strong coffee simmered and on the table a clean mug waited. She filled it, breathed the aroma, was raising it for that first desperately needed sip, when the kitchen door opened and Guthrie came in, carrying Blue in his arms. He grinned when he saw her, that broad handsome grin of his that held nothing back.

"'Mornin'," he said, gently returning the dog to her bed behind the stove. "Blue had some trouble with the porch steps, but she's doing just fine otherwise. She ate a good breakfast and I took her out to do her duty." He rose to his full height and reached for a cast-iron fry pan hanging from a hook on the wall. "I'll cook you up some breakfast. There isn't much in the larder, but I scrounged up a can of corned-beef hash and a half-dozen eggs. That'll hold you till we get to town."

Jessie sat down at the table and watched him, raising her cup again for that first swallow of coffee. Hot, strong and restorative. She took another. He opened the can of hash and spooned it into the frying pan, flattened it out and waited until it was sizzling good, then flipped it with the spatula.

"Your clothes are dry," he said over his shoulder. "I hung them behind the stove last night. They're on that chair," he said, nodding in the appropriate direction. "Your pants are ripped, you've worn holes in the heels of your socks and you'll need to oil your chaps up good. I expect you traveled far enough to have gotten sick of walking, especially carrying Blue." He fried up the hash and then cracked the eggs right into it, scrambling the concoction and cooking it until the eggs had set up. He gave her most of the food, piling it onto the only tin plate, stabbing a fork into it, then sliding the plate in front of her. "Couldn't find any bread, so no toast," he said. "Sorry." He sat down opposite her and ate the remainder right out of the frying pan. He took a big swallow of coffee from his own cup and leaned back in his chair, eyes narrowing. "Okay," he said. "Where's the cat?"

Jessie frowned. "What cat?"

"The cat that's got your tongue. You never did talk much, but you used to make words once in a while. Seems as though you might have a thing or two to say after all that's happened."

"Thank you for breakfast."

"That's not what I was fishing for, but you're welcome. Go ahead and eat. It's not fancy, but it tastes pretty good."

At that moment her stomach let out another growl, which was loud enough to get an answering response from Blue. She picked up her fork and followed Guthrie's example. He was right. The food was delicious. The best meal she'd ever eaten. She cleaned her plate and sat back, feeling the warm strength of it percolate through her. She could have eaten more. She could have eaten ten times the amount, but he was right about the larder being bare. She'd cleaned the cupboards out over the past month, using up all the food she normally had on hand. There was really nothing left except some spices and a dozen highly suspect jars of home-canned mincemeat that had to be twenty years old or better.

"My truck broke down. Fuel pump went. McCutcheon fixed it, so I can load all the boxes today," she said.

"Nope. 'Fraid not," he said with a shake of his head. "Today I'm taking you into town to get that arm of yours tended. I might make a scene, too. All those supposed professionals letting you walk out of that hospital yesterday without fixing that cast. That's shameful!"

"It wasn't like this yesterday. I'd have noticed."

"The only thing you noticed yesterday was that Blue was hurt. Today you're getting your arm fixed, unless you want it to be permanently bent like that." Guthrie pushed out of his chair and took her plate and his to the sink. "McCutcheon'll be getting out of the hospital today. We could pick him up, since we'll be there anyhow. Bring him back here. What shape is that old cabin in? Is it livable?"

"He can stay wherever he pleases. It's his place now."

"He favors that old cabin."

"It needs a good cleaning, but it's as sound as a dollar, and it has a good roof."

"He told me you could stay right here in the house," Guthrie said, pouring hot water into the dishpan.

"He might have told you that, but I'm not staying."

"He told me he offered you a good job, too."

"I have to find the mares and bring them down, that's all. Then I'm going."

"He was real worried about you. Nearly killed himself, climbing up into the pass looking for you. Even after he busted his ankle and was rolling around in that terrible pain, all he could say to me when I got to him was, 'Is she okay?'''

"I was fine. I didn't need a helicopter looking for me. I didn't need the two of you looking for me. I wasn't the least bit lost."

"'Course, he isn't going to be able to stay out here by himself. Not with that bad ankle. Too bad. I got the impression he's a private person. And he's kind of like you, the way he thinks about the land. Living out here would probably be real good medicine for him. He talked about fixing up that old cabin..."

Jessie stood and snatched her neatly folded clothes off the chair. She carried them into the bedroom and kicked the door shut behind her with a bang, leaving Guthrie to wash the breakfast dishes all by his lonesome.

"WE'RE CUTTING YOU LOOSE," Dr. Stowell said, standing at the foot of McCutcheon's bed and rubbing a kink in the back of his neck. "Your ankle is as fixed as it's going to get right now, but you'll be wearing that walking cast for a lot longer than you'd like. I guess the only thing I can add is that in future maybe you should avoid steep mountain treks on snowshoes."

"No problem. I've learned my lesson." McCutcheon swung his legs over the edge of the bed. "May I get dressed?"

"If you want to leave here looking normal, I'd certainly suggest it. Your chauffeur awaits. I'll get your release forms filled out and be back in two shakes."

"My chauffeur?"

"Actually I believe it's your nephew. He's in the waiting room...along with your niece."

"Ah, yes. Of course." McCutcheon nodded as if he had fully expected such attendance by his caring and concerned relatives.

Dr. Stowell paused at the door. "Incidentally, your niece has become somewhat of a legend here in the past two days, what with getting her dog illicitly stitched up by one of our staff doctors down in the basement yesterday afternoon and somehow neglecting her broken arm in the process. By the way, we had to perform an open reduction on it this morning—right after your surgery, as a matter of fact—to fix the considerable damage she'd done to it in the past two days.

"We've put two traction pins in it to keep the bones pointing in the right direction this time. She needs to take very good care of it. By that I mean, no more rowdy cowgirling for a while. Her orders are to take it nice and easy. As her 'uncle,' I would expect you to strictly enforce that edict."

"Oh, I will," McCutcheon solemnly reassured the concerned physician. After he'd left the room he dressed himself hastily in the same clothing he'd worn yesterday on his arduous mountain trek. It was somewhat the worse for wear, especially the left pant leg, which had been cut clear up to the crotch, but at least the clothes were dry. "And just how in hell does he expect me to do that?" he muttered as he zipped up his pants. "No one could possibly enforce any edict on that girl." He was startled by the reappearance of Dr. Stowell as he buttoned his shirt.

"Sorry," the doctor said, looking sheepish. "I don't like to ask such a thing, but my son made me promise." He reached into his lab coat and withdrew a baseball. "I was wondering, would you...?"

McCutcheon's fingers stilled. He grinned. "I'd be glad

to." And with the pen the doctor handed him, he signed the baseball.

Ten minutes later he was free to leave. Guthrie Sloane and Jessie Weaver waited in the hallway outside his room. Jessie stood flat-footed and stone-faced, her injured forearm now sporting an evil-looking metal apparatus that was connected to pins inserted into the bones of her forearm. Guthrie Sloane stood behind an empty wheelchair, which, McCutcheon assumed, was for him.

"Hello," he said, leaning on the crutches he'd barely begun to learn how to use. "Thanks for picking me up. Steven stopped in earlier and offered to do the same. He said for me to call when I was ready."

"We were here anyhow," Guthrie said. "And being as you already have a car back at the ranch, we thought it made more sense to drive you out. No point in calling him except to tell him you're all set."

"Well. Thank you." The nurse in attendance motioned for him to get into the wheelchair. He did so grudgingly, knowing from experience that hospital rules were hospital rules and arguing that he was perfectly capable of limping out under his own power was pointless. Nevertheless, to be carted out in a wheelchair, especially in front of Jessie Weaver, was the ultimate degradation. He sat obediently, feeling foolish and old and wondering if life was just going to keep sliding steadily downhill.

"You could stay in that old cabin tonight if you like," Guthrie said as he pushed the wheelchair toward the elevator. "My sister cleaned it for you today. She was going to stock the cupboards, too."

McCutcheon was overwhelmed by the magnitude of this kindness. He sat in silence while they waited for the elevator, and when it finally came and they were inside it, he said very quietly in a voice hoarse with emotion, "Thank you."

GUTHRIE'S PICKUP had a bench seat. Jessie sat in the middle—an awkward place to be in a truck with a standard transmission. She sat in silence, staring straight ahead at the empty road that stretched out before them, leading them toward the mountains of home.

Guthrie drove carefully, acutely aware of Jessie's rigid body pressed up against his in the cramped cab. She was mad. Oh, Lord, she was hopping mad! They'd had to knock her out to fix her arm. She'd protested the whole thing, of course, right from the start, but after the X rays and after the two doctors on staff had concurred Guthrie had laid down the law to her. He'd told her how it was going to be and they had squared off, right there in the emergency room and right in front of a full complement of wide-eyed staff. "You're going to do this thing!" he'd told her.

"They can fix my arm without knocking me out!" she'd said.

"No, they can't. Don't you understand what they told you? They have to cut your arm open and expose the ends of the bones. That's blood-and-guts stuff. You can't be awake for that! Now, sign the damn form or I'll sign it for you!"

"You're not my guardian!"

"I'm your best friend in the whole wide world and that makes me your guardian. Sign that piece of paper, Jess. I'm tired. You're tired. Let's get this over with so's I can take you back home."

"I don't have a home anymore. And I don't give a damn what happens to my arm!"

He'd bent over her, hands closing on her shoulders, and stared her straight in the eye. "Quit feelin' sorry for yourself! We've got to get back so's we can take care of Blue, feed and water the horses, check on the cattle. There're chores to be done and no one to do them but us. Now, sign that damn form!"

She'd signed it, all right, but the sparks had flown. She didn't like being told what to do. Hadn't liked feeling helpless. Hadn't wanted to be knocked out to have her arm cut open. Truth was, he didn't blame her one bit, but those were the breaks. Literally. And now she was sitting next to him, still reeling from the anesthesia but as tight as a bowstring and spitting mad to boot, all of which made him very uneasy. She should have been slumped against him, limp as a dishrag, dopey and drooling, the way Blue had been last night.

"Well, I swear," he said suddenly. "Wasn't that Grover drivin' that car that just passed us? Grover Vining? I thought they'd locked him up for a long time when he robbed that store in Livingston."

No response from Jessie, but McCutcheon dutifully turned his head, eyebrows raised. "He robbed a store?"

"Yessir. Robbed the grocery at gunpoint last year. Got away with forty dollars and two packs of Marlboro cigarettes and made it as far as Gallatin before they caught him. Actually, he turned himself in, didn't he, Jess?" Silence. "Yessir, he turned himself in at the gas station in Gallatin. Said he'd robbed a store and wouldn't ever get to heaven that way. Or something along those lines. So the guy at the gas station told him to go on home and sleep it off, but Grover made him call the store in Livingston. So he did. And it turned out Grover was tellin' the truth.

"Well now, the guy at the gas station in Gallatin didn't

really know what to do. Here was this dangerous robber who was insisting that he hold him there until the police could arrive and properly arrest him. But the guy got scared that Grover would pull a gun on him and do something stupid like shoot him, so he told him to git on out of there.''

"No kidding?" McCutcheon eased a cramp in his injured leg, stretched it out and bumped Jessie accidentally. "Sorry," he said quickly, feeling her flinch. "What happened then?"

"Well, Grover didn't quite know what to do. So he drove back to Livingston and went back into the store with the two packs of Marlboros, less three cigarettes, and all the money except what he'd spent on gas in Gallatin, and he gave everything back.''

"And then the cops came," McCutcheon predicted.

"Oh, hell, yes. Sirens, flashing lights, the whole shebang. They arrested Grover and convicted him of all sorts of nasty things. Grover's always been a few bullets shy of a full load, but I wouldn't consider him too dangerous. The law did, though. Didn't they sentence him to five years with all but two suspended?" Guthrie said to Jessie.

Another big silence.

"Well, anyhow," Guthrie continued, "I know that was Grover who just passed us, so he must have gotten out on good behavior or something.''

"Ah," McCutcheon said. The tension inside the truck was increasing by the moment. He was beginning to wish he'd rented a car to get himself back to Katy Junction. In fact, he was almost beginning to wish he'd never heard of a place called Katy Junction. "Maybe we could stop in town and get something to eat at the café before it closes," he suggested tactfully.

"If I know my sister, she's left something for us to eat at the ranch. But I would like to stop at the store to pick up a few things, just in case. And we should swing by your motel room, too. Collect your bags."

"I could just as easily stay there," McCutcheon offered. "It might be best if I did."

"Wouldn't make much sense, would it? Hell, you own one of the prettiest ranches in the West. You might as well start enjoying it."

McCutcheon cringed inwardly. He half expected Jessie Weaver to whip out a six-gun and shoot both of them.

He wouldn't have blamed her one bit.

CHAPTER SEVEN

THEY MADE IT BACK to the ranch before dark. Time enough to get settled in. Time enough to do evening chores. Time enough to eat. Bernie had been there. Smoke was curling from the chimney of the old cabin. Guthrie drove the truck as near to it as he could get, took McCutcheon's bags from the back and carried them inside, while McCutcheon struggled to climb down out of the truck. It was warm in the cabin, the smells of Spic and Span, wood smoke and Murphy's oil soap attesting to his sister's domestic ministrations. With the porch door ajar, the room filled with the soothing sound of the creek rushing past.

McCutcheon thumped awkwardly up onto the porch and paused there. He leaned on his crutches, looked around at the spectacular scenery and drew a deep, grateful breath. "Jesus," he said, but the way he said it, he wasn't swearing.

"I put your bags in the bedroom," Guthrie said. "Bernie's fixed the place up real nice. I'm going to get Jess situated and then I'll come back and check on you."

"I'll be fine. I'll be more than fine. Don't worry about me. This is as close to heaven as I'll ever get. You go on, take care of that girl. And thank you. Thank you for everything."

Guthrie was reluctant to return to the truck. Jess had moved over as far as she could and sat pressed up against the passenger-side door. He climbed in and slammed his door shut. "I'll tend to the horses," he said as he pointed the truck up the last stretch of road. From the old cabin to the ranch house was about one quarter of a mile. "And I'll check on the cattle, though I expect they're fine. I can carry Blue down the porch steps if she still can't navigate them. Then I'll leave you alone. I guess that's what you're wantin' most of all."

He parked in front of the ranch house, picked up the bag of groceries he'd bought at the store and followed Jessie up the porch steps. She opened the kitchen door and was met by a very lonely little dog who would have leaped up into her arms if she'd had the strength. Jessie knelt and put one arm around her.

"Blue! Hey, old girl, you're lookin' better! Come on, you must have to go outside." She stepped past Guthrie, dog at her heels, and walked back down the porch steps. The dog followed after her, moving slowly but surely. Guthrie watched until they had both made it safely to the bottom of the steps, and then he turned back into the kitchen and deposited the bag on the table.

His stomach churned with emotion and he could hardly think straight. He was so discouraged that it was hard to see the good in anything. He was still so desperately in love with Jessie Weaver, and she so obviously couldn't stand to be near him. The long summer apart had done nothing to ease her sore feelings toward him. In fact, she seemed madder with him now than she'd ever been.

His sister had left a pot of something delicious-smelling atop the stove. He lifted the lid. Beef stew. And there was a pan of fresh-baked rolls up on the warming shelf, covered over with a clean dish towel. Good girl! Jessie needed a hot home-cooked meal. She'd been through such hell. He fed some fresh firewood into the firebox and nudged the pot of stew over to warm. Then he went back outside to tend the horses. This was simple enough, just a matter of forking down some hay, making sure the water tank was full, arranging eight, equally spaced piles of grain along the edge of the corral, atop each pile of hay, so the horses could each get their share. He leaned over the top rail of the corral and watched them feed…how the pecking order asserted itself. "Hey, Billy Budd," he said to the gelding being pushed from one pile to another by the aggressive young stock. "Stick up for yourself, old man!"

None of the cattle had come in from the range, so he figured they were okay. He returned to the kitchen. Jessie had lit a lamp against the coming dusk. "You'll need to pull Billy out of the upper corral tomorrow," he said. She was filling Blue's dish with kibble and she shot him a hostile glance. "The ladies are picking on him. He's too old and he's worked too hard not to get his fair share."

"I'll take care of him," she said quietly. She put the bowl on the floor and Blue attacked it with enthusiasm.

"I got some stuff at the store. Eggs, milk, bread, butter. Survival food."

"Thanks. I'll pay you back."

"Did the doctor give you anything for pain?"

"I told him I didn't need anything."

Guthrie sighed. "How'd I know you were going to say that? You should've taken what he offered. It'd help you sleep."

"I won't need any help sleeping."

"No, I guess you won't. Not tonight, anyways." Guthrie unpacked the grocery bags and put the perishables in the propane refrigerator. "Hey!" he said. "Lookee here!" He removed the bottle of wine he found secreted within and whistled appreciatively. "It has a cork and everything! Expensive stuff!"

Jessie dropped into a chair. "Bernie," she said, staring

with morbid fascination at the evil-looking contraption on her lower left arm.

"She thinks of everything. Even the right wine for a hearty beef stew."

"It won't work."

"What's that?" Guthrie was rummaging through the empty kitchen drawers for a corkscrew.

"She thinks we'll sit here and drink it together and get married tomorrow or the day after."

"Hell, I'm all for that, but dammit all, I can't find the corkscrew…"

"Guthrie, don't you remember how awful things were between us?"

"It wasn't all bad," he said, digging in his jeans pocket for his jackknife. "Matter of fact, for fifteen years it was great. Just the last of it went wrong. That doesn't mean we can't still be friends, Jess." He used the corkscrew on his knife to pry the cork out and poured two generous measures into the coffee mugs they'd drunk from that morning. He raised his cup. "To friendship."

Jessie raised her eyes and regarded him with open skepticism. "Friendship?"

"No matter where you decide to go, what you decide to do or who you wind up marryin', I'll always be there if you should need me. I guess that's worth drinking to, isn't it?"

The faintest of wry smiles curved her lips. "To friendship," she said, and raised her cup to his.

JOE WAS TAKING a taste of his very first bottle of beer that evening at his favorite saloon in Gardiner when a familiar voice spoke at his elbow. He straightened on his bar stool and glanced sidelong into the face of none other than Senator George Averill Smith.

"Why, good evening, Senator," he said. "I didn't know you were in the valley."

"I flew in this morning for a few days at my lodge and maybe a little elk hunting on the side. Thought you might be free to take me up into the high country." The lean, vulpine senator seated himself side to shoulder with Joe and was immediately served by the bartender with a double martini. He raised it elegantly in mock salute to Joe. The big diamond on his pinkie flashed in the dim light. "Rumor has it that you saw a bear today, Joe," he remarked casually.

Joe took another long swallow of his Coors. "Word certainly gets around quick, doesn't it?"

"I heard it was a big bear. A grizzly."

"Grizzlies are a protected species around here," Joe said, studying his beer bottle.

"Grizzlies that kill and eat livestock are a public menace," the senator amended.

"Well, the thing is, Senator, Jessie Weaver didn't want to lodge a complaint against this particular grizzly, and it's her livestock that bear's been killing."

"That's because she's a tree-hugging bleeding heart. I wouldn't have thought a Weaver could ever stoop to such a level, but she's done it. I trust she survived her latest ordeal." Senator Smith tasted his drink and lowered his glass. "I've never shot a Montana grizzly, Joe," he said.

Joe nodded, reading the fine print on the side of the label.

"That kind of trophy would be worth a lot to me."

"Senator, you know Comstock's been laying for me for years. I've taken you on trophy hunts more times than I can count, and he's watched every one of them, waiting for me to slip up."

The senator nodded. Smiled. "Well, Joe, it'll be worth

an awful lot to you if you don't slip up," he said, standing. "Think about it. I'll be at my lodge and I'm counting on you to give me the answer I want to hear." He patted Joe on the shoulder as though he were an obedient dog and returned to his table, carrying the remainder of his drink.

Joe finished his first beer and started on another. He thought about the big grizzly. Killing that bear wouldn't exactly be a wrong thing. That great beast had been raising hell with the livestock on the Weaver ranch for a long time. Jessie Weaver might not approve of the killing, but her livestock would benefit.

And the bottom line was, so would he.

"YOU'D LIKE ALASKA, Jess," Guthrie said as he ladled out a bowl of stew. He set it before her and dished out another, then carried it to the table. He refilled both their cups with wine and offered her a roll from the pan. "It's pretty country. Hell, it's beautiful. Wide-open, like here, only not as many roads. Most of the people live in Anchorage or Fairbanks, so the rest is pretty untrammeled. I didn't get much of a chance to explore. Worked at the cannery, mostly, gutting salmon. I got promoted to shift supervisor after a while. The money was good, but I can still smell the fish."

Jessie pushed her stew around with the spoon and stared at the steam rising slowly in whorls. The stew smelled wonderful. Everything Bernie made smelled wonderful, yet Jessie had no appetite. She lifted her cup and took a sip of wine.

"You'd like the Yukon, too. Wilder than hell, parts of it. I camped in the Yukon one night on my way home. I heard wolves howling, Jess. A pack of 'em. Made a chill run up my spine. One day we'll hear them here, I expect."

"If people like Joe Nash and his clients don't shoot them first."

"Him and a bunch of others," Guthrie agreed, spooning stew into his mouth and taking a bite of a roll. "But times are changing. Attitudes are changing. One day we won't hate and fear the wild things so much. One day we might learn to be more tolerant."

"Not for a long time."

"Oh, I don't know. Some of the ranchers are already changing their tune about the Yellowstone wolves."

"Senator George Smith keeps them stirred up. Now, there's trash for you!" she said, firing up. "He'd like it if all wolves, mountain lions and grizzly bears were fair game so he could shoot them and put their heads on his walls. He wants to extend the bear-hunting season, expand the limit on elk and allow same-day shooting by hunters who are flown into their camps. He voted to open up the Arctic to oil drilling and he's pushing for an open-pit copper mine in the Gallatin Mountains!"

"Well, he definitely has a beer-and-bullets mentality, and he's serving the interests of the people who got him elected. I guess that's just how politics works. Eat your stew, Jess."

"I don't know why anyone would vote for that lamebrain!"

"Try one of Bernie's rolls. They're great."

"Joe Nash wanted me to file a formal complaint against that grizzly bear."

"That surprised you?"

"He has a hell of a nerve."

"That's a fact. The one thing Joe doesn't lack is nerve."

"That man has no scruples. I can't believe Ben Comstock would be caught dead flying around with him."

"Joe's a good pilot. He can spot a flea on a dog's back.

Comstock uses those skills when he needs them. One of these days, he'll bag Joe. In the meantime, he'll take advantage of him, same as you did. Joe flew you to Bozeman, didn't he? And he arranged for Blue to get fixed up, isn't that right? You expect the world to be black and white, but it's not. Not even a little. Eat, Jess. Before it gets cold.''

''Comstock didn't need Joe's skills yesterday. I was fine.''

''Nobody knew you were fine. Your horse came back without you. You could've been hurt. You've gotten hurt before. I know, it seems pretty near impossible that a gritty Park County cowgirl like Jessie Weaver could ever get hurt. But shit happens to the best of us, doesn't it?'' He stared pointedly at the alien apparatus on her arm.

Jessie glared. ''I broke my arm, that's true, but I got myself to the hospital.''

''What about the time that ornery bull knocked your horse over and you drove it off with your hat? You busted your collarbone that time. Remember?''

''That was nothing!''

''Okay, then how about the day we were baling hay down alongside the river and a big stack of bales fell on you and broke your leg? I had to carry you out to where the truck was parked. That was a long haul. If I hadn't been there when it happened, you'd have had to crawl.''

''If you hadn't been there, it wouldn't have happened in the first place!'' Jessie said. ''You drove the tractor right into all those stacked bales and tipped 'em over onto me. You broke the tractor, too, as I recall. Busted the tie-rod end. That was mighty poor driving.''

''If you hadn't been ripping your shirt off, I never would've hit that stack of hay bales. You distracted the hell out of me!''

"There was a hornet inside it. What did you expect me to do? And anyway, I'd have crawled out of there on my hands and knees if I'd had to."

"I know that. But you've got to admit that my being there was helpful. In fact, you used to like having me around. It never used to bother you a bit until you went off to college."

Jessie prodded a chunk of beef in her bowl of stew. She took another sip of wine and raised her eyes. "That's not true. My going away to college was just a catalyst for something that had been happening between us for a while."

Guthrie sighed and carefully laid down his spoon. "Here we go again. Say it. I'm a chauvinist. I was stifling you. I was jealous and possessive and all I wanted was for you to be barefoot, pregnant and in the kitchen."

Jessie flushed. "That's all true."

"I can't believe you really think that."

"Everything I did was a threat to you. If I went to the university library in Bozeman you nearly had a fit, worrying about me driving so far by myself, about me meeting someone I might, God forbid, be attracted to, about maybe discovering there was a world outside Katy Junction and maybe I might like it and not want to live here anymore. Well, you know what? You were right. All I want to do now is get as far away from this sorry place as I possibly can!"

Guthrie pushed aside his bowl. He sat very still for a few moments, as if gauging her outburst, and then he stood, ran his fingers through his tousled hair and reached his hat off the seat of the empty chair next to him. He turned it round in his strong fingers, eyeing it for a long silent moment, then glanced at her. "I was hoping things might've changed between us, but I guess they haven't.

I'm sorry you feel the way you do. I'm sorry you believe that I ever meant to stand in your way." He moved toward the kitchen door. "I'll look in on McCutcheon before I leave, and be back first thing in the morning."

"There's no need," Jessie said. "I can take care of things here. I've been taking care of things here long enough to know I don't need your help. And all your words about always being there for me no matter what were just empty words. You ran off to Alaska at the first sign of trouble, didn't you? A body can pretend to care—but can't pretend to be there."

He pulled his hat on and stared at her, his eyes shadowed beneath the hat brim. "You were the one who told me to go, Jess. Remember?" Then he strode out the door, closing it quietly behind him. Jessie sat in her chair, heard his truck start up, the tires squelch through the mud as he drove away.

She raised a trembling hand and pressed cold fingertips to her forehead. Her throat ached and her eyes burned. She wanted to cry, but she couldn't. The long struggle leading up to the cataclysmic events of the past year had hollowed her out, emptied her of the ability to feel anything remotely soft and vulnerable. She knew Guthrie still loved her, she knew that she had hurt him terribly with her words and she knew that she'd spoken those words in spiteful anger.

Anger. Of late, it was the only thing she could feel! Terrible pent-up anger about everything. That her father had gotten ill. That the insurance company had raked him over the coals. That the bottom had fallen out of the cattle market. That the medical bills had skyrocketed. That the only way she could save the land she so fiercely loved was to give it up to someone else.

Worst of all, she felt a terrible anger at Guthrie Sloane for running out on her when she had needed him the most.

McCUTCHEON was very much enjoying his evening. Sitting in a comfortably overstuffed chair, his injured ankle propped on a pillowed footstool, with oil lamp, bowl of stew and glass of wine laid out on an end table at his right hand, he was reading an old book he'd found on the shelf. It was entitled The Vigilantes of Montana, and it seemed fitting that on his first night in his new home he should be reading such an account. He was completely absorbed in the story, when he heard the tap at the door.

"Come." He carefully laid a strip of paper to mark his page and looked up as Guthrie Sloane stepped inside. "Chilly night, isn't it?" McCutcheon said. "That woodstove feels good. You were right about your sister. She thought of everything. There was a delicious pot of beef stew, some fresh yeast rolls, a bottle of red wine. Sit down and pour yourself a glass. I'm having a fine old time reading all about one of Montana's most notorious road agents."

"Henry Plummer." Guthrie grinned. "I know the book. Must've read it six or seven times in the years I lived here."

"Did you get Jessie settled in?"

"As much as she'd let me."

McCutcheon had to stifle a laugh behind a cough, but his sympathies were with the young man who stood in the lamplight, looking so glum. "She can be thorny." He pointed to the cupboard. "Glasses are in there. It's a nice wine."

Guthrie took him up on the offer and poured himself a glass. He sat down on the edge of a chair. "I've been thinking. I had an idea last night about how you might get Jess to stay on as ranch manager."

McCutcheon raised his eyebrows. "Oh? I got the definite impression from both of you that nothing would ever convince her to accept that job.''

Guthrie rested his forearms on his knees and admired the ruby hue of the wine. ''Maybe I was wrong. Anyhow, this particular idea has to do with how you happen to feel about barbed-wire fences,'' he said.

McCutcheon reached for his wineglass and settled himself more comfortably in the chair. ''Go on and tell it,'' he said. ''I'm all ears.''

BERNIE HAD PUT IN a long day and she was tired. She would have liked to have closed up early, but her customers had other ideas. Badger was chewing Charlie's ear off and showed no signs of running out of steam. That the two found so much to talk about, seeing each other the way they did on a daily basis, amazed her. She wondered how things were going with Guthrie and Jessie. She wondered if Caleb McCutcheon was enjoying his first evening out at the ranch. She wondered if, with all that had happened, Jessie would change her mind about leaving. Of course she would. She had to. How could she marry Guthrie if she left?

And she had to marry Guthrie. No other man on earth suited her the way Guthrie did, and surely no other man could ever love her as deeply. Yes, Jessie would stay. She and Guthrie would be married out at his place in late spring, or early summer, maybe, when the wildflowers were at their peak and the wild roses along the creek were in full bloom. That sweet little cabin they'd built together would be a pretty backdrop to the day. A few big picnic tables, a bluegrass band, a big bonfire when evening drew near, a big boisterous barbecue with all the trimmings. All of Katy Junction would want to attend.

What would Jessie wear? Somehow Bernie knew that it

wouldn't be a long white wedding gown, though she'd be beautiful in one. No, Jessie would opt for something simple. And Guthrie? Why, he'd look handsome in a white Mexican wedding shirt with a pair of clean black denims and some boot black rubbed into his old cowboy boots. Guthrie would look handsome no matter what he wore. Bernie couldn't understand why Guthrie's looks alone wouldn't melt Jessie. That grin of his, and the strong, calm, masculine competence. And the way he rode a horse. Oh, my, the way he rode a horse!

She envied him his cowboy upbringing. She'd spent her childhood with her mother in assorted big cities. The death of her and Guthrie's father had brought brother and sister back together again. Bernie had arrived in Katy Junction the day of the funeral, a stranger dressed in a simple black dress, standing at the very back of the crowded room, feeling frightened and out of place. Something about Guthrie had seemed vaguely familiar, but twenty years was a long time, and the tall, broad-shouldered, handsome young man bore little resemblance to the toddler she'd known. It wasn't until after the service that she approached him.

"Hi," she said, her voice trembling. "I'm Bernie Sloane, your sister. You probably don't remember me—you were so young I last saw you. You were barely walking, as I recall."

The dark-haired slender young woman standing beside him was the first to react in the silence that followed this announcement. "I'm Jessie Weaver," she said, extending her hand. "I'm so sorry about your father."

"Thank you. I am, too," she said. "I had so many questions I wanted to ask him. I caught the first flight out as soon as Mama told me. Somehow she knew he'd died, and she knew where you were living, but the only thing she ever told me all these years was that Daddy had run off on us a long time ago and taken you with him.''

Bernie vividly recalled Guthrie's expression of shock. ''Well, I'll be damned,'' he said, and then he fell speechless, trying to assimilate the fact that for some unfathomable reason his father had never told him he had a big sister. ''Lord,'' he finally said with a shake of his head. ''I don't understand any of this, and that's no lie.''

Bernie was all adrift and so was he. She gazed up at him and her eyes filled with tears. There was no telling where the truth lay, and they both realized as they stood there, speechless, that in many ways it no longer mattered. Guthrie reached out and took her hand.

''Let's the three of us go get something to eat,'' he said, ''because the two of us have some real serious catching up to do.''

Bernie had fallen in love with the area, with her baby brother again and with Jake Portis, the Ford mechanic. She and Jake wasted little time courting. They were married within the year and they settled into a sturdy little house on the outskirts of town where, shortly thereafter, they commenced raising a family. She'd managed the Longhorn for over a year now and loved it. Loved her husband and kids, too.

Now, if only Guthrie and Jessie would come to their senses...

''Bernie?''

Bernie blinked. She was standing in the middle of the room, holding a pot of coffee. Ben Comstock had just entered the café. He looked as tired as she felt, but he grinned at her when she focused on him. ''You were a million miles away,'' he said, hitching up to a seat at the counter.

''Not that far,'' she retorted, walking around the counter

and filling an ironstone mug. She set it in front of him. "I was planning a wedding."

"I won't ask whose, but if I were you I might hold off awhile before ordering the flowers."

Bernie laughed. "O ye of little faith. What brings you into town at this hour? Did Ellie kick you out?" She teased him about this frequently. Everyone knew about his enduring marriage.

"Nope. Though I will admit that she ought to have a long time ago. Do you know that in two days we will have been married forty-two years?"

"Still like her?"

"She's still my high-school sweetheart."

Bernie smiled. "Ellie's a lucky woman."

"I'm the lucky one. Thanks for the coffee. I was hoping to run into Badger. I see he's here."

"He's been sitting there talking to Charlie since before suppertime. Can I get you something to eat?"

"Nope. Ellie fed me."

"Was it as good as what I cook?"

"I'm way too diplomatic to answer a question like that." Comstock pushed off his stool and walked over to Badger's table. "Hey," he said, pulling up a chair and dropping into it. "I have a little job for you, if you're interested."

Badger perked up. "Hear that, Charlie? You're sittin' here tellin' me I'm too old and worn-out to be good for anything, and Comstock walks in and tells me he has a job for me. Who'm I to believe?"

"You interested?" Comstock raised his cup for a sip of coffee. Black, no sugar. Better than Ellie's by a long shot, but he hadn't married Ellie for her coffee-making skills.

"Hell, yes. Who is it this time?"

"George Smith's in the valley."

Badger leaned forward and lowered his voice. "The senator himself?"

"Himself."

"Here to shoot somethin' in an extra-large size, no doubt. Think he'll hunt with Joe?"

"He always does. I need your eyes and ears, but I wouldn't blame you one bit if you backed out of this one. The senator is a powerful man, and he could make life mighty miserable for anyone who crossed him. Still and all, I'd sure like to trim his ears. He's been breaking the game laws around here for a long time."

Badger puffed up with importance. "Count me in, Warden!" he said. "You know I'll keep my eyes peeled and my ears perked. Always have. Can't abide them rich trophy hunters dressed in camo, carrying thousand-dollar rifles. Never could!"

"I was hoping I could count on you," Comstock said, pushing out of his chair. "You have my phone number. If you see anything out of the ordinary, give me a call. Leave a message if I'm not home."

After he had left, Badger settled back in his chair with a smug expression. "Now, what was that you was sayin' about how old and useless I am, Charlie?"

CHAPTER EIGHT

JESSIE COULDN'T SLEEP. The ache in her arm forced her to pace the kitchen floor back and forth, back and forth. It was 2:00 a.m., and this night was proving to be as long as the night she'd spent with Blue up in the mountains. As long, but nowhere near as easy.

Guthrie had come back, and suddenly everything had changed...everything except their inability to communicate with each other. He still didn't understand why she was so angry with him, and he probably never would.

Yet in spite of her anger with him, there was this undeniable truth: he had truly loved her, and for a long time, too, if love could be measured as a meaningful emotion in the heart of a thirteen-year-old boy.

Guthrie's father had worked for the Weaver ranch back in its glory days. He and Guthrie had come as a package deal, and Jessie clearly remembered first laying eyes on them.

It had been a windy day, with a strong steady spring wind that dried the mud, made the laundry fly out straight on the line and skimmed the meadowlarks above the greening grass. She'd been pegging a load of fresh wash on the line with difficulty, struggling to hold the snapping line in one hand while she fished another shirt or pair of pants out of the basket at her feet.

The rickety truck backfiring its way slowly up the dirt track from the main road had startled her.

''We're lookin' for work, miss,'' the man had said after climbing out of the truck and politely removing his hat. ''My name's Sloane, Arthur Sloane, and that'd be my son, Guthrie. Folks in town said you might be hirin'.''

Jessie stared first at the skinny middle-aged man with the worn blue jeans and faded chambray shirt, hands gnarly with calluses, then she narrowed her eyes and peered through the cracked, fly-specked windshield at the boy named Guthrie.

''Why, he don't appear old enough to be workin', mister,'' she said. She'd always spoken frank. Her father said it was because she'd been raised alongside a bunch of mannerless cowboys. He must have heard her, that boy in the truck, because the passenger door wrenched open and he climbed stiffly out. She saw then that he stood taller than his father, and was a whole lot better-looking.

''I'm fifteen years old and I can do a man's work,'' he said. ''Same as you!''

''How would you know I can do a man's work?''

''Heard so in town. That is, if you're Jessie Weaver.''

''I am.''

''I'm Guthrie Sloane,'' he said, his young skinny chest puffing out. ''Me'n my daddy can outwork just about anybody we ever met. We lost our place when the cattle prices fell, but we didn't lose nothin' else. We're just as good as we ever was!''

''Maybe so,'' Jessie said, ''but you ain't no ways near fifteen. I'd guess if you said you were ten you wouldn't be stretchin' the blanket quite so tight.''

''I'm thirteen!'' he retorted in self-defense.

''Guthrie,'' Sloane said quietly, casting his son a warning glance. ''Miss, is your father about?''

''Nossir. But he'll be home for his dinner about noon. If you wanted, you could wait and talk to him then.''

They wanted to, all right, and her father had signed them on, both of them, and put them up in the old log cabin down on the creek.

Of course Guthrie had to go to school, same as she did. They shared the ten-mile ride in to Katy Junction, each on horseback, leaving their horses in the common corral outside the school. They also shared the same classroom, and the same ride home at the end of the day.

It didn't take long for Guthrie Sloane to start acting real strange. One afternoon, barely a month after he'd arrived, he bent low in his saddle, picked her a bunch of wildflowers blowing in the tall grass beside the creek and handed them to her, grave as could be. "One day you and me are going to be married," he informed her, "so I guess I best start treatin' you right."

Guthrie's mother had run off with another man when he was scarcely a year old, so he had no memory of her whatsoever, yet he sometimes spoke of her with a kind of wistful affection, and once he confided to Jessie that his mother never would've left if he and his dad had behaved different toward her. Jessie figured that sentiment had to have come from his father, since Guthrie as a baby could only have acted like any other baby. Oh, maybe he'd been colicky and hadn't slept through the night, but that wouldn't make a mother abandon her babe. Jessie felt sorry for him, and less apt to pity herself for losing her own mother to a legitimate illness when she was just shy of seven.

The Weaver ranch had not been totally without a woman's influence, however. One of the full-time hired hands, Drew Long, fortuitously married a buxom Mexican woman who hailed from Tucson. She ruled the Weaver household firmly but fairly, and had dispensed copious quantities of delectably authentic Mexican food for nearly sixteen years. Drew and Ramalda were the last to be let go when the ranch began to fail, and many tears were shed on both sides that sad day.

As for Guthrie, his ambitious plan to marry Jessie never wavered through high school, although the time they spent together had shrunk considerably. Guthrie's father liked the bottle, so much so that Jessie's father asked him to leave after one particularly ugly binge in the old cabin. He and Guthrie rented a battered little trailer outside of Katy Junction, though both continued to work at the ranch. Guthrie was holding down two jobs—after school at the feed store and weekends on the ranch. He put all his savings toward buying a piece of land out on Bear Creek so he could get his father out of that miserable trailer on the outskirts of town. He thought that if his father could just have his own place again he'd give up the bottle and straighten himself out.

Senior year. Jessie was accepted at the University of Colorado for a course of preveterinary studies. Guthrie took a third job stocking shelves at the Katy Junction General Store five nights a week between midnight and 2:00 a.m. to add a little more money to his kitty. He held no illusions about attending college. There was no way he could afford it.

The senior prom was held at the Cattleman's Grange Hall. She wore a cornflower-blue strapless tea-length dress and a beaded necklace that had belonged to her great-grandmother. He told her he would love her forever and that he was going to buy the land on Bear Creek, an entire section, and he was going to build a cabin on it that summer from the cedar that grew there.

"I'll help you," she told him, and she did, too, spending every moment she could spare away from the ranch over at his place, peeling logs. He built the cabin on a high, pretty spot near the creek. One corner of his land butted up to the Weaver ranch, which made it all the more special to them both. By summer's end, the cabin was complete and Jessie was no longer an innocent virgin lying awake nights, wondering how it might be with Guthrie.

By summer's end she knew what it was like to be cradled within his strong arms in the sweet grass that grew along the banks of Bear Creek; to feel the solid earth beneath her and his solid body moving over her; to look up into his dark eyes; to lie next to him afterward and watch the celestial change of guard in a sky so big and so studded with stars that it dwarfed the imagination.

She went off to college and Guthrie moved his father into the cabin on Bear Creek. Just before Christmas during her junior year, Arthur Sloane was killed when his truck left the road beyond the Katy Junction cutoff and careered into a ravine. He was drunk when it happened, and Guthrie blamed himself for not preventing it. "How could you have stopped him?" she'd asked at the funeral. Guthrie had looked beyond her to some distant place. "By being a better son," he said.

In her third year at veterinary college in Colorado, her own father was diagnosed with prostate cancer. This rocked her to her soul. One spring day after classes, she was standing in the noise and bustle of the big campus when a flock of Canada geese flew over, heading north toward Montana. Tears filled her eyes at the poignant sight and sound, and that very same day she was following them. When she reached home she found her father in the pole barn, forking hay to the horses.

"I'm home, Daddy," she said, standing flat-footed in the dim light of the barn. He had nodded, leaning on the fork, looking thin and tired.

"I can see that," he said. A long silence followed, broken by the grinding sounds of the horses eating hay.

"You're here early. I thought classes didn't get out for another three weeks."

"I'm not going back," she said. "It's too crowded there. I can't abide it. I already know all I need to know to run this ranch. I'm staying here with you."

After a bit he nodded again, said "All right," and went back to his endless chores.

What little savings her father had were quickly wiped out. He took out a third mortgage on the ranch, sold off most of the grazing leases and let the last of the hired hands go. Guthrie stayed on, pitching in all he could to take up some of the slack and asking for nothing in return. He struggled valiantly with them to keep the venerable old ranch afloat, but debt after debt went unpaid.

Her father's illness progressed more rapidly than the doctors had predicted. He tired easily. He had no appetite for the meals Jessie cooked him. Finally, one night after supper he called her into the study. The books lay spread out on the desk before him, the evidence of the ranch's decline harshly exposed in black and red ink. Weariness and defeat bowed his shoulders.

"Jessie," he said, "my life insurance policy won't make a dent in these debts. Cattle prices keep falling and the horses can't hold the place afloat. It's time to face up to it. We're going under. We've got to sell out to the developers or the bank's going to take it all."

Oh, Jessie remembered that awful night...the heated words, the tears. Remembered her rage, her grief, her denial—emotions that remained with her for the time it took the cancer to consume her father, remained potent for weeks after the funeral and came to an ugly head when Guthrie picked up her sore, blistered hands in his after a particularly discouraging day and pleaded, "Jess, please. Sell the damn ranch! Keep the buildings and enough land to run your horses on. You'll kill yourself otherwise. Your father was right. The bank will end up with the ranch and you'll be left with nothing!''

That had been the beginning of the end of her and Guthrie. She'd refused to listen to him and had, instead, redoubled her efforts to find a solution she could live with, a way to keep the land safe. And at the last moment, one step ahead of foreclosure, she had, but at a tremendous cost to her relationship with Guthrie Sloane.

She had found Steven Brown, who in turn had found a conservation buyer. Steven brought Caleb McCutcheon out to see the ranch, and the three of them spent the better part of a day in the saddle, riding up into the high country, where there were no roads at all, just game trails and old Indian traces. She showed them the cave with the strange petroglyphs, the backwater pool in the creek where the water steamed from a thermal spring, the huge Engleman spruce with her great-grandfather's initials carved in it.

McCutcheon possessed a genuine love and appreciation of wild and wide-open spaces. He didn't talk much except to ask pertinent questions. By the end of that ride she found herself liking the retired baseball player, and feeling better than she had in many months. McCutcheon was dutifully humbled by the grandeur of the land. He admired the weather-beaten but sturdy ranch buildings. He was especially intrigued by the original homestead of logs, built on the bank of the creek, and spent a long time marveling at how well it had been constructed, admiring the low ceilings with their exposed beams, the neatly dovetailed notches, the old rippled glass in the small-paned windows.

''Well, you described it to a tee,'' he said to Steven, standing on the porch of that venerable cabin. ''I'm hooked.'' He looked at Jessie. ''I'll hand over enough earnest money right now to keep the bank from foreclosing and give us the time we need to draft the conservation easements into the deed. How does that sound to you?''

After McCutcheon had left the ranch, Steven had raised his fist skyward in a primitive and triumphant gesture. ''I don't know about you,'' he said, ''but I'm feeling pretty good about things. And I'm hungry. Is there anyplace to eat in that two-horse town of yours?''

''The Longhorn. It's small, but Bernie's a great cook. I waitress there five shifts a week.''

''Join me?''

His invitation surprised her. Her response surprised her even more. ''Okay,'' she said.

He had a bottle of red wine stashed in his Wagoneer and Bernie served it to them, trying her diplomatic best to be friendly to Steven. Over the meal, observed both discreetly and indiscreetly by all the locals and no doubt the hottest topic of gossip in a long while, they discussed the different conservation easements that could be written into the deed. ''You know,'' Steven concluded, ''not many people would do what you've just done—give up all that money just to save a piece of land. You're some kind of woman.''

''I couldn't have done it without your help,'' she replied. They were raising their glasses to toast the triumph of the day when Guthrie entered the café. She saw him walk through the door, looking for his sister behind the counter and removing his hat. He came to an abrupt halt in the middle of the room when he spotted her and Brown sitting in the corner, changed direction and approached their table. Steven rose to his feet as Jessie introduced the two of them. They shook hands. It was all very awkward.

''So,'' Guthrie said, eyeing the bottle of wine, the glasses. ''Looks like some kind of celebration.''

''It is,'' Jessie said, feeling guilty and ill at ease and

resenting Guthrie for making her feel that way. "Steven helped me find a buyer for the ranch, someone who will protect it from being developed. The purchase and sales agreements were signed today. Sit down and join us."

Guthrie worked his hat around in his fingers. He gave Steven a keen, appraising stare, then turned his eyes on Jessie. "So it's done, then. You've signed it all away. The ranch buildings. The burial ground. Everything."

Jessie met his cool, disapproving gaze and felt anger warm her blood. "Everything. The ranch buildings, the burial ground, everything."

Guthrie nodded. "It was yours to give, I guess," he said, his voice maddeningly mild, but his eyes steely. He nodded curtly to Steven and then he spun on his heel and left the Longhorn.

Jessie sank back in her chair. "I'm sorry," she said to Steven.

"Is he a friend?"

Jessie picked up her wineglass, mortified to notice that her hand was trembling. She set the glass back down. "Guthrie and I have known each other for a very long time."

"I see. He obviously disagrees with your decision."

"He thought I should keep part of the ranch. He couldn't understand that if I did that, I wouldn't want to live there anymore. I couldn't bear watching the land get hacked up, bulldozed, paved over, manicured and developed. He didn't understand. He loved the ranch, too. Still does. He lived in that old cabin on the creek from the time he was thirteen. He and his father worked there."

Steven nodded. "I hope the two of you can resolve your differences."

Jessie lowered her eyes to hide the anguish in them and could not respond. They shared the rest of their meal with quiet conversation, and he drove her back to the ranch afterward. "How long will all this take?" she asked as he walked her to the door, the way she knew he would.

"I'll get in touch with your lawyer tomorrow. Arden, isn't it? We'll start working on the project. Be patient. These things don't happen overnight. The closing might not be until September, but I'll keep you posted."

"That's fine with me. It gives me time to get my act together," Jessie said. "Thanks for everything, Steven."

He smiled at her with those grave, gentle eyes. "It was my pleasure. I wouldn't mind going riding again sometime, but it'll probably be a while. I just hope I can make it up the courthouse steps tomorrow."

They said good-night and he drove off in his Wagoneer. Jessie stood on the porch for a long while, Blue beside her, and watched the sun set. She stood there until the sky turned a deep violet and the first stars appeared. She was still standing there when another vehicle drove up, a truck whose rattles and squeaks she recognized long before she could see it.

Guthrie climbed out and stood in the twilight, one hand resting on the hood of his truck.

"Did you come by just to make sure he'd gone home?" Jessie said.

He pushed off the truck and climbed the porch steps. "I came by to apologize for the way I behaved." He stopped before her, reached as if to touch her, but then let his hand drop when he read her body language. "I'm sorry. It was poor behavior."

Jessie crossed her arms and gazed down to where the creek drew a broad dark band between the pole barn and the spruce forest. She could barely make out the roofline of the old homestead, see the blocky shadow that was the big stone chimney. In a short while it would be too dark to see anything at all.

"Look, Jess, I know it's none of my business. I just didn't want to see you get taken advantage of, that's all. I only wanted to make sure you knew what you were doing, what you were signing away."

Jessie tightened her arms around herself. She drew a breath to keep from saying something she might regret, and when she spoke her voice was remarkably calm. "I'm a big girl, Guthrie. In fact, I'm a legal adult, and have been for several years. Some people even think I'm fairly smart. I know what I'm doing. You may not approve and you may not understand, but there's nothing I can do about that. We see things differently. We don't share the same dreams anymore. Lately all we do is fight, and I think it would be better if we didn't see each other for a while."

He was near enough to her that she could feel the tension in him. He turned and placed his hands on the porch rail, leaning his upper body over his braced arms and gazing down toward the barn. For a long time he was quiet, and then he said, "Is that the way you really want it?"

"Yes."

Another long silence, and then she heard him inhale, then let the breath out in a sigh. "Jesus, Jess," he said in a voice tight with pain.

Without another word, without even glancing toward her, he straightened and walked back down the porch steps. Moments later he was driving his old truck off, and the following morning he had done just what she'd asked him to do. He'd gone away and left her alone for five endless months. Yet his absence hadn't made her feel better about anything. In fact, it had made her feel worse.

When had she become so critical, so cynical? When had she forsaken spontaneous laughter? When had the joy of life left her? When had she forgotten how good the simple things could be—the smell of sweet grass, the blue dome of a big, star-studded sky, the sound of the creek running past, the feel of Guthrie's strong arms closing around her, drawing her near...

Oh, Lord, she had lost it all. Not just her father and the land, but the girl who had exulted in the wild, joyous freedoms of youth. The girl who had awakened each morning with a love of life, and the energy and enthusiasm to match the length and breadth and whirlwind pace of the day. The girl who had discovered the breathtaking magic of falling in love with her very best friend.

She paced the floor back and forth, back and forth. Her arm still ached in spite of the wine, in spite of the aspirin. But it was not just the ache in her arm that kept her awake.

It was the unbearable ache in her heart.

McCUTCHEON GLANCED at the traveling alarm clock that he'd set beside the bunk: 3:00 a.m. He sighed and laced his fingers together beneath his head. Thought about Guthrie Sloane and sighed again. Maybe he shouldn't have broken out that bottle of whiskey, but it had seemed the right thing to do at the time. The bottle of wine had long since been drunk, and their conversations had traveled down many a winding path. He liked Guthrie Sloane. There was a quiet strength about him that inspired confidence. In spite of his agony over Jessie Weaver, Guthrie was a man of substance, and he belonged to this place nearly as much as she did.

Which is why, when Guthrie was taking his leave, McCutcheon had asked him once again about the job. "If she just absolutely insists on leaving, I want you to stay on. I'd like it if you could look after the place."

Guthrie had thought about it for a while, standing there

by the door with his hat in his hand and the world upon his broad shoulders. "All right," he said. "If Jessie goes, I'll stay." He'd nodded as if his words made a kind of solemn sense to him. "But if she stays, I'll go."

"Where'll you go?" McCutcheon asked, his own sensibilities befuddled by the quantity of good scotch whiskey they'd shared.

"Home." Guthrie looked at him and grinned. It was a brave grin, but a sad one, too. "I'll go home. I guess maybe if she ever wants to see me, she can ride over. It ain't all that far and she knows the way."

"I hope it doesn't come to that. Your idea is a good one. I think she'll stay."

"I hope you're right. I surely do." He'd left then, his shoulders bent with fatigue and discouragement.

McCutcheon sighed again. Baseball. To think that his entire life had once revolved around that game. It was ludicrous to him now to even remember those times and the ridiculous amount of money he'd been paid for throwing a small white ball toward a man holding a bat.

Oh, he'd loved the game. He'd lived it long enough to believe the whole world ate it for breakfast, lunch and dinner. But one week on this ranch had changed his entire perspective. The universe had settled into its proper place, and at the core of it was this land and a young woman named Jessie Weaver. All these years he'd wondered if a woman like that could exist on this jaded planet, and now he'd found her.

A woman so centered that she rose in the morning and the sun rose with her. A woman who didn't care one whit about the way her nails were manicured or the way her hair was brushed or the way she moved when a man was watching, yet who moved through life with a natural grace and beauty that would easily shame the highest-paid models in the world. A woman who knew exactly what she was about. A woman possessing the strength and courage to play the cards life dealt her, a woman with enough conviction in her heart to move mountains.

What might his life have been like had he met such a woman in the height of his glory? Would he have recognized her for what she was, or would his youthful arrogance have blinded him?

Back then he'd been looking for a woman sophisticated enough to elevate him above his blue-collar upbringing, and he'd found that in his wife. But when advancing years and an injury had ended his career and his fame had faded, she had drifted off in search of more interesting companionship. While she was conversing with the prime minister of France, he was dreaming about a life far removed from the glitter of Paris. He was riding a big horse across a bold landscape, heading toward the mountains and into the setting sun. Their paths had amicably diverged, and in the end all that he and his wife still shared was his money.

It had taken years to discover this place and a compelling woman like of Jessie Weaver. Now that he had found them both, what next? Not only was he already married, but he was old enough to be Jessie's father. And not only was he old enough to be her father, but he happened to like Guthrie Sloane a great deal, and Guthrie Sloane was deeply in love with Jessie Weaver.

So it was enough for him just to know that a woman like her existed. It was enough to be here tonight in this old cabin beside the creek, lying in this bunk and listening to the fire snap in the woodstove, the night wind moan in the eaves, of the creek running past. It was enough for him to be warm and well fed and mildly drunk.

Lord God Almighty, it was enough. It had to be.

STEVEN BROWN WAS USED to hypocrisy. He'd been weaned on it. On the one hand, the People craved their independence, the old ways and the time of the buffalo. On the other, they couldn't live without their color TVs, pickup trucks, snow machines, clothes driers, electric lights and booze. They hated the government for putting them on the reservation and taking away their way of life. They loved the government for the way of life they had been given, and they wanted more and more of it.

He could have been working in the pencil factory like some of his friends, but instead he was sitting here in his little house in Gallatin Gateway, sleepless in the early-morning hours, thinking about all the paths he'd taken that had led him to this place. Thinking about Jessie Weaver, and how he had tried so hard to get away from the very things she embodied. Blood-and-guts stuff. She was White Buffalo Woman, walking into his life, turning it upside down, making him question all that he had chosen.

In the morning he and Pete Two Shirts would go to the Weaver ranch to find Jessie's horses and bring them down out of the high country. He would see her then, and until then he would suffer. And when he saw her, he would suffer, too, because he knew how it would be. He had seen it in her eyes when she'd climbed the steps at the ranch house and spotted Badger, then him, standing there. He had seen it, and the pain of it had been like a knife driven deep and then twisted. She was still in love with Guthrie Sloane. Guthrie had found her up there on the mountain, and she had come to terms with her feelings and wore them plainly, hiding nothing, because she was as honest as the sunrise, and as constant and enduring.

He had lost her to another man, but it was enough to have known her. And tomorrow he would see her again, and become for that small time the person he had always thought he might become but could never quite find in the maze of modern society.

It wasn't enough, but it would have to do.

GUTHRIE DIDN'T GET to his cabin on Bear Creek until well after 3:00 a.m. He was more than a little off kilter, stumbling twice as he climbed the steps and skinning his shin on the edge of the porch. He swore softly and fumbled for the door latch. The door swung silently inward and he was surprised by the warmth that met him as he stepped inside, by the fresh, clean smells that reminded him of McCutcheon's old cabin. His sister had been here, too, to make things tidy. To scrub and sweep and dust and to light a fire in the stove. She'd made the cabin nice for him to welcome him home, just in case Jessie hadn't.

If he hadn't been so tired he might have laughed. He lit the lamp, instead, and visually panned the familiar space. It would always look good to him. It would always remind him of the summer he and Jessie had spent together, working on it. They'd made a good job of it, too. She'd peeled the logs and helped him roll them into place; she'd chinked while he'd notched. They'd built the cabin together. It had been a kind of talisman of their future together, a promise of all that might be.

At least, it had seemed so to him, but then again, she'd been slated to inherit one of the finest land holdings in the state. Had she ever really dreamed of sharing this little cabin on Bear Creek with him, or had that dream been his alone? Had he imposed his own values and visions of their life together upon her? Had he stood in the way of her future, blocked all the paths she tried to take, smothered her every freedom? Had his insecurities suffocated her? Had he destroyed the very essence of the passionate, idealistic, hopelessly naive young girl he had fallen in love with so many years ago?

If so, it was too late now to erase those wrongs. All he could do was step back and let her go.

She was in such terrible torment. Perhaps by helping her achieve what she so desperately seemed to want he could make up for some of his mistakes. Perhaps only by leaving Katy Junction could she hope to find what she was searching for. He wasn't sure what that was, exactly, but he knew for certain that it wasn't a hometown cowboy who went by the name of Guthrie Sloane.

CHAPTER NINE

JOE MADE UP his mind while drinking his morning coffee. Actually, he'd made it up the night before, but he always liked to sleep on his decisions, especially the ones that could get him into the most trouble. The way he figured it, if he woke up feeling the same way he did when he went to bed, then his conscience had given him the green light. Not that his conscience was all that delicate. There weren't many things that he wouldn't do if the stakes were high enough, and the senator always kept the pot interesting. He couldn't afford to lose the senator as a client, and there were a score of other pilots who would love to step in and take Joe's place.

Of course, George Smith was well aware of that. He was not above flaunting his power and position to get what he wanted. And right now what he wanted was that big grizzly's head on his hunting-lodge wall.

Joe added another spoonful of sugar to the cup and stirred it round. Jessie Weaver's horses were still up in the pass somewheres, but she wouldn't be riding after them for a while. Not after her latest experience. Any day now a big storm could close the pass right down. The time to schedule the hunt was soon, before that bear denned up for the winter.

He'd need to provision for the trip first thing this morning. The senator liked the hunt, but he didn't like going without all the extras that gave pleasure to his days. He—

Joe—could set the whole thing up ahead of time, get the tree stand in place near the kill site, hoist all the senator's favorite treats up in the tree, set up a base camp, then fly him in and put him in place. Easy enough. Come dusk he'd fly him back to his lodge, and in the morning they'd do it all over again.

They'd keep after it for as long as it took to nail the bear, which could be as quick as a day or as lengthy as a week. It was up to Joe to make sure the hunt was successful, but that shouldn't prove too difficult. After all, Jessie Weaver's hapless horse had already as much as ensured the senator's success.

McCUTCHEON WAS SITTING out on the porch, enjoying his first cup of coffee, when the dog came around the corner of the cabin. "Here, Blue," he said. "You're looking pretty spry this morning." The little cow dog climbed the porch steps carefully, in deference to her sore ribs and the bristle of stitches in her side and flank, and sniffed delicately at his outstretched hand, her tail fanning the crisp air. Jessie appeared shortly thereafter, having walked down from the ranch house. She was surprised to see him.

"'Mornin'," she said. "How's your ankle?"

"Still there. How's your arm?"

"Good as can be expected." She was carrying a covered basket, the kind folks took on picnics. "I brought some breakfast fixin's. I can see you already made the coffee."

"Yes, ma'am, and you're welcome to a cup. It's not bad, for instant."

"Instant?" Clearly she'd never drunk the stuff and never intended to, either. "I'll make a pot of the real thing. How do you take your eggs?"

"You don't have to cook breakfast for me. In fact, I'm

not much of a breakfast eater, if I can just have my coffee."

"I brought some doughnuts."

"Now, I'd eat a doughnut without too much arm twisting."

She smiled and climbed up the steps. "I'll start the coffee."

She disappeared inside and he heard the sounds of domestic industry within. He flexed his good leg, stretched back in his chair and drew a deep breath of sweet clean mountain air. He felt pretty good, considering the late night and the amount of whiskey he'd drunk. And now, for some unfathomable reason, Jessie Weaver had showed up to make him something to eat, downright friendly in demeanor. He was beyond trying to understand what went on in women's minds. He'd given up on that long ago. He just accepted their behavior and enjoyed their company on the sunny days, and this day looked to be a sunny one for Jessie.

When she returned carrying the pot of coffee, the doughnuts and a cup for herself, he slatted the remainder of his cold instant brew over the porch rail and allowed her to fill his mug with the real thing. "I thank you," he said. He took a plain doughnut from the offering and bit into it with relish. "Actually, I'm glad you came down this morning because it saved me a long uphill hobble. I was kind of hoping to talk to you a bit about the ranch. I wanted to run something by you. An idea I had."

She leaned up against a porch post, resting her cup on the top rail. "Mr. McCutcheon, I'd like to apologize for the way I behaved yesterday," she said. "I've been thinking about how poorly I acted. It shames me. I had no call to treat you that way."

McCutcheon shook his head impatiently. "There's no

need for apologies—and my name's Caleb, in case you forgot. Listen to my idea. This might sound crazy, but I'd like to tear down all the barbed-wire fences on this land. I'd like to be able to climb on a horse and ride out over that horizon and not see a single fence cutting up the landscape. What do you think? Is that a crazy idea? Can it be done?''

Jessie straightened and her eyes narrowed suspiciously. "What does it matter what I think?''

"I respect your opinion.''

"It's a huge job. There are over sixty miles of barbed wire. Triple strand.''

"I know. It'd take some time and a fair-size crew. I was figuring we could recycle the wire. Spool it back, load it into pickups and give it to some other fool to fence himself in. Pull out the fence posts, fill in the holes. It'd probably take a couple years.''

"You'd have to leave the boundary fences.''

"For now. Some of that property might come up for sale by and by, and it's not too far a stretch to imagine this land eventually linking up to Yellowstone. Anyhow, pulling the fences is a big job, all right, and not everyone would want to ramrod it. I was hoping it might interest you enough to keep you on, at least until the job was done.''

Jessie paced the length of the porch and stared out across the river. She still held the coffee cup, though she hadn't yet tasted the brew. She stood very still for a long time, watching the long golden fingers of sunlight splinter through the craggy peaks of the Beartooth Mountains and lay themselves upon the tawny land. Then, abruptly, she swung around and confronted him. "Guthrie put you up to this, didn't he?''

Her words took McCutcheon by surprise. "No,'' he

said, and then he realized the futility of trying to fool her. "Yes. It was his idea, but I thought it was a good one. I would have come to it myself eventually. And I'm speaking the truth to you."

"Mister, in these parts, an idea like that is apt to get you run out of the county."

"Let 'em try. So what do you think?"

"I think you're crazy. It'll cost a lot of money."

"I have enough. No thanks to me, either. I had a smart mother. When I signed my first contract I gave my mother that money, and most of my salary, too. I didn't need much to live on. I was just happy to be playing ball.

"Well, by the time I got married, my mother had invested just about every penny I'd given her. My wife claimed my earnings for the rest of my career, but by then it didn't matter. My mother's investments made an unbelievable amount of money that just continues to grow. The way I see it, I might as well put some of it to good use. I have no kids, so it seems to me the best legacy I could leave right now for future generations—humans and wildlife—is as much open land as possible. And if that makes me crazy, then so be it."

Jessie regarded him with open amazement. "That's wonderful," she said.

"Could you bring yourself to work for a crazy man?"

"Maybe," she said softly. "I'll have to think about it."

Without another word, she turned and walked away from him, descended the porch steps and disappeared out of sight around the corner of the cabin. Blue sat for a few moments more at his feet and then stood. She flagged her tail and stared up at him with a questioning expression that appeared curiously intelligent. McCutcheon had never owned a dog, but the more he saw of this little one, the more he thought he might like such a companion to share this cabin with.

"Well, go on," he said. "She's getting a pretty big head start on you."

Blue gazed up at him for a few moments longer before heeding his words and following after her mistress. If he didn't know better, he'd have thought that blue-eyed cow dog had been inviting him to follow along. He settled back with his coffee and his doughnut and thought that the day was shaping up to be a pretty good one indeed, all things considered.

JESSIE STOOD in the kitchen and looked around her at the blank walls, the bare cupboards, the empty corners. Her mind raced. Should she take the job and remain on? Could she live here knowing it was no longer her place? Would she feel the same way about it now? Did her feelings really matter in the grand scheme of things?

If McCutcheon could dream about a day when this land connected to the Yellowstone ecosystem, could she be petty enough to refuse to help him achieve that dream? What a legacy it would be to leave this land the way it had been before the great herds had come up from the south. To pull down all the fences and sell off the cattle. To let the wild horses run free and the wolves howl and the elk and grizzlies and Steven Brown's buffalo, the sacred *bi'shee,* roam across it.

Wasn't all that far more important than her own sentiments?

Damn Guthrie! He'd known how tempting such an offer would be. No doubt he'd spent some time with Caleb McCutcheon after he'd left her last night. She could picture the two of them huddled together, hatching up this latest scheme. It was a clever one, she had to give him that.

Blue raised her head from her paws and whined softly, and moments later Jessie heard a truck approaching. She stepped out onto the porch to await Guthrie's arrival. He'd piled a bunch of stuff in the back of his pickup—his saddle and a whole mess of gear. When he climbed out of the cab he brought some of it with him—his old Winchester rifle, his lariat and a pair of saddlebags bulging with supplies.

"'Mornin'," he said, slinging the saddlebags over his shoulder. He turned his back on her and started down toward the pole barn.

"What're you doing?" she said.

"I'm borrowing one of your horses," he replied, not pausing.

"Oh no you're not! No way!" she said, charging down the porch steps and trotting after him.

"That bay mare," he said, halting beside the barn door to set down his rifle and sling the saddlebags over the top rail of the fence. "As I recall, you've used her a bit for roping and such. She's green broke but willing."

"I said you can't borrow a horse and you most certainly can't borrow the bay!" Jessie said, rounding on him. "She's my best horse!"

"Kestrel. Isn't that her name? Feisty, smart and tough." He ducked through the fence rails, shook out a loop and walked toward the group of mares bunched against the far side of the corral. With one flick of his wrist he dabbed the loop neatly over the bay's head before she could shy away. "Easy, now, girl. Whoa, now." He reeled her in until she was standing right in front of him, ears pricked cautiously and nostrils taking in his scent. Only when she had responded to his soothing words and relaxed did he reach out a hand to stroke her neck. "She looks good. She's muscled up a lot since I last saw her."

"I told you, you can't take her."

"I'm going up in the pass to find the rest of your mares," he said, opening the gate and leading the bay mare out. "I'd use my own horse, but I sold him when I left town, and the bastard who bought him won't sell him back to me at twice the price." He closed the gate behind him and tied the mare off to one of the fence posts. Only then did he face her squarely. He had bathed and shaved, but the deep fatigue hadn't left his eyes.

"I thought about what you said to me last night, Jess," he said, "and you're right. I've stood in your way all these years. I guess I never realized I was doing it. I wanted to keep you here—I wanted to keep you safe. I wanted you all for myself. I was suffocating you. You were right to push me away, and you were right to want to leave. So I'm going up to find your horses and bring them back, because you can't leave until they're safe, and you sure as hell can't ride yourself with that metal thing stuck into your arm.

"I should be back within a few days, a week at most if they've gone clear up and over the pass. Don't worry about your mare. I'll take good care of her. If you could just keep an eye on McCutcheon until I get back?"

He walked over to the pickup, grabbed his saddle and another armload of gear, walked back to the mare and commenced to saddle her. He did so with practiced movements and the mare, sensing his expertise, stood quietly for him.

"Guthrie, I don't need you to bring the mares down. I can do it myself when the time comes."

"It'll be winter soon. Were you planning to wait till then and use a snowmobile? There isn't a machine made that can climb that pass." He smoothed the blanket over the mare's back, settled the saddle with a gentle shake and reached under the mare's belly for the cinch.

Jessie felt hot anger course through her. "I mean it! I don't want you taking that mare! She's too valuable!"

"You probably haven't ridden her for months. Look how she's dancin' around, skittery as a deer. She should be topped off by now, but you've been too busy, I don't doubt. This little trip'll be good for her. It'll settle her down some." He looped the latigo through the cinch ring and tightened it up. "Whoa, now," he soothed as the mare stepped sideways and threw her head up with a snort of alarm.

"What about the bear?"

"What about the bear!" he retorted, startling both her and the mare. "What do you want me to do, Jess? You want me to shoot it? You want me to let it be? Just tell me. I'll do anything you want me to!"

He paused to glare at her and she glared back, but then something inside her gave and she dropped her eyes, feeling confused. "I just want you to be careful, that's all," she said in a low voice.

Guthrie straightened up and draped an arm over the saddle, clearly amazed. "You mind repeating that?"

"Those things I said last night—they're not true. Not all of them, anyway," she said, jabbing at the dirt with the toe of her boot. "I've been really angry about a lot of things for a long time, but I had no right to lash out at you that way and I'm…" She drew a quick breath, as though knifed by pain. "And I'm sorry!"

Guthrie shook his head slowly. "Kick me in the shin," he said in a wondering voice. "I must be dreamin'."

She flushed. "I'm not leaving here, Guthrie. I've decided to take the job McCutcheon offered me."

She had thought this news would gladden him and was

caught off guard by his complete lack of reaction. He turned his back on her and began bridling the mare, using a hackamore because he knew she was still green. The mare danced a bit but then held firm while he slipped the leather crown behind her ears. When he had gotten the hackamore in place he reached for his saddlebags. He tied them on behind the cantle, did the same with his bedroll, then reached up for his rifle—his father's old Winchester—and slid it effortlessly into the scabbard.

From the truck he retrieved his gloves and warm parka, which he shrugged into as he returned to the mare, still not looking at or speaking to Jessie. He untied the horse from the fence post, coiled his rope and secured it to the lariat strap. Then he took up the trailing rein and pulled the mare's head around as he stepped into the saddle. She danced again, a quick, startled sidestep that Guthrie sat quietly through. He gathered the reins in one hand and ran his his other soothingly up the mare's neck.

"Did you hear what I said!" Jessie snapped. "I said I'm taking the job!"

Guthrie stood in his stirrups to check their length and, satisfied, sank back into the saddle. He snugged his hat brim down and then reached into his coat pocket, pulled out a sheaf of folded-up papers and leaned over the mare's withers to hand them down to her. "I called the college this morning and talked to the head of the veterinary studies department. You remember him. He taught your anatomy class the first year. He said he could get you back into vet school. You'd have to scramble to catch up, but he thought you could do it. Call the number on that paper and talk to him this morning, Jess."

Jessie stared up at him…speechless, but not for long. "Damn you!" she said. "Are you playing games with me?"

"No, ma'am. I wouldn't dare play games with you."
He bent a little closer, his eyes keen. "Remember that
dream you had of being a veterinarian? You were almost
there, and you can still make it happen. Call that number,
Jess. Before you decide to take McCutcheon up on his job
offer, talk to Professor Payler. That job ripping down
fences might last two years at best. Being a veterinarian is
a lifelong career, and your father was right. You'd make
a damn fine one."

Before she could respond, he reined the mare around,
touched his heels to her flanks and jumped her into a
smooth lope. "You're an idiot, Guthrie Sloane!" she
shouted after him. "An imbecile! I hope that grizzly eats
you!"

He never turned his head. He sat easy in the saddle, his
broad shoulders mocking her as he rode away. For some
irrational reason it made her even angrier that he could
ride so well. Nobody in the whole wide West could set a
horse the way Guthrie Sloane could.

Not even Clint Eastwood.

JESSIE'S BEHAVIOR totally floored Guthrie. For one thing,
he'd been sure she'd never take that job. For another, he
never thought she'd ever apologize for anything she ever
said to anyone, no matter how awful or wrong it was. And
then that part about the bear, and about him being careful.
Had she really said those things? How much could a person change in just a few short hours? The entire encounter
might have completely unsettled him, except that her send-
off had been fairly normal. That, and her protests over him
taking the bay mare.

Who, as a matter of fact, was an absolute joy to ride.
Her ancestry was written all over her in the beautiful dish
of her face, the width between her large, intelligent eyes,

the short-coupled strength of her back and her tough yet slender legs. It came through in her gait, as well, for she had the smooth, tireless lope of a Spanish Barb. No wonder Jess had been so protective of her. He'd been riding her a scant two hours and already he figured she was worth a great deal of money, that value not just solely based on her bloodlines.

Jess had trained her well. She had a way with all animals, but with horses she could make a kind of magic. This little mare might be green yet, but soon she'd be dazzling some fortunate high bidder who might live anywhere in the world.

"She needs to go back to school," he explained to the mare. "I don't know why it took me so long to see that, but it's the only way. She needs to get beyond this place. Beyond you and beyond me. She needs to get past the anger she feels about everything right now. She needs to finish up her education. She's too damn smart to stick around here just to pull down some barbed-wire fences."

He listened to his own words and laughed. Hell, for years he'd dreaded her going away to school, and now he was telling one of her horses that it was the only thing for her to do. To leave here for at least one year, maybe forever. "But if she comes back when she's finished because she chooses to be here with us, that'll really mean something," he said softly into the mare's flickering ears.

It was the kind of day that swept across Montana in a vivid panorama of strong winds, deep blue sky, tawny grasslands and looming snowcapped mountains. The sun strengthened and softened the chilly air, melted the frost from the grass, rose higher and coaxed a mist off the surface of the tumbling creek he followed. He heard a flock of Canada geese overhead, heading south just as fast as they could go, leaving their wild northern haunts and winging stalwartly toward the barrage of hunters' guns that would dog them all the way home and keep more than a few from making it. "Good luck," he said, because that was what Jess always said when the geese flew over, heading south in the fall. Good luck!

He felt good, better than he had since he'd gone to Alaska this past spring. He felt as if he could eat food again and taste it, sleep again and not be tormented by hopelessly dark and lonely dreams of loss. He reined the bay mare to a rapid walk as she began to ascend Dead Woman Pass.

Running the legs off her wouldn't do. Jess would never forgive him.

THE RIFLE WAS a Weatherby .357 Magnum, packing a big enough wallop to knock down an elephant, let alone a thousand-pound grizzly. The senator took good care of his guns, and he was especially fond of the Weatherby. His only regret was that the elephant he'd shot with it several months prior had to be forfeited to a pride of lions patrolling that area of the game preserve. The African government frowned on the killing of its elephants. There was no way he could have returned home with the great beast's head to mount on his wall.

Still, the kill itself had been satisfying. Whenever he picked up the Weatherby he felt an almost sexual thrill. The anticipation of the hunt always did that to him. Now he looked forward to pitting his wits against the big bear. Looked forward to the moment the bear moved into range and he could target the kill. Looked forward to the moment his finger would squeeze the trigger and the bear would take the full charge of the massive bullet. Looked forward to mounting the bear's head on his wall. He'd already made a place for it, next to the lion and the tiger. What location could be more appropriate than that?

All that remained was for Joe to pick him up. He was ready and waiting and had been since before dawn. He'd fully expected that Joe would call and tell him to get his gear together. Joe Nash had never let him down.

If he knew what was good for him, he never would.

CHAPTER TEN

THERE WERE LOTS of things a person could do with just one good arm, and Jessie had discovered many of them since she'd broken one of hers. One thing she couldn't do, however, was braid her hair. The metal pins in her forearm kept getting snagged in her dark tresses every time she tried. At length she gave up and drew her hair back into a loose, if somewhat lopsided, ponytail. Long, flowing hair might befit other women, but for a working cowgirl it just wouldn't do. Not that she was going to be much of a cowgirl for a while.

She stood on the porch looking out toward the mountains while the morning slipped away from her, the sheaf of papers that Guthrie had handed her before riding off held firmly in her hand. She had read them over and over, her convictions swinging erratically between staying here and accepting the job that Caleb McCutcheon had offered, and going back to school, then pursuing a career in veterinary medicine. She'd spent the morning cursing Guthrie's apparent duplicity on the one hand and blessing his selflessness on the other. Had he been toying with her? Trying to get her goat?

No. Guthrie was many things, but deceitful wasn't among them. He must have had a change of heart, a change of attitude. All these years he'd rebelled against her leaving here, and suddenly he was encouraging her to go.

The strange thing was, now that he was urging her to leave she no longer wanted to. She wanted to unpack all the boxes stacked in the shed, return her mother's, her grandmother's, her great-grandmother's things to their proper and time-honored places in the old ranch house and settle back into the comfortable routine of living here. Only, this time it would be different. There would be no constant gnawing anxiety about how she was going to make ends meet. That would be McCutcheon's worry now. She could buy what she needed, hire whom she pleased and see that the ranch was run the way it should be, no expenses spared.

Instead of spending her money on veterinary school, she could invest it in land. She could buy Dan Robb's place, the one Bernie had told her about. It didn't amount to much, but it did abut the Weaver ranch and one corner of it connected with the Gallatin National Forest. It would be another piece in the jigsaw puzzle that would ultimately tie together Yellowstone, Gallatin National Forest and the Weaver land, and create one of the largest contiguous unfenced pieces of open space in the West.

Compared with that dream, what chance did veterinary school have? No, she wouldn't make that phone call. Her mind was made up.

And yet… Could she deny her lifelong ambition to become a veterinarian? Her two summers in Arizona working for Lorraine Carey had shown her just how satisfying such a career could be. Dr. Carey specialized in equine sports medicine and worked out of her truck, traveling from ranch to ranch and practicing the kind of medicine that old-school vets like Dr. Cooper hadn't even heard of. She also had access to one of the most advanced surgical clinics in the United States. She'd let Jessie observe two of her operations on racehorses. The experience had dazzled her.

Could she give up any chance of ever having such a career and not live to regret it later?

Jessie narrowed her eyes on the mountain peaks and tried to visualize herself in ten years, in twenty. What would she be doing when her hair was starting to gray and her childbearing years were past? What would she be doing when she was sixty? Would she be standing here on this porch, looking out at these solid, unchanging mountains? Would she still be all by herself, fighting the endless battles that life threw at her and growing more embittered and cynical with each one?

Where would Guthrie be? What would he look like when he was sixty? Damn the man, he'd be just as handsome as he was today. More so, even, with his hair streaked with silver at the temples, his long body just as lithe as ever. Guthrie would age the way all true cowboys did, and the years would give him a depth of pragmatic wisdom and wry humor that would make others seek him as they did shade and a cool drink on a hot afternoon.

Would they be together, she and Guthrie, when they were old and gray?

As hard as she tried, she couldn't see into the future.

But she could see something else. A man walking toward the ranch house, limping along with the aid of a pair of crutches, Blue dogging his heels. Caleb McCutcheon must have grown tired of sitting on his porch, watching the river run by. He thumped and swung along at a brisk pace until he reached the bottom of the steps, where he paused and grinned up at her. "I'm getting pretty good at this," he said. "I was wondering if you'd made up your mind about the job."

Jessie's fingers tightened on the sheaf of papers. "I've been thinking about it."

"I never told you what the salary would be."

"It doesn't matter."

"Well, it ought to. People should feel they're getting paid what they're worth."

"Is that how you felt when you signed all those baseball contracts?" Jessie said.

McCutcheon threw back his head and laughed appreciatively. "I felt like the most ridiculously overpaid person on earth!" he admitted. "But I signed my name all the same. And I kept the money, too."

"All right, then. How much are you willing to pay?"

"Well, I've thought about it for a long time. It'll be hard work, but nothing you aren't already used to doing. There'll be weeks when you put in eighty hours, and times in the dark of winter when you'll barely pull forty."

"It's seven days a week, on call twenty-four hours a day, summer and winter."

"True enough. Animals like to be fed in winter and watered, too, and I haven't been here very long, but it seems they're always getting into some kind of trouble. Seven hundred."

Jessie gripped the papers so hard they scrunched up. "Seven hundred *dollars* a week?" she said.

"That's right."

"Seven *hundred?*"

"Yes."

"You could hire two full-timers for that amount of money!"

"I figure you're worth four full-timers any day, and I'd be lucky to get you for that price."

Jessie turned and stared out at the mountains. A hawk wheeled high against the hard blue sky, scanning the tawny land for some promise of its next meal. "Guthrie came by here this morning."

"He told me last night he was going to try to bring your mares in."

"Did he also tell you that he wanted me to go back to school?"

The expression on McCutcheon's face said plainly that Guthrie hadn't. McCutcheon pondered her words. He leaned against his crutches and stared at the ground for a moment before squaring up to her. "Let me get this straight. He doesn't want you to take this job?"

"He thought I should go back and finish up vet school. He knows that's what I wanted back before my father got sick." McCutcheon shook his head, apparently too bewildered to speak. Blue stood beside him, peering questioningly up into his face, her tail flagging gently. "I guess it's something he thought about all night long, after he left your place," Jessie continued. "He even called the vet school this morning to talk to one of my professors about it." She held up the sheaf of papers. "I honestly don't know what to do. One minute I want to stay here and rip out fences, the next minute I think maybe he's right. Maybe I should go back to school."

McCutcheon drew a deep breath. "Then I'd suggest you finish your education. You can always come back here. I meant what I said about you belonging to this land. This place isn't going anywhere and neither am I, not for a long time, I hope."

"But the job! Pulling the fences! Who would help you with that?"

"Oh, don't you worry about this crazy old man. I have all the bases covered. Last night Guthrie agreed to take the job if you turned it down."

For a moment McCutcheon's words were too unexpected to digest, but then Jessie's jaw dropped and she felt heat flush her face as a surge of hot anger boiled through her blood. ''Guthrie!'' She crumpled the sheaf of papers into a ball and flung them at her feet, seething. ''No wonder he wanted me to go back to school! He wanted that seven hundred dollars a week for himself! Well, he isn't getting it! Mr. McCutcheon, if your offer still stands, I accept!''

''Well…'' McCutcheon rubbed his jaw. He sensed he had gotten himself into a pickle and he had no idea how to climb out of the brine. ''I don't believe Guthrie wanted to take the job from you. Hell, he didn't even know what it would pay. He just didn't want to leave me in a bind if you should go. Anyhow, I'm a man of my word. The job is yours…if you're sure that's what you want.''

''It is! I'm going to start unpacking right now. By the time Guthrie gets back with my mares, things'll be back to normal around here, and if that doesn't set well with him, then he can just pack up his things and run right back to Alaska!''

STEVEN LOOKED forward to seeing Jessie, but the idea of spending an unknown quantity of time on horseback, looking for her mares up in the high country, left him feeling a little off balance. He remembered how lame that last horseback ride with McCutcheon and Jessie had left him. He might be a full-blooded Crow Indian, but he'd take his Jeep over a horse any day. In fact, he wished he were sitting in it now, instead of riding in the passenger seat of a very old pickup that Pete Two Shirts drove down the ranch road. The truck's vinyl seat was cracked and shredded, the tires were bald, the paint was blistered and rust had worked its way into every possible crack and crevice. The vehicle had no suspension to speak of and conversation was possible only in raised voices. The horse trailer hitched behind looked pretty much the same as the old truck, but inside it were two solid horses, if what Pete had told him was true. And there was no reason it shouldn't be. Pete Two Shirts was renowned for his knowledge of horses.

"So," Pete said, downshifting and easing the truck to the left to avoid a deep rut, "this girl—Jessie Weaver. You like her?"

Steven gazed out the mud-spattered windshield and said nothing.

"She likes you?" Pete said.

Silence.

"So. When we find the mares, will she like you better then?"

"You talk too much," Steven said.

"And you don't speak. That's not like you. You must be in love."

Silence.

"Once, we were like brothers," Pete said. "You'd tell me stuff."

"I still tell you stuff."

Pete maneuvered the truck around a rock. "It's not the same. You've gone on a long journey, took another name. You walk in the white man's world now." He shook his head. "You've changed."

Steven looked at his friend for a long moment before facing front. The truck was climbing the last knoll toward the Weaver ranch. He could see the old weathered ranch house. Jessie was standing on the porch, watching their approach. He felt something tighten inside him, as he caught sight of her. "I haven't changed that much," he told his friend.

"Prove it," Pete said as he pulled the truck to a gentle stop just below the porch and cut the engine.

Steven wrenched open the door and jumped down. He

looked up at Jessie and felt that painful twist of emotion again. "I brought my friend Pete Two Shirts and two good horses. We'd have gotten here sooner, but Pete's son was sick—he had to take him to the clinic. But we're here now, and we can find your mares."

Jessie stepped to the porch rail. A breeze flagged the end of her lopsided ponytail. She smiled faintly, revealing a hint of something good and gentle, and glanced toward the truck, where Pete sat waiting. "Thanks, but there's no need for you to take another ride, Steven," she said. "Guthrie's gone up to bring the mares down. He left less than an hour ago."

Steven nodded, thumbs hooked in the rear pockets of his jeans. "Does he want help?"

Jessie shook her head. "He'd be insulted if you offered it. Come inside. I'll make a fresh pot of coffee."

Steven looked down at the ground, then shifted his gaze to where the mountains walled off the sky. "My name isn't really Brown," he said, studying the skyline. A long silence followed his words and he lifted his eyes to her face. She watched him and waited with a quiet patience that he greatly admired. "I changed it when I went to law school," he said. "I didn't want to deal with the prejudices, the old feelings. I thought Brown was a good name."

"Brown's a fine name," she said, "but it's no better than your own, whatever that might be."

Steven studied the scuffed ground at his feet. He thought for a moment and then glanced up at her. "Young Bear," he said. "Steven Young Bear, Crow Indian of the Wolf Clan, who doesn't like riding horses too much but who very much admires a woman named Jessie Weaver."

His words brought color to her cheeks. Her eyes were dark and turbulent. She shook her head. "Steven, I…"

He raised one hand. "That was not said to make you uncomfortable. You're an extraordinary woman. I only pay you homage. If you ever need anything, I'm only a phone call away. You have the number. And remember, you said you wanted to see the buffalo herd. The *bi'shee*. I'll show you any time you want."

Steven spun on his heel before she could respond and climbed into the passenger seat of Pete Two Shirts's old pickup. Pete started the truck, backed it up skillfully with the trailer in tow and headed down the ranch road. A long time passed, long enough for them to reach the main road and turn north toward Bozeman. "Well," Pete said, staring straight ahead as he drove, "you proved it, I guess."

GUTHRIE DIDN'T THINK he'd find Jessie's mares the first day out. In fact, he kinda doubted he'd find them at all, especially since Fox had such a big head start and an active loathing of captivity. Given the choice between suffering through a harsh winter without promise of food or shelter and being offered a snug barn, a good bait of feed and fresh water, she'd choose the wild way every time. The odds were in her favor that she'd survive, too. But Jess liked having her broodmares down near the ranch when the bitter winds blew and the snow piled up, and he didn't blame her. Fox might, but Fox was a wild horse, and some wild horses thought differently about certain matters of civilization.

There was always the possibility that the horse Joe Nash had spotted at the grizzly's kill site was Fox, and that nagged at him, for if the wily red mare was dead, her band might be scattered to hell and gone in the foothills.

If Jessie's prize stallion hadn't been struck by lightning, none of this would have happened. The gray had brought the mares down each fall of his own volition, driving the

stubborn reluctant Fox before him using his teeth and his
hooves. He had kept his band safe from predators, holding
them in the valley, close to the home ranch, close to Jessie.
She had been inordinately fond of that intelligent, rugged
horse, and he had trusted her enough to bring his band of
mares to her willingly each fall.

The fates seemed to have conspired against her—taking
her father, taking her brave but gentle gray stallion, taking
her ranch and her heritage, all within a year's time. No
wonder she was angry and raged against everything.

"Whoa, now." He drew rein and the bay mare flexed
her graceful neck and blew. He rubbed a gloved hand over
the crest of her neck and felt the tension in her ebb. "Easy,
girl. Let's stop for a breather." He swung out of the saddle
and loosened the cinch, then gave the saddle a shake to
unglue it from her sweaty back. The climb up into the pass
had been tough, but the young mare hadn't shirked. It was
past noon now, and they were at least an hour shy of where
Jessie had found Blue. He thought he knew the place she'd
been told of, but there were many side ravines angling
down out of the pass, and pinpointing any one of them
with certainty was hard. The only thing he was sure of was
that it was on Montana Mountain.

She hadn't asked him to find the kill site. She hadn't
expressed any wish to learn which of her mares she had
lost, but Guthrie knew she was wondering. Knew Jess
wanted to know. Even if he never located her little band
of broodmares, he had to at least bring her that information. Finding the place Joe had described from the air and
Jess remembered from the ground was important for him.
He wasn't eager to have a run-in with the grizzly, especially so near a kill site, but the mare would give him
ample warning if the big bruin was anywhere around.

Horses were scared to death of grizzlies, and with good enough reason.

Grizzlies could kill horses.

MCCUTCHEON SAT on the porch of the old cabin and watched the sparkling waters rush past. He wondered if a girl like Jessie Weaver could ever care about a man like himself. He wondered if she could ever look at him in the same way she looked at the mountains, at the big blue dome of the sky, at the hawk that wheeled high above, at the horses that ran free across the face of land she loved. He wondered, idly, if his wife would ever give him a divorce.

McCutcheon sighed wistfully, then laughed. "Old fool," he said to himself. The little cow dog thumped her tail at his words. Blue had followed him back to the cabin after his conversation with Jessie earlier in the day. It was as if she needed to make sure he got where he was going, and then she needed to be sure he stayed where he was supposed to be. He wondered, again idly, if Jessie had charged Blue with baby-sitting him. Such a thing would not be beyond her or the dog.

And then he wondered where Guthrie was, if he had reached the place that Jessie had lost her horse and had found Blue injured. Wondered if Jessie knew how painfully in love with her Guthrie Sloane still was. Wondered if Jessie realized that she was still in love with Guthrie, or if maybe her emotions were all tangled up with another good man, as well. Steven Brown, for all his quiet reserve, was plainly smitten with Jessie Weaver.

McCutcheon shifted in his chair, arranged his injured ankle on the footstool and pondered the painful paths of love. Had he ever truly trod them the way these three young people had? No. Love to him had meant something completely different, and he had chosen a different path. Perhaps *chosen* was not the word. Perhaps saying he had stumbled upon a different path and then groped his way along it as best he could would be better.

In retrospect, it was not the way he would have chosen had he been given in the impulsive days of his youth the wisdom of his years. Nonetheless, it was the way he had chosen, and any regrets he had were of his own doing. After all, a man made his own bed, and hadn't ought to complain about lying in it.

JESSIE HUNG the painting just so and then stood back to contemplate the story it told, laid out in the spare but masterful strokes of an artist's brush, bound in its gilt frame against the plain whitewashed walls of the ranch's living room. She had grown up looking at this picture. How many hours had she spent gazing at it, letting herself be transported to another place, another time?

She could hear the plaintive lowing of the cattle, the sounds of their hooves striking the dry earth and their long twisted horns clacking together. She could taste the dust that rose in the hot air, smell the killing drought that accompanied the dust, feel the torture of longstanding thirst, see the shimmering wall of mountains on the distant horizon above the bony backs of two thousand head of Texas longhorns—mountains that taunted with the promise of shade and clear, cool water but never came any closer as the days slowly passed.

Llano Estacado. The Staked Plains. Home of the Comanche, and a harsh and hostile barrier that had to be crossed if a man was to bring a herd of cattle from a place called Texas to territory known as Montana.

She had crossed it with her great-grandfather a thousand times and more, both in daydreams while entranced by the painting and again in the turbulent dreams that swept her up in the middle of the night and stampeded her into another time, another reality. She had been there. She had suffered, but she had survived, and she survived still, to stand in the great room of the old ranch and look upon the canvas that had been painted more than one hundred years ago in tribute to a man with a vision, a man whose blood ran in her veins.

"There," she said, speaking quietly to the ghosts who gently haunted the room. "I've put it back where it belongs."

Her anger at Guthrie had faded a little with each box she had laboriously unpacked, using her injured arm more than she should but unable to resist the urge to make the home place comfortable and familiar again. She had paused in midafternoon to drink a cup of hot coffee and soak up the warmth of the waning sunlight while sitting on the edge of the porch steps. He would be well up into the pass by now, perhaps near the place she had found Blue. Would he try to identify the dead horse? She hadn't asked him to, yet she knew he would. When he came back he would be driving her mares into the valley before him, because she knew, also, that he wouldn't return until he located them. No matter how long it took, Guthrie always got the job done.

Once, when he was seventeen, he was gone for over a week on a three-day job out at the line camp on Piney Creek. He was checking fence, and he came upon a stretch that had been cut and ripped out to allow cattle from Bureau of Land Management grazing leases to stray onto Weaver land, which had far better grass. Not only had he meticulously repaired the long stretch of damaged fence, but he had driven the trespassing cattle, some 115 head, fifteen miles across country to their respective head-quarters.

Jessie smiled, remembering how he looked when he'd ridden up after that job. His lip was cut, his eye was swollen shut, his nose was broken and he could hardly climb down out of the saddle, but he hadn't said two words to anyone about what happened. It took a trip to town to sift out the story, and Badger liked to tell it still, how Guthrie had driven that herd through Dick King's yard, trampling his wife's flower beds and ruining the vegetable garden to boot. He'd called Dick out and the two of them had at it there in the yard, right in front of King's young wife. Jessie just assumed Guthrie had come out the poorer of the two, but Badger had set her straight. "Oh, our boy's top dog—make no mistake. You think Guthrie looks bad you should see Dick King! I highly doubt his cows'll be straying onto Weaver land any time soon."

Guthrie had never backed down from a fight. He didn't go looking for trouble, but when it came to his door he faced up to it. The only fight he'd ever run from was the one with her, and then he'd run clear to Alaska to avoid it.

Maybe they needed to start over again. Maybe Guthrie was right. Maybe friendship was the beginning they had to return to in order for their hearts to find their way back home.

CHAPTER ELEVEN

BADGER WAS ON a mission. He'd offered his services to both Bernie and Ben Comstock, and the mission Bernie was sending him on played neatly into his determination to keep a sharp eye on suspicious happenings in the valley. The more legwork he did, the greater his chances of helping the warden. Driving out to the Weaver ranch played right into his secret plans, though Bernie had cast doubt on just how secret they were when she handed him the cardboard box filled with tidily packaged home-cooked delights. "Take this out to Jessie, will you, Badger? And for heaven's sake be discreet!" she'd advised.

What had she meant by that exactly? Had she overheard the conversation between the warden and him? Was she warning him not to run afoul of Senator George Smith? Or were her words simply a gentle prod, a woman's way of asking him to see how things were going between all parties involved and asking him to report back to her at his earliest convenience? He was not above doing both, knowing how Bernie wished for a happy resolution to Guthrie and Jessie's estranged relationship, and how Comstock wanted to nail Senator George Smith and his sidekick, Joe Nash.

Oh, yes, Badger could do both, and gladly enough, too. Nobody wanted Jessie and Guthrie to get back together more than he did. Hell, he'd been there the day that girl was born. He remembered it well enough even after all these years. How Jessie's mother had taken it hard, hard enough so's to make any man set back and think a bit before delving again into the mysteries of a woman. How the midwife, a woman of some fifty-eight years and countless births, had come out of the bedchamber as pale as the sheet that had swathed that quiet child, and how she had drawn back one corner of the bloodied cloth, and in the awful tension that was that night he had caught a glimpse of Jessie's face, and that moment had stayed with him forever.

He loved her in a way that was somehow more profound than her own father's love, for he had stood on the family's outer edge and seen the rise and fall of her empire; seen, too, the stuff that she was made of, this quiet but passionate child, as the hardships suffered over the years had shaped her into the strong young woman she had become.

The same was true of Guthrie. The boy had come to this place and had changed it and been changed by it in many of the same ways Jessie had. Both of them were moving toward some as-yet-unknown future, but their futures must surely be bound to each other and to the land. Nothing would make sense otherwise. Badger believed that all things happened for a reason. His mother had told him that when he was knee high to a grasshopper and his mother had always been right.

Badger drove his truck down the rutted ranch road, one hand on the wheel, the other steadying the cardboard box that rode in the passenger seat. Yessir, they'd eat well tonight. Maybe they'd eat together, Jessie and Guthrie and McCutcheon, and maybe they'd ask him to stay on and enjoy the feast. That'd be real nice, just like old times. Well, not quite, but he had fond memories of the meals he'd taken at that old kitchen table, hearty meals cooked by Ramalda, that big Mexican woman Drew Long had married. Jessie had helped her out some from time to time, but the love of standing over a hot kitchen cookstove did not abide in that girl. She'd far rather be out from dawn to dusk riding some half-wild mustang, chousin' cows and chasing after her untamable dreams.

At fourteen Jessie had been about as much a tomboy as a girl could be. "I don't much care for housework, Badger," she'd announced to him one day whilst hurriedly saddling her horse. Ramalda was up on the porch, calling for her impatiently. It was laundry day, and Ramalda fully expected Jessie to pitch in, but the girl had other plans. "Housework is for married women and I don't expect I'll ever be married."

"You'll break Guthrie's heart if you tell him that," he'd cautioned, stepping into the saddle. Jessie was already astride, impatient to make her escape before Ramalda caught her.

"He already knows," she'd said, snugging down her hat. "I told him flat out I was never gettin' married."

"Oh? And what did he have to say about that?" Badger asked as they snuck around the corner of the pole barn and reined their horses down along the river.

"He thinks I'll change my mind, by and by. I guess he just doesn't understand how it is. Face it, Badger. Why would anyone want to be married?"

"Your parents were married."

"Yes, and look where that got my mother."

"Your mother didn't die because she got married," Badger said, knowing where this conversation was headed.

"She died because she had me. She wouldn't have had me if she hadn't got married."

"She died long after she had you. You had nothin' to do with your mother's death. She died because she got sick."

"She got sick because I brought that sickness home from school with me."

"She got sick because she got sick, Jessie. And in a few years' time you'll be talkin' different about marriage."

"Nope. Not me. It'll never happen!"

Badger chuckled, remembering how adamant she'd been, jogging along on her horse, chin uptilted in that stubborn way of hers. Of course, a few years later she was madly in love with Guthrie, wandering around all starry eyed, helping him build that cabin over on Bear Creek, counting the children they'd have together on both hands. She even had names picked for them all. She was so swept up in that boy that she nearly forgot about such a thing as college.

Hell, maybe she shouldn't have gone away to college. Maybe if she and Guthrie had pitched camp together right out of high school things'd be different today. Maybe none of that bad stuff would've happened. Maybe she'd be happy now, countin' her babies on one hand and her blessings on the other. Or maybe she and Guthrie would have gone their own ways no matter what when the ranch failed. Hard to tell which way the heart is going to turn when it's being tugged this way and that.

Take McCutcheon. He was reputedly a married man, but his wife lived in another country most of the time. Where was the sense in that? Maybe that was just how rich people lived. McCutcheon sure had a lot of money. Why, he was so wealthy, rumor had it he gave a lot of it away to charities. Such a concept was beyond Badger's grasp. If he had enough to keep hunger at bay and pay his daily dues, he counted himself lucky.

It helped if a man lived simple and had plain tastes. McCutcheon seemed as if he could live as plain as Badger did and be happy enough. Maybe choosing a simple path was different from being forced down it due to circumstance. Some folks would probably keel over in a dead faint if they had to use an outhouse or take a bath standing in a galvanized washtub. They'd forgotten that a short while ago everyone lived that way and thought nothing of it.

Well, maybe a few thought enough of it to invent such things as flush toilets and hot showers and the like. Not bad inventions at all, come to think of it.

The truck slowed as it climbed an incline, and Badger downshifted. He always liked the last stretch of ranch road the best. He liked the way the road rounded over this gentle knoll, crested in a grove of tall Engleman spruce and then all of a sudden there it was, stretched out as far as the eye could see—the high climbing valley, the river winding through it, the ranch buildings nestled at the foot of Montana Mountain and the big sky reaching forever.

Even after all these years the beauty of this mountain valley still tugged at him. That it wasn't Jessie's home anymore was hard to imagine. To him, it would always be the Weaver ranch, and he would remain tied to it the way Jessie was, the way Guthrie was, the way anyone who had ever sweated and toiled and struggled and loved the land was bound to it. The land got in a person's blood the way the spawning stream got into a salmon smolt. Salmon might spend years at sea, but they always knew where home was. They could taste the waters where they'd been born.

Badger cut the truck's engine and unfolded his creaky frame cautiously as he climbed out of the cab. Getting old wasn't the hard part. The hard part was getting around. Things didn't function quite up to snuff, but by God he could still ride a horse, and pretty good, too.

Jessie and the dog came out of the house and the kitchen

door banged behind her. She smiled at him from the porch. She appeared tired but more at peace then she had in a long while. "Hey, Badger."

"Bernie sent me over with some chow. I guess it's edible." He wrenched open the passenger-side door and lifted out the box. "Enough here for an army."

"Well, we don't have an army. Guthrie's gone up into the pass, looking for the mares. If he's lucky he'll find them in a week or so."

"If I know that boy, he's found 'em already and he'll be home for supper, hungrier'n a grizzly in springtime." He climbed the porch steps slowly and nodded as Jessie opened the kitchen door for him. "Say!" He set the box on the kitchen table and swung around in a complete circle, taking in the room with visible appreciation. "The place feels like home again. You fixin' to stay?"

"Yessir. McCutcheon offered me a job."

Badger grinned unabashedly. "That's real fine! I can't imagine this place without you."

Jessie smiled again. "So tell me what's been going on, Badger. It seems like years since I've thought about anything but losing the ranch. Now I just want things to get back to normal."

"Well, most of the talk in town is about you. In fact, I should probably get back right away to tell Bernie you're staying."

Jessie laughed. "She sent you on a mission, didn't she?"

"She'll be tickled pink with my report."

"What else?"

"Oh, not much. Nothing much ever changes in Katy Junction."

Jessie studied him for a long moment, her eyes narrowing and her head tipping to one side. "Huh," she said.

She turned away, poured two mugs of coffee and set them on the table with a decided thump. She then proceeded to poke through the packages within the cardboard box until she found the one she was looking for. "C'mon, Badger. Let's you and me eat some bear sign and get us good and fat," she said, dropping into her chair and opening the bag of doughnuts. She picked one, raised it for a big bite and chased it down with a swallow of strong black coffee. "Okay," she said, settling back in her chair. "Spill the beans. You've got mystery and mayhem written all over that sly old face of yours."

Badger removed his hat to cover his unsettled state. He sat down gingerly and drew his mug toward him. "I don't have a sly old face," he said, injured.

"What is it. Is it Comstock? Has he asked you to keep an eye out for Joe Nash and his hunting clients?"

Badger's jaw dropped. "How'd you know?"

Jessie grinned. "The elk have been bugling up in the high country for a while now and the aspen have nearly all dropped their leaves. If Comstock's got you on patrol, he must smell a rat. Who is it, Badger? Could it be the almighty Senator George Averill Smith himself? He always shows up right around this time of year looking to shoot something big, and he always hires Joe to squire him and his big fancy gun around."

Badger was disappointed that she had guessed so easily. He chose a doughnut from the paper sack, contemplated it for a moment, then bit and chewed. "Well," he said, shaping his words around the yeasty sweetness, "Comstock asked me to keep my eyes peeled, and that's all I'll say about it."

"He'll never catch Joe. A fast helicopter is a mighty hard act to follow."

"Maybe." Badger swallowed, gestured with the remainder of the doughnut. "But if we can just pinpoint his whereabouts…"

"What's he gunning for this time? Sheep, goats, elk?"

Badger's shoulders rose and fell. "Dunno. Just something big."

Jessie sighed. "Something big. Some men have to kill something big to feel big themselves, I guess." She raised her mug, tasted the strong brew. "I'm on your side, Badger—you know that. I'll tell you if I see anything even remotely suspicious. Why are you looking at me that way?"

"I was just thinkin'," Badger said. "Wishin' that I could've told Guthrie before he rode up into the pass. A man up high like that—he can see a long ways. He can see things we can't, down here in the valley. Why, up high in the pass, he can see the sun set over the Pacific and rise over the Atlantic. Guthrie could spot Joe Nash's helicopter easy enough, I guess. I'm just wishin' I could've told him to watch for it, that's all."

JESSIE WOKE UP with a start just past midnight. The green luminescent hands of her bedside clock silently mocked her. To think about what Badger had said and put it all together had taken her seven hours. Joe Nash, Senator George Smith—both on the trail of a big animal to shoot. Guthrie, riding up into the pass to fetch her mares down, riding up toward the kill site of a very big grizzly that Joe himself had spotted just two days prior.

She sat up in the darkness, her heart rate trebling and a cold sweat chilling her skin. Joe had mentioned the bear several times in her presence. Joe had keen eyes. He could measure the size of a creature at a distance of half a mile, and come within an ounce of its weight. If Senator George Smith was paying a lot of money for a chance to knock down a big animal, then that grizzly up in the pass had probably been earmarked for the senator's big gun about the time Joe Nash first set eyes on it. It didn't matter that the threatened grizzlies were off limits to hunters.

Big grizzly for the senator meant big bucks for Joe. That was the bottom line in their world.

Jessie swung her legs over the edge of the bed. She could hear her heart beating in the stillness and her mouth was suddenly quite dry. The entire universe stood still to hear the name she breathed into the silence of the night.

"Guthrie."

Guthrie had ridden up to bring her mares down, ridden up into the pass where Blue had been injured. He would find the kill site, determine which of her mares had died there. He would ride right up into the thick of it, with Joe Nash counting on that dead mare to draw the grizzly back in, counting on the fact that Jessie would be out of commission with her arm broken the way it was. Counting on the money Senator George Smith would pay him when he had that grizzly's head to mount on the wall of his disgustingly opulent hunting lodge. Oh, Lord, it was all so plain.

And she had been the cause of it all. If she hadn't lost her horse, none of this would ever have happened. Joe Nash would never have been asked by Ben Comstock to look for her and he would never have seen the grizzly. That bear might be shot because of her, and Guthrie would somehow be right in the midst of it, the way he usually wound up in the midst of everything.

All because of her!

HE KEPT THE TINY CAMPFIRE burning long after he should have rolled into his blankets and drifted off to sleep. He stared at the yellow flames licking up around the chunks of resinous softwood, smelled the sweet tang of wood smoke, cradled his tin cup in his hands and sipped hot coffee. He was thinking about the wild horses and about how they had led him on a wild-goose chase clear over the pass, only to double back and climb into this high alpine valley where they grazed on the wild grasses and drank the clear glacial waters of Horseshoe Lake. He had spotted them at sunset, the tail end of the band disappearing into a dense grove of softwood at a dead run.

Instead of following them, he had pitched his camp in this pretty place on the shore of the little lake, near the base of a tree big enough to climb should a grizzly pay an unexpected visit. He'd gathered driftwood for his campfire until darkness closed in and the stars spangled the dark arch of sky overhead. He boiled a small pot of coffee and ate a ham sandwich packed that morning, content to sit cross-legged in the small warmth and light of the little campfire and reflect upon his journey.

He had not looked for the kill site after coming upon the fresh tracks of the band of mares, but instead had focused on locating them before nightfall, and in that respect he had been successful. Whether or not they would be in the valley come morning remained to be seen, but the graze up here was still remarkably good and he hoped they would tolerate his presence and spend the night. He had picketed the bay mare close by and her company was a comfort. The mare had done well today and had showed an enthusiasm for travel that Guthrie admired in a horse. He had fed her a generous bait of sweet feed and rubbed her down well before turning her out to graze. A few days of traveling like this and the mare would settle in and become a real good trail horse.

Guthrie poured the last of the hot coffee into his cup. The moon was rising over the rim of mountains to the east of the high valley, one day shy of full. It was big and bright and he could clearly see the craters on its surface. He watched it until it had cleared the horizon and lifted into the night sky. Somehow the beauty of it intensified the empty, aching feeling inside him. He wished that Jess were up here with him, camping in this high, wild place, just the two of them, tucked up close beneath the glow of that big Montana moon.

He wished that she were sitting beside him on this log, that she would listen while he spoke and that she would speak and he would listen, and that they could give and take the words between them that would help make things right again. He wished that they could lie together beneath this bright canopy of the moonlit heavens and move the universe with the power of their love. He wished that she still loved him, and he wished that he knew how to make her love him again, but he realized that such a thing was not possible. She had moved beyond him, outgrown him, evolved to become so much more than anything he could ever hope to be. He could not hope to keep apace of her. He would no longer even try.

The only thing he could do for her now was be there for her when she needed a friend, help her out all he could and try not to let his heartache show.

SENATOR SMITH COULDN'T sleep. He was afraid of the darkness, afraid that if the fire died to ashes all the big creatures that ruled the night would creep upon him silently, and so he sat upright, his back braced against the trunk of the big red cedar, and wondered what had possessed him to ask Joe Nash to let him spend the night out here alone. There was the ever-present threat of being caught, of course, and the fewer flights Joe made to this place, the better. Nobody else knew he was up here, not even Joe's boss, who'd been told by Joe that the senator was just spending a couple days elk hunting out at his remote camp.

Joe had set up a nice tree stand for him, and brought all the prerequisites to keep him comfortable for a week or better. It made no sense for Joe to return tonight, after setting him up so well. He had told Joe to pick him up at sunset tomorrow, and that would be time enough for him to sit in the stand for an entire day and watch for the grizzly.

When a grizzly would return to a kill was hard to say. He'd seen no sign of the bear today, but the helicopter would have frightened it away. At dawn he would climb back up into the stand, which was a good safe distance from his campsite, and he would wait for the bear, and the bear would come.

That was the thing about all creatures. They had to eat. If their behavior wasn't motivated by mating rituals, it most surely was by their stomachs. If only all things were as predictable as that, life would be a lark.

A twig snapped and the sharp sound jolted him to his very foundations. Adrenaline surged. He reached for his rifle, eyes wide. Could it be the bear? Might it have smelled the supper he'd eaten?

He rose to his feet, gripping the Weatherby. After a while he realized that his entire body was clenched with fear, that his hands were gripping the gun so hard they were shaking. He forced himself to relax. The fire would keep the wild things at bay. He knew this. He was, after all, a big-game hunter. And yet a small noise in the wilderness had made him act like a fearful woman.

Contempt coursed through him. He returned to his seat by the fire and threw more wood on it. The flames licked up and brightened the surrounding woods. He saw no eyes glowing at him through the darkness, but his imagination kept him awake for the rest of the night and he had used up every last piece of firewood by morning.

DAWN, and she had been up for hours, had drunk an entire pot of black coffee, had laboriously stuffed her saddlebags with gear, had checked her rifle, stuffed her parka pockets with extra cartridges, carried her saddle down to the corral and told Blue that she would have to stay home. Dawn, and she was saddling Billy—hard slow work with only one good arm. Billy was rested up and rarin' to go, as ready as a horse could be, but he stood pat for the saddle and lowered his head to take the bit. It was as though he was trying to help her, to hurry the process along. The bay gelding seemed as eager as she to be back on the trail again.

Dawn, and she rode Billy down to the old cabin by the river and called McCutcheon out of his bed. He thumped out on the porch in his long johns, braced himself on his crutches, looked at her setting there upon the horse and nodded. "You're going up there after him, aren't you."

"It's a feeling I have," she told him, "and I've always trusted my feelings. I'd thank you to look after Blue while I'm gone. She'll stay right here with you. Badger'll be coming by with food, I expect. If he doesn't, there's plenty up to the main house, and you could call Bernie if you have to. I shouldn't be gone long."

"You shouldn't be going at all, but I guess that won't stop you. You think he's in some kind of trouble?"

"I think he might need my help. He most always helped me when I needed it, so I guess maybe it's my turn now."

McCutcheon nodded again. "I'll watch Blue for you," he said. "You be careful."

"I will." She reined Billy around and lifted him into a

lope. The day was just taking shape, the dim light defining the high mountain peaks, giving substance and shape to the land. It was cold, and Billy's breath gusted from his nostrils like twin frost plumes as he ran off his initial burst of exuberance at being on the trail again. She reined him in before they reached the faint trace that began the ascent into the pass. It wouldn't do to tire him out now, when the whole day and that high pass stretched ahead of them, to climb and conquer.

HE SPENT a good night by the shore of Horseshoe Lake, and when he awoke, the mare, Kestrel, was watching him. She stood at the end of her picket line, ears pricked, nostrils delicately taking in his scent. He sat up and she lowered her head cautiously. "Easy, girl. Easy, Kestrel." At his softly spoken words the tautness in her vanished. She raised her head again, her ears flickered, and she shook her head and neck like a big dog before continuing to graze.

There were live coals buried in the ashes of his night fire, and with a few handfuls of tinder he brought the fire back into service and put the coffeepot on to boil. Luck was with him, for the sky promised fair weather for the day ahead. With a little more luck he would find the band of mares and by nightfall would be returning them to the valley below, to Jess. Perhaps by doing so he would gain some small favor in her eyes.

Perhaps not.

Either way, he was determined to bring those wily mares back down. They were too good to risk losing to the brutal winter that would savage this high valley, and the graze was still good enough now that they might wait too long themselves to head back down. It wouldn't be the first time good livestock was lost to poor judgment and rapidly changing mountain weather. It was up to him to make sure that didn't happen.

Jess. He had awoken in the middle of the night thinking he heard her voice calling his name. A wishful dream it must have been, yet so real he had sat bolt upright in the darkness. To think that she would have followed him to this high place seemed foolish now. Not that she couldn't, for she'd ridden these mountain haunts all her life and they were as familiar to her as they had been to the Indians who'd once called them home. But between her arm with those metal screws sticking out of it and the fact that she could barely tolerate his company, he figured he wouldn't be seeing her any time soon.

He drank his coffee while squatting on his heels beside the little fire, admiring the way the pale-yellow light of dawn glossed the waters of the crystalline lake and touched the very tips of the snowy peaks with a clear, bright light. It was quiet, so quiet he could hear the splash of a trout rising clear across the lake. Civilization felt a million miles away, yet only yesterday afternoon he'd heard a helicopter tracing along the western flanks of the mountains and he'd wondered if Joe Nash was flying some elk hunters into a remote camp. Guthrie had mixed feelings about Joe, but the man had never crossed him, and in spite of his somewhat shady reputation he was a good enough pilot. He'd helped Jessie out, too, and that had gained him some points. Truth was, if he'd thought of it, he'd have asked Joe to scope out the whereabouts of those wild mares. It would have saved him a lot of scouting.

But no matter. He'd caught up with them on his own, and if they'd left the valley during the night he wouldn't be far behind. Unless, of course, he sat here drinking his coffee all morning long, admiring the scenery and day-dreaming about Jess.

Guthrie rose to his full height and poured the remains of his coffee on the coals of the fire. He made sure the fire was cold out before saddling the mare. He led her to the shore's edge to drink before bridling her, liking the way she took her cue and then lifted her head and gazed at him with those dark intelligent eyes, velvety muzzle dripping water. He wondered if Jess would consider selling him the mare, but the thought was fleeting.

He tightened the cinch, sheathed his rifle in the saddle scabbard and stepped aboard. The mare danced a few spirited steps and then quieted. He stroked her neck, shifted his weight and reached higher to rub behind her ears. No, Jess wouldn't part with this horse, not with Billy getting on in years. All Jessie's horses were good, but this mare was special and Jessie knew it. She'd keep Kestrel and count herself blessed.

He reined the mare around and she stepped out willingly toward the place that he had seen the mares the evening before. With any luck, they'd still be there.

CHAPTER TWELVE

HOW MANY TIMES had she ridden this trail on Billy, on old Seven, on a tough little horse called Mouse when her feet still dangled twelve inches shy of the stirrups? Yet still it surprised her, thrilled her, awed her and humbled her. She could never ride up into these mountains and not feel the magnificence of this great land. And even now, caught up in a clench of anxiety over Guthrie, she had to pause from time to time to sit for a few moments and absorb the vastness of it, breathe the very essence of what it was. Did Guthrie feel the same way about it? Perhaps he did but manifested the emotions differently. Perhaps a man couldn't express his feelings the way a woman could, and perhaps a woman just couldn't understand such reticence.

He could be so silent, so implacable. She would look at him and not know what he was thinking. It maddened her, because she had longed to be a part of him. She had loved him so painfully that it had frightened her, yet at times he was so distant, almost like a stranger. Like when he'd been turned down for the loan on the land along Bear Creek. For days he'd been noncommunicative and downright abrupt, yet for days he'd kept the news to himself, not telling her about this huge disappointment in his life, about the humility of having a banker say to him that he didn't think he'd make good on the loan. He'd wanted that section of land so badly. He'd wanted to build a cedar cabin

on it and move his father there. He'd worked so hard toward that goal and the banker had turned him down. Guthrie Sloane, the banker believed, was not a good risk.

Oh, Lord, she'd been so in love with him that his rejec-
tion had nearly driven her over the edge of the canyon.
She hadn't known the why of his brooding until one afternoon when he'd driven up to the ranch in that old rat-
tletrap truck of his father's. He'd taken the porch steps
three at a time and swept her up in his arms, grinning ear
to ear. "I got the money!" he said, holding her close.
"That paper-backed fool in Livingston turned me down,
so I went to another bank in Bozeman, and I got the
money! I'm buyin' the land, Jess. The papers are signed.
It's as good as ours!"

She'd been glad enough at his news, but the hurt of his
prior silence still rankled. Why hadn't he confided in her?
She was a part of his life, wasn't she? Everything he did
affected her. His thoughts, his actions, his ideas, his opinions—they were the stuff of her life. She resonated with
him, and in doing so discovered facets of herself that gave
into her a more complete sense of being. Wasn't it the
same way with him? Why would he want to withhold anything from her?

She still remembered the times they'd had together
when all was right and things were as they should be. She
still remembered how he could make her laugh, how he
could make her love.

Those memories were sweet, but they were painful, too.
There was no going back. If they were to find anything
like that again, it would necessarily be a melding of those
turbulent times with the sweet ones, an amalgamation that
would preclude the naive and youthful passion that had
swept them up initially and deposited them all these years

later like stones on a glacial moran, worn smooth from exposure to the harshest of elements.

Could they ever look upon each other in the same way? Would they even want to? People changed. Feelings changed. Sometimes there was no retrieving what had once been so precious and it was better to move on and let time dull the bitter memories and heal the raw wounds. Maybe in moving forward another life would beckon.

Another love…?

MCCUTCHEON DIDN'T WAIT for Badger to arrive from town to check on him. He dressed, fumbled his car keys out of his pocket, whistled up the dog and thumped his way on crutches clear to the ranch house, where his car was parked. It was an automatic, after all, and he only needed one foot to drive it. Lucky his left ankle—not his right one—was busted.

He drove to town, Blue sitting beside him on the buttery-soft leather passenger seat, looking well pleased with herself. He left her in the car and hobbled into the café, glad to see Bernie's familiar face behind the counter. Badger was there, as well, sharing a booth with a friend, and half a dozen locals sat drinking coffee and chewing the fat. It was 8:00 a.m. and he figured every morning was pretty much the same at the Longhorn. Same faces, same booths and bar stools, same times. People were creatures of habit.

"Mr. McCutcheon!" Bernie smiled as he lurched up to the counter and slid onto a stool. "What can I get you?"

"It's Caleb, please. Coffee for starters. And then breakfast—eggs, bacon, home fries, toast. Scramble the eggs or fry them—I'm not particular."

"Hotcakes?"

"Sure."

Bernie filled an ironstone mug with robust-smelling brew and nudged it toward him. "How's Jessie doing?" she asked.

"Well, actually, that's the reason I came into town," he said, lifting the mug for a taste. "She was fine when I saw her last, which was about three hours ago, but she was heading up into the pass to find Guthrie."

Bernie frowned. "What on earth possessed her to do that? Guthrie probably won't get those mares back down for a couple days. She's supposed to be laying low and taking it easy, same as you!"

"I know that, and so does Jessie. But she had a feeling something was wrong, so she went off to find him."

Bernie looked pensive. "She had a feeling...?" She gave his breakfast order to the cook and then gazed pensively into space for a few moments before riveting her eyes on him. "Guthrie's my brother, you know," she said.

"Yes."

"She said she had a feeling...?"

"Yes."

"Guthrie's pretty competent. He can take care of himself."

"I don't doubt that for a moment."

"Of course, if she had a feeling... I mean, things can happen..." Bernie's smooth brow furrowed. "She shouldn't be riding up there, anyways. No matter what she's feeling. Not with that arm of hers."

"No, I guess she shouldn't."

"Well." Bernie walked to the end of the counter, refilling coffee cups, then returned. "I'm not sure what we can do. A vehicle can't get up there, and neither one of us can ride a horse. Jessie and Guthrie aren't exactly overdue or missing, so calling the warden seems premature. But still…'' Bernie paced the length of the counter and back. ''If Jessie had a feeling…''

McCutcheon sipped his coffee and wasn't surprised when Badger approached the counter. The old cowboy didn't beat about the bush. ''I couldn't help but overhear,'' he said. He rubbed the stubble on his jaw and his eyes narrowed on McCutcheon's face. ''She said she had a feeling?''

''That's right, and she said she trusted her feelings.''

Badger rubbed his jaw some more, then nodded. ''Huh!'' And then to Bernie, who had been listening on the other side of the counter, he said, ''Can I borrow your phone? I guess maybe I ought to give the warden a call. When Jessie plays a hunch, it's usually for real.''

''Wait a moment, Badger,'' Bernie said, refilling McCutcheon's mug with fresh coffee. ''Maybe we're reading this all wrong. Maybe Jessie went up there to spend some time alone with Guthrie, to try to sort things out between them. Maybe the feeling she was having was of a romantic kind.''

Badger snorted and shook his head. ''Fireworks ain't exactly been exploding between the two of 'em lately. At least, not the kind you and I are hopin' for. No, ma'am. Romance ain't why Jessie went.''

''Well,'' McCutcheon said slowly, ''I don't know her the way you do, but she did seem genuinely worried.''

'''Course she was worried!'' Badger said.

''But *why* would she be worried?'' Bernie asked, giving Badger a pointed stare.

''Because.'' Badger picked up his mug and took a sip, pausing long enough for everyone listening to get fidgety. ''See, we talked last night, Jessie and me. About some things…''

''Badger!'' Bernie set the coffeepot down abruptly and

reached to take his wrist in a surprisingly strong grip. "Tell me what you know. Everything!"

Badger met her eyes and for a few moments maintained his stoic expression, but then his shoulders slumped. He knew when he'd met his match. "All right," he said. "But first I better call the warden and let him know what's goin' on."

JESSIE'S BAND of broodmares had left the high valley sometime during the night, working their way slowly westward through the pass. It would be ironic, Guthrie thought, if they brought themselves back to their winter pastures with no help at all from him. He didn't push Kestrel to catch them up, but rather took advantage of the situation and enjoyed the slow, panoramic descent. It came to him, as the warmth of the morning sun began to work the kinks out of his muscles, that perhaps something else was motivating these wily mares. Perhaps that close encounter with the grizzly had spooked them enough to want to return to the safe and familiar haunts of their upbringing.

Jessie's little band of mares might appear wild, but in fact each and every one of them had been gentled in their early years and had put in their time as working cow horses on the ranch. Jessie had kept the finest of the mares, and when they had passed their prime she gave them into a life of relative freedom, up until recently running them with that gentle gray stallion she had so favored. Each spring when the mares foaled she would keep them in the fenced meadows alongside the creek, and when the foals were big enough to be handled she would do so, hazing the mares into the corrals near the pole barn in order to spend time with the young ones.

To watch the mares around Jessie was a treat. They

would put up a big wild front when first corralled, snorting and tossing their heads and racing around the enclosure with their foals pressed hard against their flanks, dust flying. And then Jessie would walk out into the middle of the corral with a pan of oats and shake it, and the mares would stop and face her, heads thrown up, ears pricked, nostrils flaring salmon pink.

The fire was still in their eyes but was tempered by the remembrance of gentler days, and by the remembrance, too, of the girl who had been kind to them, and had given them no cause to rebel against her. Their genetic compulsion to be free was gradually overcome by an equally powerful compulsion to be near Jessie, to waft the scent of her, to feel her hands work their magic in all the right places and to hear her soft, soothing voice.

In no time flat the mares would be lipping oats from the pan, while the wide-eyed foals watched and took in this human, who would become so formative in their lives. By the second day, the foals would allow Jessie to touch them. By the third day, they were following her around like long-legged pups. And the mares were equally tractable. At weaning, Jessie took complete charge of the foals and let the mares resume their idealistic lives.

The vast scope of the Weaver ranch had allowed her to do this, and had contributed greatly to the uniqueness of her horses. They had more vigor and spunk than the more conventionally housed horses, and it showed in everything they did. How would she manage now that she had lost the free range her mares had so coveted? Or did that really matter? Was the uniqueness all due to Jess? That was possible. Lord, that was probable. She herself was unique.

Guthrie reined in the mare and eased himself in the saddle. He took off his hat and ran his hand through his hair. Once, he'd called Jess his Montana Rose, thinking she'd take it as pure flattery, being as how she loved the wild roses that grew in the untamed places she so favored, but she had laughed at him. "That fits, I guess," she'd said. "I'm thorny as all get out!"

Thorny. That was how McCutcheon had described her, and he was partially right. Jess was sharp. She could cut a man to the bone with her tongue. She was quick to judge and quick to condemn. But Lord A'mighty, when she loved, she loved with all her heart, and her heart was easily the size of Montana. The things she cared about she would fight and die for. She had the courage of her convictions and the simple faith of a child who believed that good would always prevail.

The world would eat her up. It would destroy her. A part of him wanted to keep her in Katy Junction forever to protect her. But she had already faced the worst battle without him and had done the most selfless and courageous thing that anyone could ever do. She had given up what she loved more than anything to keep it from being destroyed.

He had failed her completely. If only he had had the financial ability to help her, he might have saved her world, but the truth was, he was just a simple hometown boy, with the bank account to match. McCutcheon and Steven Brown had it all over him, and that was written in black and white for anyone to see. Guthrie had done all right, by Katy Junction standards. He had a pretty good piece of land, a fine cabin and the means to keep them and make a modest living. But a modest living did not support the dreams Jess had of a west that knew no boundaries, had no limits and sprouted no fences.

A West that had no place for the simple dreams of a homespun cowboy.

SHE HAD TO REST Billy more often than she wanted, for
he was not a young horse, or even in his prime. He was
well past it and ready for retirement. He had paid his dues
ten times over, and anything he gave her now was out of
the stalwart goodness of his gritty heart. She stood at his
shoulder and scratched his withers where he liked to have
them scratched and gazed down, down, into a valley she
could never look upon in quite the same way again, a
valley that was no longer any part of her in reality, yet a
valley that had been the very making of her. She now knew
how the Crow and the Bannock and Blackfeet had felt
when they had been pushed from this land, and she wondered if that anguish would ever go away, if time would
soften the raw, rough edges of the pain.

Nagging doubts assailed her. Had Guthrie been right?
Should she go back to school? The money she had realized
after the debts on the ranch had been paid was enough to
keep her comfortable for a good long while, but not forever, especially not if she bought another sizable piece of
land. If she bought Dan Robb's place she would have
enough room to keep her mares comfortably ensconced
and enough money to finish up her education. Perhaps that
education was the key. Perhaps it would buy her more
land, and give her into an existence that would make sense
to someone who loved working with animals and who
loved the wide-open spaces. Maybe… Maybe Guthrie had
been right. Perhaps she should have called her professor
and talked to him about it….

And then there was Guthrie. She could no more deny
her feelings for him than she could deny her attachment
to this land. He was a part of both, and in spite of her
anger with him she still loved him. Most likely she always
would.

Damn the man! In spite of her resolve to go it alone

after he'd run off to Alaska, she felt herself caving in, weakening, wanting and needing the calm, quiet strength he had always offered her. Maybe he was the most close-mouthed cowboy ever born, but he was honest and loyal, and as Badger had told her time and again, Guthrie Sloane was all wool and a yard wide. And he loved her. Wasn't that enough? *Wasn't* it?

SENATOR SMITH HADN'T meant to fall asleep. He had kept a vigil ever since climbing into his tree stand at dawn. The bear would come. It would come, and he would be ready. The chair he sat in was comfortable. Not all tree stands were this luxurious, but as much as he enjoyed the hunt, he didn't enjoy the hardships that normally accompanied it. He liked a good slug of brandy in his morning coffee. Cream cheese and lox on his bagel.

And, cursed he'd be if the world ever found out, he loved cold beans-and-franks right out of the can. He ate his breakfast up in the tree stand and kept the Weatherby close at hand as he did. After his second cup of coffee, liberally laced with a very fine old brandy, he relaxed a bit and leaned his shoulders against the rough tree trunk. It was quiet. Early quiet. The sun hadn't risen yet, and the morning swell of birdsong was only just beginning. The bear was hungry. George could sense it. Feel it. The bear was on the move. On the prowl. Heading up to the kill site. George Averill Smith would be ready.

"Come on, bear," he whispered. "Come to Big Daddy..."

The brandy warmed his stomach. His eyelids felt heavy. No sleep last night. Not much the night before. Damn that blond nymphomaniac his aide had set him up with. She'd wrung him out and left him begging for mercy. Still, she'd had her talents. She could do things with her tongue and fingers that he hadn't thought possible... Remembering brought a surge of sexual awakening and he shifted in his chair to ease the sudden pressure in his groin.

"Come on, bear! Come to Big Daddy."

He cradled the Weatherby in his lap, kept his burning eyes on the kill site. An hour passed. Long yellow streamers of sunlight broke over the rim of mountains and lay across the valley far below. The shadows lightened, grew shorter. No sleep last night. Tired. He settled more deeply in his chair. He'd know when the bear came. He had an instinct for such things. The bear might be silent, but it had a presence. A smell. An aura. An undeniable energy. He'd know… A nap… All he needed was a nap….

MIDMORNING, and it was Kestrel who alerted him to the place he was looking for. The tracks of Jessie's mares led down the narrow trace, past the gully that opened to his left, and it was toward this dark ravine that Kestrel looked. Her head came up, her ears pricked, her nostrils flared as she wafted some strange scent, and he felt a wave of tension ripple through her as he drew rein. "Whoa, girl," he said softly. He reached a hand to his Winchester and drew it from the saddle scabbard to check that it was loaded, and of course it was—he'd checked it first thing that morning, too—but a man riding into potential trouble couldn't be too careful.

The Winchester had been his father's rifle and it was a fine gun, a classic model 70, .270 caliber, big enough to handle anything, but Guthrie hoped he wouldn't have to use it. There were three reasons for that. Number one, he didn't want to kill the grizzly. Number two, Jessie didn't want him to kill the grizzly. Number three, he wasn't sure that if he *had* to kill the grizzly, his skills would be up to the task.

True, grizzlies had been bested by legendary mountain

men wielding nothing more than Green River knives, but Guthrie had no such illusions about his prowess. He hunted, but only to supplement what for a long time had been a very meager larder for his father and him. Some of Jessie's philosophy had definitely rubbed off on him, for he felt as if he, too, was a part of the earth, and that he was the equal of all living things, no better and no worse. When he killed, he killed humbly, and he thanked the animal that had given its life to sustain his own. Beyond that he had never ventured. Sport killing had never been a part of his life. Perhaps if he'd been raised differently he'd have different views, but between the sustenance philosophy of his father and Jessie's strong spiritual ethics, he had become what he was, for better or for worse.

Oh, he could shoot well enough if it came to that. He liked to target-practice. Many was the hour he and Jess had spent shooting pistols, rifles and shotguns down at the sandpit south of the ranch, pretending all sorts of scenarios at first, as youngsters, and then pretending nothing at all, just competing fiercely against each other. She was a damn good shot. She had a keen eye and a steady hand, and her reflexes were quick. But he was her match, and he could get her dander up enough to best her at least half the time. Oh, yes, the minute Jess started acting pushy, bossy, uppity or mad, it was a sure sign she was off balance and felt threatened. He could read her pretty good after all these years...yet in some ways, and especially of late, he felt he barely knew her.

Did anyone ever truly know another?

The young mare stepped out when he heeled her, but she did so reluctantly, muscles bunched, ears flickering, the whites of her fine dark eyes flashing. Guthrie kept the Winchester balanced crosswise in front of him until the game trail narrowed down and then he propped the butt against his thigh and held it pointing skyward, hand wrapped through the trigger guard.

The trees closed around them, shut them off from the big sky, compressing their view to a narrow, twisting tunnel. At one point the mare had to slide on her haunches down a steep talus slope of loose rock and shale, and at the bottom she nearly jumped out from beneath him with a snort of alarm as the rocks cascaded behind her in a clattering landslide.

"Whoa, Kestrel. Whoa, now, lady." He reined her in a tight circle. She was explosive, ready to blow at the slightest provocation. He lowered his own energy level as best he could in an effort to soothe her and murmured calming words into her flattened ears. She steadied and her whirling dance slowed, but her haunches were still bunched beneath her and her breath came in snorts. "Whoa, now. Easy, easy..."

A lift of the rein and she sprang forward, chin tucked against her chest. Sweat lathered her dark shoulders. She never once lost her footing in the loose shale as the trail climbed again. She sprang over a blowdown as nimbly as a deer, never missing a beat. Lord, what a horse! Had the situation been any different he would be enjoying the hell out of this ride, but his nerves were drawn as taut as hers as he scanned the dark woods for some sign of a dead horse or a big, territorial grizzly.

Abruptly the forest receded and the trail humped over a great dome of bare rock, tracing a narrow fracture that angled steeply upward. The mare lunged, head down, and scrambled for a foothold. He bent over her withers and gave her a free rein, but halfway up the steep incline he stepped out of the saddle to help her, one hand gripping the pommel while the other sheathed the Winchester. He took the reins and led her up the narrow ledge, wishing she were barefoot, for her iron shoes offered poor purchase. Wishing, halfway up, that he'd had the good sense to tie her off down below and come ahead on foot. Wishing, suddenly, with a dark, uneasy feeling of impending disaster, that he'd left her back at the ranch with Jess.

He would have stopped then and there if he could have, but the mare couldn't turn around in this treacherous place. He had no choice but to continue upward.

As they crested the dome he slipped and went down on one knee, and at that very moment a single rifle shot rent his world apart. The sound exploded over him, slammed through him, scared the hell out of him. Kestrel screamed and knocked into him even as he struggled to gain his feet. Her body crashed sideways and eight hundred pounds of horseflesh rolled over him. Together they tumbled back down the rocky dome, tangling in each other as they descended, one of them already dead, and the other reasonably sure he was well on his way.

CHAPTER THIRTEEN

SENATOR SMITH SCRAMBLED from the tree stand with the Weatherby slung over his shoulder. He descended triumphantly, hand over hand down the ladder, heart pounding with excitement. He'd come awake at the very moment the bear had crested the ledge of rock above the kill site. The dark bulk of it had surprised him, caught him off guard for a split second until the adrenaline had kicked in and he'd raised the rifle to his shoulder. It had been a difficult shot, but a good one—damn good! He'd hit the bear square as it lunged over the rock a good hundred yards distant. He'd gotten his grizzly, all right! Nothing could survive the wallop the Weatherby packed. Not even the biggest horse-killing grizzly on the roof of the continent!

He was on the ground now, running in a half crouch toward the ledge, past the dead and mostly eaten horse, creeping now, carefully, carefully... There was always the possibility that the bear was only wounded and was lying in wait for him just over that crest of rock...

Rifle held at the ready, he advanced. Stopped and listened. There was a faint rattle of loose stones far below, but other than that, nothing except the wind. Three more cautious steps and he was on top of the ledge, looking over the rounded curve to where the trail came up out of the forest.

For a moment it didn't register. His eyes widened and a strange blankness came over him, and for what seemed like a very long time he just stood there on the rim of the great rock, looking down.

Shock.

It struck him like a blow, knocking him back a step. His breath left him in a rush and nausea boiled up and brought the bitter taste of bile to his mouth. He nearly dropped the rifle as he went down on one knee, hard.

"No!" he said, gasping for air. "No!"

A dark horse was lying at the very base of the rock ledge, facing downhill, motionless and dead. There was something else, too. Something other than a horse. Something that looked human lying apart from it in a sprawl. Quite motionless, quite dead.

For the longest time he knelt on the cold hard stone. The sun rose high enough to spill into the clearing and the chill air instantly warmed. He became aware of a loud rattling. He'd been hearing it for a long time. He raised his head and realized that the noise came from him. Came from his teeth chattering. His hands were shaking. His whole body was shaking. He stood and his knees barely braced enough to hold him upright.

Maybe he had imagined it. Maybe if he looked again he would see the great dark grizzly.

But he knew, even as he took those few fateful steps, even as he peered with horror once again over the edge, that he would once again see the horse and the man. That he would see the newspaper headlines, the live newscasts, the federal courtroom, the prison walls and the bitter, bitter end of his political career.

The end of his life.

He knew that when he looked over the edge again he would be staring into the abyss, and the abyss would be staring back at him.

JESSIE STOPPED for lunch in a fine, high spot with a far view of the valley below and the Gallatin Mountains to the west. Billy was grateful for the break and was grazing on the sparse browse. A snake had decided to join her, slithering out of a crack in the rocks to sun itself nearby. It wasn't a rattler, but nonetheless she increased the distance between them. Guthrie use to tease her about her fear of snakes.

"I don't know why you get so worked up about 'em," he'd say. "Look how big you are compared with that little thing."

"That little thing packs enough venom in its fangs to kill both of us!" she'd retort.

"Venom? Why, I doubt that serpent even knows the meaning of the word. I bet you could teach it a thing or two, were you to be inclined to talk to a snake."

They seemed to have spent the last year of their relationship sparring, trying to best each other, to have the last word, to win. Win what? What kind of foolishness was that? The verbal parrying had been enjoyable at first, but it had transformed into a kind of war. Why?

The wind had picked up and was roaring through the stunted trees, keening over the jagged peaks. Montana's wind had a soul. It had a spirit. It could blow the thoughts from a person's mind and fill it with a kind of music that was wild and powerful and primitive and incredibly beautiful. She used to think that if one could gather the world's population in this high place and let the wind blow over it, through it and around it the way it had in this valley for a millennium and more, all evils would be swept forever from the human mind.

Today the wind stampeded like a herd of buffalo over the land. She snugged her hat down and leaned against Billy's shoulder and let it cleanse her soul, her spirit, as she ate her meager lunch. She chewed on a strip of tough beef jerky, which she'd dried herself, sipped coffee strong enough to float a spoon, and never heard the rifle shot that was only a half a mile from where she rested. Never heard it because the Montana wind picked it up and carried it away on the thundering hooves of the sacred *bi'shee*.

WHEN HE OPENED HIS EYES he could see two things, one living, the other dead. He saw the mare Kestrel, and she was quite dead, and he saw a raven, perched near the top of an Engleman spruce, watching him from forty feet up. It was a large bird, with the unmistakable beak and beard of its kind. When he looked at Kestrel he felt a huge sense of loss, of guilt. When his eyes shifted to the raven he felt an irrational kinship.

Jessie liked ravens. She said they were smart. Called them the Creators. Listened to them and admired them, but always from a distance, because they were such shy birds, wary of humans the way most intelligent creatures were.

For a time the dead mare and the raven became the focus of his world, and the reason for him to wonder why he was where he was…and who had shot Jessie's beautiful mare.

LUNCH-HOUR RUSH was nearly over at the Longhorn and Bernie was closing out the shift, trying to concentrate on the figures scrawled across the guest checks, but worrying too much about Jessie and Guthrie to keep her mind on her work. McCutcheon had left hours ago to keep vigil at the ranch, and she ferverently hoped that the warden would stop by soon or at least call in response to the message Badger had left on his answering machine. She struggled to tally the figures while listening with one ear to Badger and Charlie haranguing each other. When she caught the gist of their conversation, she gave up on her figures.

"You? You're thinkin' to ride up into them mountains after the two of them?" Charlie was clearly incredulous.

"I may be in my seventies," Badger admitted, levering his old bones off the bar stool and smoothing his mustache with his forefinger, first one side, then the other, "but I can still ride a horse."

"Sure you can," Charlie said. "But how far?"

"Farther'n you, you old fart. Always could, too."

"The hell you say! As I recall, the only time you'n me ever rodeo'd, I was the one who brought home the winnings. All you got was a bunch of busted ribs and a sore head."

"I drew a rougher bronc. If you strained your brain a whisker, you might recall that, as well."

"Well, we was a pair, all right, when we rode for them outfits. We neither of us shirked."

"Nossir, we didn't, you're right about that, but you're still an old fart."

"So you say, but that only makes you an older one."

"Mebbe so. You comin' or not?" Badger hooked his thumbs in his back pockets and scowled at his friend.

Charlie reached up for his hat. "You kidding?" he said, pushing off his bar stool. "Wouldn't miss it."

Bernie was ready with provisions. She'd quickly filled two flour sacks with the stuff and sustenance of a long journey, and handed one to each of them. Her eyes were grave. "I'll keep trying to contact Comstock," she said. "I'll tell him where you've gone and why." She watched the two old men leave the café, both of them bent with the years, arthritic and bowlegged. She shook her head. It seemed foolish to her, the two of them setting out on such a questionable mission, but once they made up their minds to something there was no stopping them. At any rate, Comstock was sure to be home soon, and he'd call the Longhorn when he got his messages.

Bernie settled in to wait.

CALEB MCCUTCHEON was not a horseman. He'd had visions aplenty of himself sitting tall on a horse, but in actuality he hadn't the vaguest idea how to even go about saddling one. He leaned against the top pole of the corral and pondered the horses within while Badger and Charlie threw their ropes over two likely prospects. As they led the submissive beasts up to the fence McCutcheon made his proposal.

"Say, why don't you rope one for me while you're at it. I'd like to come along with you boys."

"Nope," Badger said, shifting a wad of tobacco from one cheek to the other and smoothing the saddle blanket over his horse's back.

"I know my ankle's busted, but the horse has four legs. I won't need to do much limping around."

"Nope," Badger repeated, settling the saddle with a shake, flipping the stirrup up over the seat, then bending to reach beneath the horse's belly for the cinch.

"I'll go crazy hanging out here."

"Well, I'm sorry for that, but there's nothin' else for it." It didn't take any time at all for those two codgers to pack up their gear and haul aboard. McCutcheon felt his spirits sink as he watched them ride out. He waited until the distance had shrunk them to toys, and then he heaved a great sigh.

"Well, Blue," he said. "Looks like it's just you and me."

But as he was stomping back down to the cabin, swinging along pretty good now on his crutches, an idea came to him. A clever idea. He might have patted himself on the back if he could have, but instead he made for his Mercedes and the very handy cell phone that lurked within.

"HEY, JOE!"

Joe jerked awake with a rude start. He'd been napping in the warmth of the sun, shoulders slumped against the corrugated metal of the hangar, long-billed baseball cap pulled over his eyes. Dreaming about a girl who lived outside of Jackson Hole in a house trailer shaded by a big gnarly cottonwood. A girl who was always glad to see him. A girl he hadn't visited in a while. Her name was Carlotta, and she could—

"Joe!"

He straightened, pushed his hat back, yawned. His boss was coming out of the hangar, wiping his hands on a greasy rag and appearing inordinately pleased about something.

"Got a call just now," he said. "That guy you flew to the hospital. Caleb McCutcheon. The rich-and-famous baseball player. He wants an aerial tour of his new property."

"Yeah?" Joe stood, brushed the crumbs of his sandwich from his lap. "When?"

"Now. Today. Soon as you can get out there."

"Huh?"

His boss frowned. "You gettin' hard of hearing?"

Joe's stomach tightened. "Kind of short notice, isn't it?"

"What's the matter? You got nothin' on the books that I can see. You too busy taking a nap to get out there and earn your keep?"

He flushed, took his cap off and whipped it against his pant leg. "No, it's just that I thought maybe this afternoon

I should check on the senator, make sure everything's okay. That hunting camp of his is pretty remote…"

"Hey, this guy's loaded! Get out there. Charm him. He could be a good long term account for us, especially if he hunts. The senator'll be all right roughing it at his camp for a day or two. It's good for him. Builds character. If he calls in for anything, I'll radio you."

"Right."

Joe pulled his cap on, adjusted it. Squared his shoulders. Turned and began walking toward the Bell JetRanger.

Wondering to himself how in hell he was going to get out of this one.

RAVEN, BRING JESSIE…

Raven.

Who? An image. A face. Jessie. Her voice soft. Her hair like heavy black silk flowing through his fingers. Yes, it was Jessie… She was here… but where? Gone. Jessie gone…

The sun was hot. Thirsty. Water. He needed water. Raven, create water.

The bird was still there, black, big, watching. Waiting, perhaps, for him to die.

The smell of blood, sweet, coppery, thick and sticky wet beneath him. A hand lying on the ledge, fingers reaching for something. Was that his hand? Move fingers. Fingers moved. That was his hand. It was attached to him. Belonged.

Awareness seeped into him. How long had he been here? A dullness fogged his mind. Couldn't think clearly. Couldn't focus. Could only lie in stillness and contemplate his thirst, his tremendous, agonizing thirst.

Raven, bring Jessie.

He watched the large black bird for some response. Some indication that it had heard his thoughts.

Raven, bring Jess!

Nothing. No movement. Was the bird real? Was any of this real?

Raven moved with a suddenness that startled. Spread its wings and sprang from the branch. He heard the strong, rhythmic swish of its feathers as it climbed, climbed...

Gone.

And yet he was not alone. A rock bounced down the dome of stone. A scattering of pebbles. A small cascade of gravel. Footsteps, slow, cautious, slipping, skidding.

Human.

Descending toward him. To the place where he lay beside the dead mare.

Instinctively he closed his eyes, overwhelmed with fear, knowing the footsteps weren't Jessie's, knowing that a terrible danger approached and that he was helpless to defend himself against it.

GEORGE SMITH UNDERSTOOD what he had to do in order to save himself. He had spent the past few horrific hours debating different paths to take, and ultimately he had chosen the only path open to him, the only one that gave him any future at all.

He crept carefully down the steep ledge toward where the horse and the man lay. There wasn't much time. In a few short hours Joe Nash would be flying to meet him at the camp, and the pilot had very keen eyes. Unless he hid both bodies well, Joe would spot them, and his political career would be finished. But if he could somehow cover them, scavengers would soon destroy all evidence that the horse had been shot. The grizzly alone could do that in one feeding, but there were coyotes, wolves, ravens, a host of hungry others that could do the job.

There was hardly anything left of that black horse back at the kill site, hardly enough for the bear to bother with. In a very short time there would be nothing left of this horse, either. It would look as though the horse had slipped and fallen, crushing the man and killing itself in the long steep tumble to the bottom of the ledge.

He intended to cover the horse and the man with trees and brush, stones and gravel, deadwood and blowdowns dragged from as far away as he could manage so as to avoid disturbing the site as much as possible. In a week's time Mother Nature would take care of everything and he could get on with his life.

Luck was with him, for when he reached the horse he saw that his bullet had struck the animal between the eyes and had exploded the top of its skull. There was no other mark on the horse. No entry or exit wound to worry about. He turned his attention to the man. A cowboy from the look of him, regrettably young and well built, apparently out elk hunting by himself. He could see the stock of a rifle wedged beneath the horse. Yes, a hunter on a lone journey up into the high country, saddlebags stuffed with provisions, bedroll lashed behind the saddle. Nobody would be missing him for a while.

George had dealt with plenty of dead animals but never before had he confronted a human body. With a certain amount of distaste he bent to grab the man's booted ankles. He backed down the slope, dragging the limp, bloodied body until it was lying beside that of the horse. He dropped the legs and wiped his hands on his pants over and over, as if by doing so he could erase his terrible deed. He couldn't let himself go to pieces over this. Too much was at stake. All that blood... The man was dead. It was too bad, but the senator had no intentions of sacrificing his own life, too.

He began the arduous task of gathering enough brush to cover both bodies. He would need a lot of brush, and he didn't have a lot of time.

SHE HAD HOPED to find Guthrie before dark, but as time passed her hopes dimmed. Billy was tired from the climb and their pace had been slow. For some reason Guthrie had taken a different trail from the one that led directly over the pass. It threaded along the flank of Montana Mountain and then climbed steadily to the northeast before tucking down into a high mountain cirque and a pretty place called Horseshoe Lake. Was he heading there on a hunch? Did he think the mares might be up in that valley?

It was possible. The graze was usually good, and there were several routes in and out, something wild creatures appreciated, especially when they thought they might be cornered by predators. One of the trails hooked back up with Dead Woman Pass; another led down toward the valley, bypassing an old line camp on Colley Creek. Yet another circled the lake and followed the outlet down a steep ravine that emptied into the east branch of the Silver. Which route had Guthrie taken?

She contemplated his day-old tracks. There was little else she could do but follow after them.

Or was there? She reined Billy in and sat for a few moments in deep thought. If her hunch was correct, Guthrie would eventually go to the place Joe Nash had spotted the dead mare. Supposing she went directly there and waited for him? It would be risky, because if Joe had put the senator over the kill site in order to get a shot at the big grizzly, she'd have to be very careful not to be spotted by the senator or run foul of the territorial grizzly. But she would be able to warn Guthrie before he rode right into the thick of things.

Yes, that's what she would do. She wasn't far from there now. In a bit she would need to find a safe place for Billy and tether him securely while she went ahead on foot. The thought chilled her, but she shrugged off the fear, not allowing it to take root. This was all her fault. She had gotten Guthrie into this mess and it was up to her to make sure he came out of it all right.

She'd never be able to live with herself if anything happened to Guthrie because of her.

JOE HAD MANAGED to calm his roiling nerves by the time he landed the helicopter at the Weaver ranch, and nodded a curt greeting to the man who stumped out of the ranch house on crutches.

"How's old Blue feeling?" Joe asked as he helped McCutcheon into the chopper and handed his crutches to him.

"Pretty good, considering. I think she enjoys babysitting me." As he strapped himself in, McCutcheon divulged his interest in an aerial overview. "I'd like to get a feel for the size of the ranch. Where the boundaries are. How much is grazing land, how much is forested, how many cows are wandering over it. Horses. Buffalo. Grizzly bears. You know."

Joe nodded. Adjusted his sunglasses. "Yep. I think I have a pretty good idea what to show you. You bring a camera?" McCutcheon shook his head. "Too bad. The light'll be real pretty in an hour or so. Good for taking pictures."

"There'll be other times. Right now I just want to see it."

Joe nodded again and popped a stick of Big Red chewing gum into his mouth. "Okay," he said. "Scenic tours are my specialty."

Half an hour later McCutcheon had to admit that Joe Nash really knew his stuff. Not only could he fly with a grace that would shame some birds, but he had an intimate knowledge of the land, its geography, history and wildlife, and in spite of McCutcheon's ulterior motives for staging this flight, he found himself enjoying Joe's running commentary, his skilled observations, his keen eyes.

"Down there?" Joe said. "That's one of those longhorn crosses of Jessie's. Look at the horns on that cow! They're really something! Sometimes they curl around just like corkscrews!" McCutcheon hadn't even spotted the cow yet and Joe was already onto something else.

"Those trees there? That tall one, the dead snag atop that hogback ridge? Right in that spot back in 1878 the Crow killed three whites. Killed 'em hard, too. Stirred up all kinds of bad feelings. I guess they thought the whites needed to die, and who knows, maybe they did. They were hide hunters after the buffalo. Slaughtered thousands of them and took their hides, left the rest of the animal to rot. The Indians interpreted that as pretty rude behavior. They relied on the buffalo for just about everything. The buffalo was sacred to them."

McCutcheon couldn't spot the dead tree on the ridge, but he appreciated the history being related to him. "I guess the Indians had a right to dislike us," he said.

"Yep," Joe replied, chewing on his gum.

"I wonder if they still do."

"Why shouldn't they? We took everything they had."

McCutcheon suddenly felt gloomy. Why not, indeed?

"I could show you places where they camped in the valley. Right on your own land. Tepee circles."

"I'd like that," McCutcheon said.

"See that trail climbing up the mountain there? Prospectors laid in that trail. There's a mining camp, or what's left of it, just over that pass to the left of that rock slide. Just a bunch of rotten timbers now, but back in the late 1800s a lot of men lived there, thinking they were going to strike it rich and be on easy street the rest of their lives. Some of them are buried up there. No grave markers, just piles of stones. Kind of lonely. Some folks say that place is haunted, but I don't hold with that."

"No?"

"Nossir." Joe shook his head emphatically. "I don't believe in ghosts."

"Well, I haven't made my mind up either way, but I'd kind of like to see where we looked for Jessie that day," McCutcheon said. "It felt like we'd walked a hundred miles on snowshoes, Guthrie and I. I'd like to view it from the air. Put it into perspective."

"Ah." Joe nodded, the late-afternoon sunlight glinting off his sunglasses. "Okay," he said, banking the chopper. He chewed harder on his gum to quell the ripples of unease in his stomach. The senator wouldn't show himself unless Joe landed. That was the code. He needn't fear discovery from McCutcheon, a man whose eyes were so untrained that he hadn't seen a single thing Joe had pointed out. No, there was no reason to be nervous about this. No reason at all.

He lowered the nose of the chopper and throttled her up.

PAIN. He'd felt it plenty of times before, but never like this. It was everywhere, it was excruciating and with every passing moment it worsened. Nothing he did, no small movements he made to ease his position, lessened it. He had forgotten the mindless torment of thirst and wished only for some release from the pain.

Fleeting thoughts splintered through the pain. He had heard a rifle shot. Footsteps. Human footsteps. Someone had shot at him. Killed Kestrel. Who? Why? A man's face. A glimpse, just a glimpse... Familiar.

Dark. He was covered beneath layers of something. He smelled the resiny tang of pitch. Moved his hands. Felt branches. Why was he beneath a pile of branches? Was it night? Was he dead? Could there possibly be so much pain in death?

He was curled on his side in the fetal position, but he couldn't remember anything of how he came to be here, in this dark place, and in so much pain. All he remembered was the report of a rifle, and the sound of human footsteps... And that face. That familiar face. Just a glimpse he'd had, but it haunted him...

Raven. There had been a raven. He remembered wishing for Jess. For water to slake his terrible thirst.

Jessie. He had killed her prize mare. Ridden her up a slope too steep and she had fallen...was dead. Or had she been shot? Rifle shot. Yes, he remembered the rifle shot. Jessie would never forgive him for losing Kestrel. She would hate him forever. She had coveted that mare, that beautiful horse. Kestrel...dead now, all that blood... Blood everywhere... Death.

He clenched up against the pain, gritted his teeth against it. A sound escaped him, a small sound that squeezed out of his throat.

Mustn't make any noise.

Those footsteps... Who? That man's face... So familiar... Dangerous... Might come back...

Quiet! Mustn't make any noise...

CHAPTER FOURTEEN

BADGER'S BONES ACHED, but damned if he was going to let on. He leaned over the shoulder of his horse, spat a wad of tobacco juice, straightened, wiped his whiskery chin on his jacket sleeve and glanced behind at Charlie. "Charlie, for cripes' sake," he said, "do I have to send to Bozeman for an oxygen tank, or are you gonna make it?"

Charlie racked himself up in his saddle, pretended outrage on his face, and kicked his horse into a rough jog that must've felt as though it was herniating the last of his spinal discs and dislodging all them fancy fillings in his teeth. It looked mighty painful from where Badger was sitting, and he was sure enough familiar with what painful looked and felt like.

"Me? You're worried about me, old man?" Charlie said as he closed the gap between them. "You should see yourself. Why, I've seen dead men who looked better'n you do right now!"

Badger snorted and faced front again. No doubt Charlie was telling the truth, but he wasn't about to let on anything of the sort. "We're makin' mighty poor time, for a pair of top hands."

"Been a few years, Badger, since anyone could'a called us rounders."

Badger braced his shoulders and squared up. He didn't feel old. Oh, sometimes he did, but mostly he just felt the way he'd always felt. Like he could still sweep a little girl name of Lizzy Kinney off her feet, and work the day hard from sunup to sundown. He wondered what had ever become of Lizzy Kinney. Lord, she had surely smote him back when he was a young buck. But the war had come along and swept him away, and when he returned to Katy Junction sweet little Lizzy Kinney was two years gone, spirited away by some traveling salesman with a smooth tongue and a cowlick that even Charlie remembered.

Charlie had been the only constant in Badger's life. Charlie had been his anchor. His sounding board. His best friend. All these long years they'd worked together, drunk together, played cards together, argued together, and they still called themselves friends. That was something, in this day and age. Men had walked on the moon, but that miracle had nothing on their friendship. If the world went to hell in a handbasket, the one thing that Badger could always count on was Charlie.

Two old men in the twilight of their lives. Could anything be more pathetic? Could anything be more profound? Lizzy Kinney was just a sweet memory, but Charlie was a solid presence right behind him, ready to back him up any which way. He was all twisted up with arthritis, absentminded and forgetful and had one foot in the grave, but by God, he was there.

Badger spat again over his horse's shoulder and counted himself damn lucky to have such a friend in his life.

JESSIE WAS NEARLY to the place where she had found Blue. Nearly to the spot where that faint game trail led off the well-traveled one, when she heard a noise. It was the sound of a horse approaching, coming down the main trail toward them. She reined Billy in and sat for a moment, listening. Guthrie? She was downwind from whatever, and it played to her advantage. She reined Billy hard to the right and drove him into the brush and woods to one side of the trail.

Waited there quietly.

Heard more noises, more sounds. More than one horse. A group of horses coming downslope, down the trail toward them.

Unshod horses.

She swung out of the saddle and laced Billy's rein to a spruce. Stepped quietly forward, close enough so that she could see the trail, could watch the approach of the horses. Hope quickened her heartbeat. Might they be her own little band of mares? Could Guthrie have found them and be herding them back down into the valley?

She felt an electrical jolt when the first horse came into view.

"Fox!" The name passed her lips unbeknownst to her, a whisper of disbelief, of joy, unheard by the red mare that descended toward her. She felt a surge of gladness and relief and feasted her eyes on the beautiful Spanish mustang she had feared never to see again. Fox, followed by the others, all carefully picking their way among the loose stones as the trail dropped steeply. They passed one by one and might have kept right on going except for Billy. He let out a plaintive whinny that stopped them all in their tracks. Fox swung about on the narrow trail, head thrown up, ears pricked. Jessie stepped out into plain view of the mares. "Hey, old ladies," she said. "Hey, Fox, you beautiful wild thing you. Decided to come home, did you?"

There was a good bit of head tossing and eye rolling, a stomp of alarm and a snort from one of the mares, and then Fox pivoted on her haunches and continued down the trail, the rest following on her heels. Jessie watched them go and shook her head, giddy with relief. Coaly was missing. A black mare, one of the oldest of the little band and barren for the past four years.

Well, all of life was a risk. Letting the mares run free exposed them to certain dangers and hazards, no doubt about that.

"I'd rather be killed by a grizzly in the mountains of Montana than hit by a bus in New York City," she said softly, watching the mares out of sight. She returned to where Billy was tethered and slapped his shoulder with affection. "Good-looking bunch, huh?" she said. "Don't worry, you'll be socializing with them soon enough." She led him back out onto the trail and stood for a moment, wondering where Guthrie was. Surely he was trailing them down. He couldn't be far.

She swung into the saddle and sat a few moments more, waiting. Glancing back up the mountain, she saw a raven wing in a wide loop over some curiosity. Perhaps the raven was over the kill site. Perhaps it had spotted the dead horse, or a hungry grizzly. Jessie watched and pondered, marked the spot, and then decided to follow along after the mares. Guthrie would catch up before dark, she was certain.

Finding her with the mares would be kind of a joke on him.

SENATOR SMITH HAD EASED some of his anxieties with what remained of the excellent brandy, and by the time he heard the chopper approaching he was reasonably certain that he could carry off the deceit. No one would ever suspect anything. When security finally found the man missing, no evidence would remain of any wrongdoing. He would return to Washington and keep his head down for a while, stay away from his Montana lodge until next spring when fishing season opened. If Joe wondered why he gave up on the grizzly, he'd tell him he'd been called back to Washington for a special Senate hearing. Too bad, but those were the breaks when one was an important politician.

He lifted the bottle for a final swallow before tucking it away inside his down vest. The chopper was coming over the ridge now but veering southward, not heading for the landing spot, a clearing near his camp with a diameter barely big enough to set the Bell JetRanger down in without tangling its blades in a forest of trees. George sat up, listening. His gear was packed. He was ready. It was time. The sun was sliding low, hovering over the Gallatin Mountains. In a short while dusk would descend, and after that, darkness, when all the big predators came out to prowl.

But, unbelievably, it sounded as if the chopper was flying away from his location. He stood up, uneasiness building within him. Yes, the sound was definitely fading, blown away by the constant wind until nothing remained of it.

He was alone…and yet he was not alone. Not one quarter of a mile away from him a dead man lay beside his dead horse, and somewhere in his darkening world a large grizzly grew more hungry.

"YOU CAN SEE the spot we put down to pick you up," Joe said, hovering the chopper and nodding to a clearing below. "I figured we'd catch hell trying to land there, but this thing isn't as big as it sometimes seems. 'Course, in a big wind you need to give yourself an allowance, about twice the diameter you need. This mountain flying can be real tricky in dirty weather."

"I can imagine," McCutcheon said. "So right now we're not far from where you spotted the dead horse?"

"Nope. We nearly flew right over it a moment ago, same mountain, different gully."

"Does this mountain have a name?"

"Montana Mountain. That's where you were. On Montana Mountain."

"Can you show me where the horse was?"

"Sure. It's getting dark, you won't see much, probably. But I'll try to point it out."

Joe had no intention of showing McCutcheon the exact place. He pivoted the chopper and climbed up the slope, dipping over a ridge and picking up the faint trace of the game path. He followed it only briefly before peeling to the left and tracing into a dark ravine, but in the few moments he'd watched the trail he'd seen something that had jolted him to the core, something perhaps no one else would ever notice, but it had stood out as plain to him as a streak of lightning searing a night sky.

"Down there. See it?" he said, pointing to an imaginary spot in the thick tangle below.

McCutcheon peered, shook his head. "You're right. I can't see a damn thing!"

"We better be heading back. It's getting late."

"I was kind of hoping we might catch sight of Jessie's mares," McCutcheon said.

"Not today. Maybe some other day if you want to look for them."

"It'd be a big help to her, just knowing where they were."

"No doubt."

Joe's mind raced. What he had seen troubled him. At the base of that steep rounded ledge where the old trail through the pass came out of the woods he had spotted a pile of dead branches, a big pile. Anyone who spent any time at all in the woods would notice something like that instantly. Something out of place. Unnatural.

Had the grizzly killed again? Was that new pile of brush covering up the senator?

"Hey!" McCutcheon burst out, startling Joe badly. "Look!" He stabbed a finger down below where the main trail snaked. "Isn't that a bunch of horses?"

Joe steadied his pounding heart, chewing hard on the piece of used-up gum. He nodded, sweat springing onto his forehead. "Yup," he said. "Seven. Followed by a rider." He felt sick to his stomach. Big brush pile. Damn! Would a bear have dragged *that* much brush to cover a kill? It seemed unlikely. And who was that rider following after that band of mares? Couldn't be Jessie. Might be Guthrie, though. How high had he gone? Could he have run afoul of the senator up on the mountain?

"By God! That's good to see. Those must be Jessie's mares, and they're heading in the right direction." McCutcheon was grinning. Joe looked over at him and forced himself to grin back, wondering if McCutcheon had deliberately withheld telling him that someone had gone up searching for the mares, or if he really hadn't a clue.

In spite of the chewing gum, Joe's mouth was powder dry.

THERE WAS NO WAY they would make it down into the valley before dark, but Jessie wasn't worried. The moon would be full tonight, a hunter's moon, and it would cast enough light for the horses to navigate the trail in safety. She wouldn't hurry them. If they wanted to graze their way back home, that was fine with her. Guthrie would catch up all the quicker. It tickled her to think of the expression on his face when he saw it was she who was trailing along behind the mares. "What took you so long?'' she'd say, and she knew that he'd just shake his head and grin that faint, wry grin of his.

Maybe they'd camp out together, let the mares keep going on their own. Yes, that'd be a good idea. It would give them time to talk things out. There was nothing like a campfire to coax the words out of a person. They could boil a pot of coffee, share the food in their pockets, gaze into the fire and just talk.

Or maybe… Jessie felt the heat come into her face just thinking about it. Campfire memories, Guthrie use to call them. A long time had gone by since they'd made any. Used to be that any excuse was a good one for kindling a fire. Didn't have to be coming dark; the moon just needed a circle of stones, a bed of hard pan, a little tinder and match, the flames licking up, the sweet tang of pine smoke, Guthrie's eyes catching hers above the flickering dance. The little campfires came to symbolize their passion for each other. Guthrie use to joke that it was a wonder there was any deadwood left in the forest.

Maybe they would never find their way back to that special place in their hearts, but Jessie felt a softening, a warming within herself where for a long time there had been only bitterness and anger. It would be good to sit near a fire with Guthrie again, even if all they ever did was talk.

She pulled Billy out of a stumble, hearing a sound down the trail even as she did, a sound very much like a human voice swearing. Billy's head came up, ears alert. She reined him in and listened.

"Cuss it all, Charlie, don't spook 'em!" an old voice rasped. "Let 'em drift on by. Just let 'em ease past us. There, there now. Good lady, Fox. On by, girls, on by. The barn ain't far now, you worthless old hay burners."

Badger and Charlie! What were they doing up here?

She nudged Billy forward and played catchup with the mares, barely spotting the riders in the thick gloaming. "Badger?" she called out.

"That you, Jessie?"

"Charlie?"

"You betcha. Thought we'd come up and give you a hand."

She drew abreast of them and reined in, grinning with gladness, weak with relief. "I'm glad you did. Did you see that chopper a while back?"

"That we did. Flew right over us. Figured Joe Nash was taking the senator back to his lodge for the evening. I guess you read things the way I did, with that big grizzly bear and all. Where's Guthrie?" Badger said.

"Behind me. I figure I'll go back up a ways, find a good camping spot and wait for him. That is, if you don't mind taking the mares down for me."

"Glad to oblige." She caught the flash of Badger's teeth as he grinned. "You two behave yourselves, hear?" he called after her as she swung Billy back around and headed back up the trail.

NASH WAS in a real pinch. By the time he let McCutcheon off at the Weaver ranch it was too late to go back for the senator. No way could he set the Bell JetRanger down in that clearing in total darkness. It would have to wait until morning. He returned the chopper to the airstrip and drove to town. He needed a beer or two or three, something to take the edge off.

Who had been looking for Jessie's mares? When asked, McCutcheon had been deliberately obtuse, playing ignorant about the goings-on right under his own nose. Said he didn't know where Jessie or Guthrie were, over to Guthrie's place, maybe. Who knows? He wasn't their keeper.

And so forth.

But someone had gone up to look for those mares and had found them, and was bringing them back down. Had that rider also stumbled across the senator?

And then there was the brush pile. That big damn brush pile out in the open where a pile of brush would never be unless a man stacked it there. Men built brush piles when they were clearing land. They wouldn't go into the woods, haul a bunch of dead stuff out and make a huge pile way out in the middle of the wilderness at the base of a barren rock ledge, unless it was going to be a signal fire of some sort.

Signaling who? And why? It was so close to where the senator's tree stand was. So close! Big brush pile! Damn!

Joe drank four beers sitting on the bar stool and each beer had the opposite effect of what he was hoping for. By the time he left the bar he was wound up tighter than a violin string and he knew for certain that there would be no sleep for him this night.

HE WANTED to build a fire, but it was too dark now to gather the wood for it. There was no way he could stay on the ground so near the kill site without a fire to keep that huge grizzly at bay, so Senator George Smith went back to the tree stand and climbed the ladder with the Weatherby slung over his shoulder. He would sleep cold and in the dark, but he would sleep safe, because grizzlies couldn't climb trees.

For whatever reason Joe had stranded him here—and there had to be a pretty good reason—he was certain that in the morning the chopper would return for him. If it didn't, he would walk out by himself. He'd brought a cell phone in case of emergency, but he wouldn't use it unless he had to. Cell phone calls could be monitored.

No, he'd hike out. He could stash the Weatherby when he made it out to the road and bum a ride from some rancher who wouldn't recognize him, not with two days of stubble on his jaw and dressed head to toe in hunter's camo. He'd just be another hard-luck elk hunter who had abandoned the camp to assuage his thirst for a beer in town. Once he reached the road he could walk to his hunting lodge if worst came to worst. To hell with Joe Nash. He'd make sure the bastard never flew again if he didn't come for him in the morning. He'd make sure that worthless pilot burned in hell.

He sat in the dark with his back against the tree trunk and his knees drawn up against his chest. It was cold. He felt a twist of revulsion when he thought about that man lying beneath the pile of brush at the base of that ledge. Even if his inclination had been to help, there was nothing he could have done. Head busted open, all broken up, blood everywhere. That long fall all tangled up with a horse. The poor bastard had been doomed from the moment he'd rolled out of bed that morning.

It had been his day to die.

JESSIE MADE CAMP on a bench just off the main trail. In the near darkness she gathered an armload of dry wood and kindled a tiny, tiny fire, just big enough so that Guthrie would see it when he rode by. With water from her bottle she put a little pot of coffee on to boil, and then set about making Billy comfortable, stripping the gear off him, rubbing him down with a twist of dry grass, giving him a bait of the sweet feed she carried in her saddlebag. There was enough browse to hold him overnight, but he'd have to work for it. In the morning she'd feed him the rest of the grain, and she and Guthrie would ride back down out of the mountains together.

Odd that he hadn't shown up yet. She leaned back against her saddle and ate the last hard-boiled egg, pondering what might be holding him up. She sat up straight as a dark thought flashed through her mind. Suppose... Just supposing he had found the mares and started them back down the trail toward the valley, and then decided to check out the kill site? And suppose when he got there, something bad had happened?

She swallowed. Leaned forward and tucked another piece of wood into the tiny fire. No, that was a foolish thought. The chopper had already come and gone, so the senator had undoubtedly been whisked away to his private hunting lodge for the night. She shifted the billy can over the flames and the water began to boil. But...supposing Guthrie had shown up before Joe Nash? What might the senator have done if he was up there trying to shoot a trophy grizzly and Guthrie stumbled onto the scene? Might he have shot Guthrie?

Hardly likely. Committing murder didn't seem like the stuff of senators. No, he'd cower and hide and hope Guthrie didn't see him.

And if Guthrie did? The senator would be in trouble, but it was the kind of trouble he could bribe and buy his way out of. He wouldn't be the first senator to be caught doing something naughty and have it all swept neatly under the rug. Besides, he could always say he was hunting black bear or elk. Unless he was caught red-handed with a dead grizzly, the senator wouldn't get into any trouble at all for hunting up on the mountain.

She was needlessly worrying about things that hadn't happened. Couldn't happen. Wouldn't happen. Guthrie was all right. He was just taking his time. Maybe he was camped up above her somewhere, in a pretty spot with a little creek rushing past. He had no idea she was up on the mountain. Maybe he was eating his supper even as she was eating hers. Maybe he was watching the way the moonlight illuminated the mountain peaks and then slowly poured into the valley basin and filled it with a milky-blue glow.

Maybe he was thinking about her the way she was thinking about him, and wondering what the future held for them both.

BADGER AND CHARLIE made it back to the ranch before midnight, and McCutcheon was up to the main house. He had the lamps lit, and when he heard the hoofbeats he came out onto the porch, leaving the door ajar behind him, and stood there while they choused the weary mustangs into the corrals. After they had seen to the horses, forking them hay and making sure the water tank was full, they headed up to the house to wrap their hands around the mugs of hot strong coffee they knew McCutcheon would have waiting.

"There, by damn," Badger said, dropping into the nearest chair and tossing his hat upon the table. "That's a good day's work for a couple of old farts."

Charlie followed suit, too tired to speak, and they let McCutcheon stomp awkwardly around on one crutch, carrying the coffeepot to the table, then the mugs. There was a pot of soup atop the stove and he carried that over, too, and a couple of bowls and spoons and what was left of a loaf of bread. "Bernie came by early this evening," he explained as they dug into the soup. "I told her Jessie's horses were on their way home."

Badger glanced up, mouth full, eyebrows raised. He swallowed. "Now, how in hell would you know a thing like that?" he protested. "That's my story to tell!"

McCutcheon's smile was smug. "Hired myself a chopper. Joe flew me all around the ranch this afternoon and we spotted the horses toward the tail end of the day being pushed by a rider. Saw the two of you not far below there. We figured you'd meet up before too long.''

Badger and Charlie stared at each other. ''Well,'' Badger said with grudging admiration. ''I guess a'horseback ain't the only way to get around when your ankle is busted. We saw you fly over. Figured it was Joe fetching the senator down for the night.''

''Where's Jessie and Guthrie?'' McCutcheon prodded. ''Why aren't they with you?''

''Guthrie was higher up in the pass, so Jessie sent us down with the mares and stayed up on the mountain to wait for him. I expect they'll camp together tonight.'' Badger shoveled the soup in. It was delicious, just like everything Bernie made. He reached for the ladle and dished himself up another bowl. ''She sure was glad to get her mares back. Fox is just fine. Looks like the only one missing is an old black mare name of Coaly.''

''Coaly was a top cuttin' horse in her day,'' Charlie said, sopping up the last of the soup in his bowl with a thick slice of bread.

''Bear bait now.'' Badger chewed on another slice of bread. ''We all gotta die sometimes. I'd rather go that way than tied to a wheelchair in some damn nursing home.''

''You'n me both,'' Charlie agreed, barely able to keep his eyes open.

''So, if our hunch was right and the senator was up there trying to bag that big grizzly, and you were monopolizing Joe Nash's time,'' Badger said to McCutcheon, ''then the senator could still be up there.''

''I hope so,'' McCutcheon said. ''I hope he's shaking in his boots thinking about that huge bear coming out of the dark at him.''

Badger nodded. "It's a known fact that bears get a whole lot bigger in the night."

"So do a man's fears," Charlie said, yawning hugely.

They all seemed well pleased with the thought.

THE BEAR DID COME in the night, but it came silently, not standing on its hind legs roaring out a challenge, eyes glowing red with rage. It came up the game trail and caught the scent of two things: a man and a horse. The man was to be avoided. The horse was to be eaten. To get to the horse, the bear had to come very close to the man. An animal can tell much with its keen sense of smell, and the bear knew that the horse was dead and the man was alive, but hurt. It approached with caution, quiet for so large a creature, yet the man heard it coming. Heard the roll of gravel beneath its great paws. The snap of a twig. Heard the sound of its lung-deep breaths wafting the cold night air.

Guthrie was past caring about the bear. Past fearing it. He listened, but it was with the detached calm of a distant observer. He remembered an Indian legend about the grizzly. Heard Jessie's voice relating it to him in the flickering light of one of their campfires.

Jessie was beautiful in the firelight. She was beautiful in the harsh light of high noon, but in the firelight her beauty became ethereal, otherworldly. He was mesmerized by her, caught up in the heady pleasure of being in her presence and listening to her calm, gentle voice speak the words of another culture, another spirituality, another part of herself. She moved over the earth with the same respect and embraced the same basic doctrines of her Crow and Blackfeet ancestors. She never took more than she could give, and gave everything of herself when she could.

She told the story of the great bear, and all the pain,

cold, thirst and fear slipped away from him as he lay listening. The darkness became filled with starlight, filled with the strengthening glow of the moon, filled with beauty, with peace, with magic, so that when the bear came and stood over him he felt only a kind of awe that he could share this high wild place with such a magnificent presence. If he could do one thing more before he died he wished he could write the magic of this night on paper somehow, so she could read it and understand how it was.

But perhaps she would know. She had a way of knowing, a way of sensing things, an intuition that surpassed anything he had ever experienced. Perhaps even now she knew what he was feeling. What he was thinking.

Dying wasn't so hard, but leaving Jess behind was unimaginably painful. He had promised to be there for her when she needed him, and now he was lying here in about as big a mess as a man could be in. There didn't seem to be any way out of it. When the bear began knocking aside the great pile of brush that covered him and the dead mare, he said aloud,

"Hello, Grandfather..."

CHAPTER FIFTEEN

SHE FINISHED the tiny pot of coffee and fed the last of the firewood into the fire. It was late, well past midnight. Billy was dozing on his tether, standing hip shot and relaxed in the moonlight, lower lip sagging and twitching as he slept. She pushed to her feet, a vague uneasiness building within her. She stared out across the valley and her soft breaths plumed visibly in the frosty air.

This thought came to her as if uttered in the silvery silence:

Guthrie's in trouble!

The raven she had seen earlier had foretold it. The raven had shown her the place. It was suddenly as plain to her as the broad face of the moon shining down. He was in trouble and she was sitting here drinking coffee, waiting for a man who would never come.

The dark thought galvanized her into action. She packed her gear with feverish haste, saddled the startled and disgruntled Billy, sheathed her rifle in the scabbard and smothered the coals of the tiny fire with the remains of the coffee and handfuls of sand and gravel. She wasn't far from the game trail where she'd found Blue. She'd bring Billy as close as she dared and then go ahead on foot, just as she originally planned.

She only hoped she wasn't too late. She had wasted so much time waiting, thinking he'd be right along. She'd squandered precious hours and somehow had to make them up.

Billy was tired, but he was game. She led him at a brisk uphill climb, turning and twisting with the trail, stumbling now and again over loose rocks and tree roots. In the moonlight everything looked ghostly—the rocks, the trees, the mountain slopes, the sky itself. It was as if they were traveling in a strange dream state, fumbling their way through a nightmare.

Damn her arm! It had commenced to ache in protest, and the fingers on that hand were tingling and numb, but Guthrie needed her, and she kept climbing toward where she knew he was because she needed him, too, the way she needed food and water and sunshine and the high wild places where the wind blew free.

She needed him and she loved him.

Tears stung her eyes as she jerked Billy's lead rein. Hurry! Hurry! Her lungs gasped for breath and her thigh muscles burned, but her arm was warmer now, the tingling had left her fingers, and she unzipped her parka to keep from getting sweaty. Here! Here at last was the game trail she sought! She turned onto it, and as soon as she did, Billy threw his head back and snorted. He planted his feet in stubborn refusal to go on.

"Okay!" Cursing her weak and clumsy fingers, she tied him off with a tether rope, giving him enough slack to move about. She loosened his cinch and slipped his bridle off, then draped it over a nearby branch. She slid her rifle out of the scabbard, slung her saddlebags, bedroll and water bottle over her shoulder. "Wait for me here, old friend," she said, stroking Billy's shoulder in a brief farewell.

On her own now, alone, traveling down that narrow trail, brush and tree branches closing in, snagging against her. Stumbling in the darkness as the trees blocked off the moonlight. She could hear her breathing, raspy in the stillness of the night. When she paused to catch her breath and fish the little flashlight out of her saddlebag she could hear her heart pounding in the stillness, and it sounded as loud as an Indian war drum.

Oh, Lord, had she ever been this afraid?

A bear in the darkness. A grizzly. A senator with a big gun. And somewhere in the midst of it all, Guthrie was in trouble.

Jessie took a fresh grip on her rifle and pushed on.

HE WONDERED if his mother would have loved him better if he'd been born blond like his sister. Bernie had such pretty hair. Flaxen, shiny. His was dark, ordinary hair. Maybe his mother would've thought him cuter if he'd been towheaded like his sister; else why had she taken Bernie with her and left him behind?

He wondered if a mother knew when her child died, if she felt a severing of some deep, primal connection to herself. Would his mother know? Would she awaken in the morning, sit up in her bedroom that overlooked the Pacific Ocean and mourn to her current lover, "Oh, I never should have left that boy, and now he's dead!"

"One letter," he said now to his mother. "One visit. Would that've killed you?"

The bear raised its head and whuffed, a great lung-deep sound of alarm, and rocked back on its haunches. Man moved. Man spoke. The bear hated Man, feared Man, had been hurt by Man before and remembered the hurt. This man bled, but he was alive and moved, made noise, might still cause pain. Man was still too close. In the interest of survival the big grizzly shuffled off, its great bulk casting a shadow in the moonlight, its musky smell permeating the chill air.

"One letter," he said as the moonlight flooded over him once again. "One damn letter. Would that've killed you?"

So DARK! The darkness was thick, suffocating. Jessie stopped. She stood on trembling legs and gripped her rifle with hands that shook. She couldn't see a thing beyond the narrow beam of the flashlight. How far was she from the kill site? Where was Guthrie? She sensed that both were very close.

Gradually her breathing slowed and steadied, and the loud drumbeat of her heart faded. Night sounds surrounded her, small noises made big by the stillness. The rustle of a mouse sounded like the footfall of some giant creature and caused her to pan the flashlight quickly in an arc. Calm, Jessie told herself. Be calm. The darkness is nothing to fear.

Yet she knew that in this darkness lurked the bear that may have killed one of her mares and had definitely wounded her cow dog. In this darkness lurked danger. Morning light would not diminish that danger, but it would reveal it to her and end these gruesome imaginings magnified by the night.

A murmuring came to her. The wind moving through the trees? No, the sound had more substance than the wind. Deeper. An animal growling? No, softer. Consonants and vowels shaping into words. A voice. A man's voice speaking in the darkness, faint, so very faint. She craned to hear, but all was quiet now. No sounds, not even the stir of a mouse among the woods duff. She began to think she had imagined it, and then she heard it again, this time clearly.

"Too late," the voice said, anguished. "Too late!"

Ahead of her, and not very far. She took a cautious step,

then another, reaching out with the tiny flashlight to keep from walking into branches, holding the rifle in her right hand.

"Won't be any more, no more!"

The voice was nearer and the words ran together in an almost drunken slur, but the voice was familiar, and her heart jumped with gladness to hear it.

"Guthrie!" She spoke his name sharply and waited, motionless, for some response.

"No more. All gone…"

A few more steps and then she spoke his name again, fear giving a shrillness to her voice. "Guthrie!"

Silence. She extended the flashlight as if it were a sword and continued forward cautiously. The narrow tunnel of the trail opened out. She saw the glow of moonlight reflecting off the rounded curve of ledge up ahead.

"Don't know what I did wrong…"

The voice was right in front of her now. She panned the flashlight slowly toward the voice and she saw Guthrie. He was lying on the ground beside an enormous pile of brush, half covered over with it, curled on his side, hatless, knees drawn up. The beam of the flashlight illuminated his face. His eyes were half-open, glassy, and his face was covered with dried blood.

Hurt. Terribly hurt. Guthrie was hurt.

She couldn't speak, couldn't move for a few horrified moments, and when she did it was to fling aside her rifle and gear. She fell to her knees next to him and frantically began lifting the brush away, feeling for the driest of it and breaking off brittle branch tips. She made a little pile of tinder beside where she knelt, reached in her parka pocket for a match, struck it on her jeans and gently fed the flame beneath the little pile of twigs. The resin in the dried spills sputtered, smoked, caught and flared. She fed bigger pieces onto the tiny pile. The flames climbed, the fearsome darkness was pushed back, golden light danced off the nearby tree trunks.

She continued to remove the brush from him carefully, piece by piece, until he lay revealed in the strengthening firelight. She knelt beside him again and touched him ever so gently, touched her fingertips to his temple, smoothed bits of twigs from his blood-stiffened hair. "Guthrie," she breathed, bending over him, feeling as though she were in the midst of some horrific nightmare that she would surely wake from at any moment. His eyes opened at the sound of her voice and he gazed at her in the flickering light.

"I did it all wrong," he said, his words running into each other. His breathing was fast, shallow. "All of it. Everything. She left me, and so did you."

"That's not true. I'm here! I'm right here beside you, Guthrie. It's going to be all right." She retrieved the bedroll, undid it and laid it carefully over him. Felt briefly for his pulse, which was rapid and weak. Scrambled to the fire and added more fuel. Dragged her rifle and her saddlebags and water bottle back to his side. "It's all right. You're going to be okay. You hear me, Guthrie? I'm right here and I'm not leaving you."

She fumbled with the buckles, threw back the leather flap, reached inside for the first-aid kit…but what would she do with it? How would she tend wounds she couldn't see and didn't begin to understand? What had happened to him? Had he been shot? Had the bear attacked him and then tried to cover him over with all that brush? Such a huge pile of brush! She unzipped the cordura bag and stared blankly, with a rush of growing panic, at the abundance of medical supplies within.

"Raven came," he said. "Brought you, just like I asked…"

"Guthrie, don't talk. I'm going to get you warm and fix you something hot to drink. Just lie still."

There was enough water left in her bottle for a pot of bouillon.

"You came, and told me the story about the bear walker. And then the bear came and stayed awhile."

Jessie froze and stared at him. "Did the bear cover you with brush?" she said.

He shook his head weakly. "The bear uncovered me. And then we talked." His eyes watched her, more lucid now, focusing on her, comprehending her presence. "Kestrel's dead. My fault."

She bent lower. "Hush!"

"I shouldn't have brought her up there. We were almost to the top. Should've left her down here. My fault."

Jessie rocked back on her heels. She picked up her flashlight and shined the narrow beam into the depths of the brush pile. Her breath caught in her throat when she saw the bay gloss of horse hide. Kestrel. Hidden beneath a huge brush pile. Hidden, covered over. But how…? Fear curdled her blood and rendered her completely incompetent. The mare had fallen, rolled on him. Crushed him. Kestrel was dead and Guthrie was all broken up inside, and there was nothing she could do! It could be his liver, his spleen, his kidneys, all manner of broken bones and ruptured organs. What could she do! Help was so very far away!

And how had all this brush come to be here? Had the grizzly done it?

"It's all right," she heard herself say. "All that matters is that you're alive, and we're going to keep you that way. You made me a promise, remember? You said you'd always be around when I needed a friend. Well, as it happens, right now I need one real bad, and like it or not you're it. Besides, we have an argument to finish. I figure that'll take us the rest of our lives. Years and years.''

She emptied the remainder of her water bottle into the billy can and put it on the fire to heat, dropping four bouillon cubes into it. She could treat him for shock, keep him warm, get some warm, salty fluids into him. She could bandage the lacerations on his head and face. She had a powerful pain medication in her kit. She had sutures and antibiotics and splints and bandages, but she didn't have anything that would magically stop internal bleeding.

She raised her hand to her face, surprised to feel that her cheeks were wet. She hadn't realized that she was crying. She brushed the tears away and glanced to where he lay.

He was watching her, but his gaze was losing focus and drifting away. "No more fighting, Jess. No more," he said, and closed his eyes upon a great weariness.

THIS WAS UNDOUBTEDLY the worst night the senator had ever spent. Sleep eluded him as he stood watch over the moon-washed landscape and his mind rehashed the day's events over and over again. "Stupid, stupid, stupid!" He had shot without identifying his target. It was one of the most shameful and dangerous crimes a hunter could commit, and it was the first time he had ever done it. Oh, he could come up with a thousand excuses, but none of them worked. The truth of the matter was, he had screwed up royally and would pay for it for the rest of his life. Every time he picked up a gun, every time he thought about hunting, every time he closed his eyes to sleep, he would see that dead man and he would remember his inexcusable stupidity.

Once beyond that awful moment he'd had no choice in his actions. He had to protect himself. That man was probably nothing more than a small-time rancher or hired hand. His life was insignificant compared with a senator's life. A senator could make a difference. He could change the future for the better. He was powerful; he was important. He mattered far more in the scheme of things than some hick-town cowboy.

Sacrifices were made every day in order to benefit the majority. This was just another such incident. Unfortunate, but most were. The important thing was that he get things back to normal as quickly as possible. That he not dwell on this or let the memory of it ruin his life. Guilt had no place in his life.

Half-convinced, Smith raised his eyes toward the east in anticipation of the long-awaited dawn. What he saw, instead, caused the blood to rush from his head. He felt faint and dizzy and for a moment he thought he might pass out.

A light was softly shining on the trees fringing the stone ledge. The light came from below and it flickered like the light of a campfire, and yet there could be no campfire in that place. A man was hidden beneath the brush pile, a man who was dead. There could be no fire, no light, and yet…there was!

His breath came in shallow gasps. He pushed to his feet, one hand braced against the rough bark of the tree, the other grasping the Weatherby. It was unbelievable! The whole thing was unbelievable! What should he do? What would he see if he walked to the edge and peered over? Would it be as awful as before, or would it be even worse? Could anything *possibly* be any worse?

This couldn't be happening to him. He was a good man. A great politician. People looked up to him, admired him, feared him and emulated him. He might even run for president someday, and here he stood in the tree stand, all clenched up with irrational fear, feeling weak in the bowels and totally out of control.

The only way to deal with such a paralyzing fear was to confront it.

He climbed down the tree stand, hand over hand, rifle slung over his shoulder. Crept as before toward the edge of the great rounded dome of rock where the narrow shelf of trail came up and over, and as before he held his rifle at the ready and moved with great caution until he was standing at the very edge, peering over and down. His heartbeat clubbed in his ears. He blinked his eyes and squinted. Yes—yes, there was a fire in the very place he had built the brush pile to cover the man and the horse. It glowed against the tree trunks and upswept branches at the base of the ledge, danced and taunted, threw sparks skyward to join the moon in the broad arc of the heavens.

A campfire.

Not only was the man still alive, he was well enough to have built a fire, perhaps even well enough to recover and identify the person who had shot his horse, concealed him beneath a brush pile and left him for dead!

The senator stood on top of the rock dome, stricken with the enormity of this latest turn of events. Dawn was fast approaching. He had little time now to plot a new course of action, but there seemed to be only one thing he could do to save himself.

He began a slow and cautious descent toward the light of the fire.

TENDING GUTHRIE was easier while he was unconscious. She was able to clean his lacerations without worrying about hurting him. When the gash on his head was tidied up to her satisfaction, the hair trimmed neatly from its edges and the wound amply flushed out, she decided to suture it because it was a good four inches long, running from behind his left ear toward the top of his head, and deep enough to reveal the gleam of bone. She had ten individual sutures with needles in her kit and used every last one of them, holding the little flashlight in her teeth to illuminate the area as best she could.

Her work was slow and clumsy because her left hand was weak; the wrist and forearm didn't flex at all, and her fingers tingled with the cold. She had to keep pausing to throw more wood on the little fire, but she finished with the feeling that at least she had done something to better his condition. She wrapped clean gauze around his head, binding a sterile dressing over the wound, then sat with his head in her lap, near enough to the fire to keep it going, to watch the bouillon broth and to wait for him to awaken.

If he did.

There was, of course, the possibility that he wouldn't, that the internal bleeding would continue, the shock would deepen and he would slip into a coma and die. "But you won't," she whispered to him, smoothing the hair back from his abraded forehead. "You wouldn't dare break your promise." His face was a mess. As if he'd been dragged facedown over sharp rocks for a long ways. "Oh, Guthrie." Her throat tightened and she blinked away tears impatiently. She couldn't let herself cave in. He needed her to be strong. She couldn't let him down.

A sudden nearby rattle of loose stones startled her and she looked up, adrenaline surging through her. The firelight had blinded her night vision. A great monster could loom and she wouldn't see it until it stepped into the circle of light cast by the fire. She reached for her rifle and drew it near, then slid out from beneath Guthrie and laid him gently on the ground. She stood and squared off toward the sound. To fire the rifle with any degree of accuracy would be nearly impossible. Her left arm and hand were unable to steady the rifle to get off a good shot. She would need to rest the rifle barrel on something, but what?

More noise. More rocks and scree scattering down the steep defile. She sensed something large moving around the edge of the camp, something apart from the rattling stones. "Bear walker!" she whispered over the pounding of her heart. If screaming would have helped, she'd have screamed at the top of her lungs, for her nerves were drawn taut. She couldn't stand still another moment without doing something, so without further delay she braced the stock of the rifle against her hip, pointed the barrel skyward and pulled the trigger.

The noise was deafening. The rifle shot cracked open the night, reverberated off the mountain slopes, rocketed into the distance and then echoed back over the ringing in her ears. A great rush of sounds followed on the heels of the rifle shot, sounds that she couldn't separate, couldn't identify at first. Big sounds, nearby. A deep woofing noise like a huge startled dog, and then something very big running quickly away, scattering more scree behind it.

The bear. The grizzly had been coming toward their camp, had gotten very close! Too close! Quick! More wood on the fire! She bent and flung several branches over the coals. Fresh flames licked up. In her panic she was lucky she hadn't knocked over the billy can with its precious broth. She laid on more firewood with greater care, her hands shaking, and then squatted near the warmth and the burgeoning light, rifle balanced across her knees, listening, listening...

THE SENATOR CREPT down the steep rock ledge. He kept a grip on the Weatherby and keened his eyes on the dancing firelight. His pulse pounded in his temples. His mouth was dry. His knees barely braced up to the steep descent. He paused to steady his breathing. Wouldn't do to hyperventilate. Had to keep his wits about him. Had to do what needed to be done. He…

A rifle shot shattered the silence, startling him so badly that he lost his footing and fell hard on his left hip, a jolt of pain stabbing up into his lower back. "No!" he gasped, struggling to rise. The man couldn't have heard him coming. Couldn't have known he was out here.

But he heard something else now, something lunging toward him up the steep trail. In the murky blue moonlight he could see the great bulk of something monstrous. He pushed up and slipped again, lost his grip on the Weatherby, and it slid away, rattled down and down, toward the bear he had come here to kill. The bear whose head was to have graced the wall of his hunting lodge. The rifle struck the bear's foreleg, bounced off and continued down toward where the dead horse lay.

The senator was almost on his feet now, almost, but too late! The bear was upon him. It barely slowed its uphill lunge. It was scared and it was angry, and with one powerful swipe of its massive paw it swatted the senator aside as if he were no more than an insignificant piece of chaff.

It was quick, there was no pain, and no time to be afraid. Just the way the senator would have liked it.

CHAPTER SIXTEEN

JOE hadn't slept a wink all night. He was as edgy as a cat, wired from lack of sleep and anxiety. He paced his kitchen while the coffee brewed, drank a cup on the way to the airfield, and was more than a little dismayed to be met by his boss in the hangar before he had even shrugged into his requisite leather flight jacket, before the sun had even properly risen.

"Got a call from one of your clients last night!" Boss said, fairly swaggering with excitement.

Joe's heart rate trebled. The senator? "Oh?"

"He liked the flight yesterday. Wants you over there again first thing this morning. He says this time he'll bring his camera and he's packed a lunch. What did I tell you? This is going to be a good account. That man's richer than anyone else in this star-crossed valley."

Joe stared. "McCutcheon?"

"Who the hell do you think I'm talking about? Your chopper's all fueled up, I saw to it myself. Go on, crank her up. He's waiting on you."

McCutcheon? But he'd seen all he wanted to see last night, hadn't he? He knew the horses were back and everything was okay. What else could he want to see? Joe unwrapped a stick of gum and shoved it in his mouth as he walked out to where the chopper squatted on its landing pad. No more hunting trips for the almighty senator. Let him find someone else to squire him around on his little trophy expeditions. The stress of the past few days had aged Joe ten years. It wasn't worth it.

He'd stick to scenic tours and legitimate elk hunts, and to hell with everything else. To hell with it!

IN THE COLD CLEAR LIGHT of dawn Jessie Weaver slept. It was not a long sleep, or a restful one. She had spent the night keeping the little fire going and Guthrie warm, feeding sips of bouillon into him when he waked and willing him with all her soul and spirit to stay alive. After the moon had set she'd drifted off, her back braced against the trunk of a tree, her rifle close at hand and Guthrie's head cradled in her lap. She had a dream and in it she was riding Fox, the wily red mare.

They were high in the mountains, when a raven flew overhead, quarking and croaking, dodging artfully this way and that, playing the updrafts and the sudden gusts of mountain wind, but when she reined in the mare to watch, the raven swooped suddenly down, its wings swishing loudly. It carved a tight arc around them, before winging down, down, toward a figure far below.

A man stood on an outcrop of rock, below which loomed an immense free fall of space clear to the valley floor. She was filled with a sense of dread, for she knew that he was about to fall off the edge and into that void. Fox tossed her head, eager to be on her way, but the raven flew down toward the man and Jessie watched, transfixed and horrified.

"Guthrie, no!" she said.

For it was Guthrie who stood on the edge of that precipice, who wavered between life and death and who seemed to want to choose death over life. But why? Down the raven flew, down and down... And then she became the raven, sluicing through the air on powerful wings, reaching out to him, catching him just before he slipped and fell into the bottomless void.

"Guthrie!"

She came awake with a jerk, her mouth dry and her heart pounding. She felt a movement within the cradle of her arms and legs. He stirred. Was alive. Relief flooded through her and she bent her head over his, cursing the day they had parted company, turned their backs on each other and gone their separate ways. Remembering the very moment it happened, remembering that she'd been the one to speak the fatal words.

Remembering all and regretting deeply, but too late now to return to that place in time and take it all back, make it all right. Too late! Guthrie was alive for now, but would he be alive to see the sun rise over the Beartooth Wilderness they both so loved? "Guthrie." She breathed his name and traced her fingertips across his forehead. "Guthrie…"

Last night seemed like a nightmare, like something that couldn't have happened, and yet it had. She was here, Guthrie was here, the bear had been here. The senator might still be on the prowl with that powerful gun of his, looking to shoot something, but she had fired her own rifle last night, and surely the senator would have heard it. He would have known to pull his horns in, to cower and hope no one ever discovered his foolish transgression.

Perhaps he wasn't here. Perhaps he'd left on the chopper last night with Joe Nash…if indeed he'd been here at all. Maybe they were wrong about the senator, though she doubted it. When her intuition spoke loudly to her, she listened, and it had already told her all she needed to know.

When Joe Nash returned, he would set his chopper down somewheres nearby, and that would be the only chance to get Guthrie out in time to save his life. But first she had to find the place Joe would put the chopper down, and that meant leaving Guthrie, something she was loath to do. What if he died while she was away from him? What if he died wondering why she had left him? Yet if she didn't find the place the chopper would land, he might die anyway.

What was she to do?

She spoke his name softly, her fingertips lightly touching his face, feeling the stubble of his beard. She bent closer. "Guthrie." At the sound of her voice he moved. His eyelashes fluttered and he moaned.

"Guthrie!"

His eyes opened and he stared blankly up for a few moments, then shifted focus, searching for her. Finding her. Looking at her for a long silent moment. "Jess," he said finally. "What...?"

"Don't try to talk. Listen to me. You rode up here two days ago to find my mares and you had an accident. You're hurt, but you're going to be all right. Joe Nash might be flying close to this spot pretty soon. I have to try to signal him so he can take you out of here. I'll be gone a little while, but I won't be far, and we'll come get you. You're going to be okay, Guthrie. Do you understand?"

He gazed up at her in the dimness. "Jess," he said again. His voice was weak, faint. "I heard a rifle shot. Big, powerful rifle. And footsteps after." He formed the words slowly, carefully, but as their meaning registered she felt the hair on the back of her neck prickle.

"I fired a shot last night to scare the bear away," she said. "You must have heard me moving around...."

"He was here. The senator. Shot Kestrel by mistake. Must've thought she was the bear. Covered us both up with brush."

Her indrawn breath was sharp. "Oh, Guthrie, no!"

"Don't go out there, Jess. He could still be nearby."

"No!" Jessie exclaimed. "Why would he do that? I can't believe he'd do that!"

"Joe must have flown him here, set him up over the kill site to shoot that bear." Guthrie's hand closed around her wrist. "Don't go out there!"

"But if the senator shot Kestrel by mistake, why wouldn't he help you if you were hurt? Why would he cover you with brush?"

Guthrie's grip on her wrist weakened and his hand slid away. "He must've thought I was dead," he said, struggling for breath. "I heard his footsteps. He dragged me. I saw him." His eyes pleaded with her to understand the gravity of their situation. "I *saw* him."

The horror of his words overwhelmed her. She sat in shocked silence, trying to calm her racing thoughts. "I heard the chopper late yesterday," she said. "It must've been Joe coming to pick him up. Why else would he have flown over here? He's already picked the senator up, Guthrie. The senator's gone!"

He reached for her again but didn't have the strength. "Don't go up there, Jess. Please."

She reached to squeeze his hand. "It'll be okay. I'll be careful, I promise. I have to check things out, don't you see? If the senator's gone, we're in big trouble, because it means Joe Nash won't be coming back, and I'm counting on him to fly you out of here."

She took her rifle, since Guthrie was too weak to use it even if she left it behind and she doubted the bear would come near their campfire. In any event, she didn't travel far. She rounded the brush pile with the stealth of a hunter, deliberately averting her eyes from any glimpse of Kestrel. She was unable to comprehend the actions of the senator. He must be insane! He must—

Not fifty feet from where she'd left Guthrie she stopped short in her tracks, hands tightening on her rifle, breath catching in her throat. On the far side of the brush pile, at the very base of the rock ledge, lay the senator, and next to him, within arm's reach, was a big fancy rifle. He was sprawled on his back, with his arms outflung and his eyes staring up at the early-morning sky, but he was far beyond seeing it.

Jessie moved forward cautiously and paused again, heart hammering against her ribs. Across the left side of the senator's face were several parallel gashes. From the angle at which he lay it looked as if his neck had been broken, and it looked as if the great bear might have broken it.

For the reality of what she was seeing to strike home took a few moments. On reluctant tread she approached the body and knelt, laid her rifle down and pressed her fingers against the flesh at the base of his neck. The skin was still vaguely warm in spite of the freezing temperatures. The senator was dead, but he hadn't been dead for long. The noise she'd heard last night hadn't just been the bear prowling nearby. The senator must have spotted their campfire. He'd been creeping down the ledge toward it, carrying that big powerful rifle, when both her rifle shot and the bear had surprised him.

"Fair play," Jessie said without remorse. She shivered with a combination of cold and tightly drawn nerves, and glanced around, wondering where the bear was now. The thought spurred her into action. She stood, reaching her rifle off the ground, and walked back to the brush pile.

"Guthrie?" she called out. "I'm right over here. I'm going to get your gear off the horse." She laid her rifle aside and began pulling the brush off the pile. To expose Kestrel, that beautiful young mare that Jessie had held in

such high regard, didn't take long. She bit her lower lip
as she worked the saddlebags and bedroll free and tugged
Guthrie's water bottle loose. His father's old Winchester
was jammed beneath the dead horse. She didn't have the
leverage with only one good arm to free it or the saddle,
so she left both behind and returned to their campsite on
the far side of the brush pile with the saddlebags, the bedroll and the water bottle.

Guthrie was relieved to see her. She dropped to her
knees beside him and lay her burdens down. "You don't
have to worry about the senator anymore. He's dead," she
said flatly. "Looks like our bear killed him. And you were
right. Kestrel was definitely shot."

"My fault. I shouldn't have taken her…"

"Guthrie, we have to get you out of here. I have to get
Joe to help us. He'll definitely be coming back for the
senator. I don't know why he already hasn't!"

"How did you get here?"

"On Billy. I tied him off down below."

"Fetch him. I can set a horse…"

"No, you can't! You're all busted up inside!"

"Get Billy, Jess, or I swear I'll crawl off this mountain
on my hands and knees if I have to."

Jessie rose to her feet. Guthrie was out of his head.
Irrational. "All right," she soothed. "You lie still and I'll
bring Billy, but I warn you, Guthrie, if you move so much
as an inch, you won't have to worry about that bear eating
you."

Billy wasn't far, but reaching him seemed to take forever. She had no intention of leading him to Guthrie. She
had another idea of how to use Billy to save Guthrie, just
in case Joe Nash didn't come back.

It was certainly worth a shot.

McCUTCHEON WAS restlessly pacing the length of the porch when he finally heard the helicopter approaching. Sunlight was already flooding over the rim of mountains to the east. Badger and Charlie hobbled out onto the porch and stood with him, watching the Bell JetRanger draw nearer.

"He came straight here," Badger confirmed. "We'da heard if he'd snuck up on the mountain to fetch the senator down."

"Yessir," Charlie agreed. "And we was listening all the while, sure enough. He ain't been up there."

"So that means if our hunch is right, the senator still is," McCutcheon said.

"Him and his big fancy gun," Badger said, and spat over the porch railing.

"Don't forget about Guthrie and Jessie," McCutcheon said.

All three looked at one another as the chopper set down. "Hell!" Badger said.

"Okay, here's what I'll do," McCutcheon said. "I'll feel him out and we'll go from there. One way or the other, we'll get Jessie and Guthrie home safe. As for the senator..."

"The grizzly can have him," Badger said.

SHE WAS RIGHT about Guthrie. He'd tried to drag himself down the trail on his hands and knees, but he hadn't gotten far. He was propped up against the trunk of an aspen, face gray with pain, forehead clammy with sweat, his breathing rapid and shallow. He gazed foggily at her when she knelt beside him. "Where's Billy!" he said, gasping the words. "I can't crawl too much farther."

"Damn you, Guthrie! You were doing good! You were getting better and now you've gone and undone it all!"

She knelt in his face and glared, angry and scared and hating the feeling of helplessness that engulfed her.

"Where's Billy!"

"You're not riding a horse! You're staying put. Lying still. Waiting for help. You hear me? No more of this. I can't take any more of this! I can't take you being hurt. Guthrie, please, please listen to me. I have my rifle. That bear won't bother us if we keep a fire burning. Joe Nash will come looking for the senator, and if he doesn't, someone else will. He was a senator, after all. Sooner or later someone's bound to miss him. You're going to get down off this mountain, but you aren't going to crawl and you aren't going to ride. You hear me?"

He let his head tip back against the aspen trunk and his eyes closed. Gradually his breathing slowed. He nodded. "Okay."

Jessie slumped. She raised her hand and pressed palm to forehead, blinking hard. What a nightmare. When would it end? "Billy's fine," she heard herself say. "I sent him home with a message. I wrote it on a scrap of paper, bound it over the saddle horn and turned him loose. He knows how to get home. The way I figure it, he should be there just shy of suppertime."

JOE set the chopper down badly. He hadn't hit the skids that hard for over a decade. For a moment he sat chewing his gum and wondering what the hell was happening to him. He didn't have very long to wonder. McCutcheon stumped out toward the chopper on one crutch, a big canvas bag of something slung over one shoulder, a camera over the other. Joe cut the engine and the blades feathered down.

"I brought lunch," McCutcheon said over the diminishing noise. "Enough for both of us. And a camera with a lot of film. By God, it'll take all day for me to use it up. But your boss said you were free and I don't know of anyone else who gives such a good aerial tour.'' He tossed his crutch in the open door, followed it with the canvas bag and handed the camera to Joe. ''Easy. She's fragile.''

Joe winced and chewed harder. What a friggin' note, to have to squire this rich dunderhead around, while somewhere out there the senator waited on him. The senator had the power to make his life holy old hell, and Joe was thinking he probably would, too, given that he'd been a little tardy in picking the important politician up.

''Well, sir, what's your pleasure?'' he said to McCutcheon as the man buckled himself in.

''I'd kind of like to get a picture of that big grizzly you saw,'' came the unexpected answer.

Joe was glad for the sunglasses that hid his surprise fairly well. He fumbled for a fresh stick of gum.

''Huh. Well, no promises on that score. Grizzlies aren't exactly hams in front of a camera. At least, none of the ones I've ever seen have exhibited that tendency, though I'm told some of the Yellowstone bears are pretty tolerant. I suppose we could get lucky.''

''If we do, I'm ready.'' McCutcheon patted the camera fondly.

''Anything else you'd like to see while we're at it?''

''Well, actually, I was kind of hoping we'd catch sight of Jessie and Guthrie. Seems they spent the night together up on the mountain. They should be heading down by now, and I'd kind of like to make sure they're okay. Guthrie's sister is a chronic worrier. You know the type.''

Joe drew a deep breath as he fired the engine back up. Good godamighty, he felt on the verge of complete and utter ruination. How could he possibly function competently under such stress? Gum. Chew lots of gum. Try not to think about that big brush pile. Maybe... Maybe the senator had bagged the grizzly and built that brush pile to conceal the great bruin's body.

It was a good thought, but Joe had little faith in it.

"YOU REMEMBER that play we were in?" Jessie said, absentmindedly watching the smoke from the fire curl upward. "How the whole school had to memorize a part? You were Romeo and I was Juliet. I forgot most of my lines and so did you."

"No, I didn't. I remembered them all. We only had to memorize that one scene, and when I got stuck all I had to do was look at your beautiful face and the lines just came to me." Guthrie's own words came slow but steady, and stronger than they had been.

"Yes, and you made every single one of them up. That's cheating. The crowd came to hear Shakespeare and instead they heard the original poetry of Guthrie Sloane."

"Crowd? Hell, Jess, all the parents in that audience times ten wouldn't constitute a crowd."

Jessie smiled and shifted her position slightly against the trunk of the tree, easing a cramp in the small of her back. She glanced down at Guthrie, who lay beside her, sandwiched between their bedrolls, head and shoulders propped against a fallen log. "Well, it was like a lot of people to me. I hated it. All of it. The stage, the bright lights, the lines I had to learn, Mr. Becker's constant scowl, all those faces in the audience waiting for some kind of magic to happen, and you looking at me as if you were about to burst out laughing at any moment."

"Well, you gotta admit it was funny."

"It wasn't! It was awful! And that dress I had to wear!"

"It was a gown, and you were beautiful in it."

"Drink some more soup," she said, leaning over him.

"Just a little. That's good." She lowered the tin cup and tears prickled in her eyes. He was still so weak. He could barely raise his hand to help steady the cup. She'd never seen him as anything but strong and self-reliant. "Oh, Lord, Guthrie, it seems as though we've known each other forever. I can scarcely recall a time when you weren't there."

Jessie let her head tip back against the rough bark of the tree trunk, remembering other days. The sun was high; the late-October warmth was light, clean, crisp and pleasant. For the moment Guthrie was resting easily, but he had been slipping in and out of different worlds, here with her one moment, drifting away the next. Most of the morning had been this way. He would become anxious and ask about things that had no basis in reality. Reach for her, try to hold on to her, his fingers grasping her wrist, her parka, but with no real strength. She would soothe him as if he were a child, bending over him, her voice gentle and calm.

Inside, she was anything but. She was overwhelmed with her own anxieties. Where was the bear? Where was Joe Nash? How long could Guthrie go on in his deteriorating state? And if he died, what would she do? A part of her could not think about such an outcome. Pushed it away. Kept the darkness at bay through sheer denial. Guthrie would be all right. He would always be there for her. Nothing would ever change that. Not a horse falling on him. Not a big grizzly. Not an important senator. Not anything, ever.

"Did you call your professor, Jess?" he said, startling her. She gazed down at him. Just to look at his face hurt her.

"Yes," she said. "I spoke with him right after you left. It's all set. I'm going back to school."

He blinked, trying hard to focus on her face. Drew a shallow breath and let it out slowly. "Liar," he said.

Jessie looked away. A gust of wind tossed the treetops and blew smoke from their little fire into her eyes. Where was Joe Nash? Where was the chopper? Flies were probably crawling all over the dead senator by now; the sun's warmth would have brought them out. "I was too mad," she said. "When McCutcheon told me you agreed to take the job if I didn't, I figured that's why you wanted me to go back to school."

"You think pretty highly of me, don't you?"

"I was wrong." Jessie met his eyes and winced at the hurt in them. "I'm sorry. I'll call the professor, I promise."

"And you'll go back to school. Promise me that, too."

"I'll go back to school if you take the job for McCutcheon and rip out all those damn fences."

"Promise me you'll go back no matter what I end up doing."

"No."

"Damn you, Jess."

"Damn me all you want! I got you into this mess and I'm getting you out of it. Dying isn't one of the things you're going to end up doing, Guthrie. I won't allow it!"

JESSIE SPENT most of the morning gathering wood. She was sure they wouldn't have to spend another night up here; but better to be prepared. If worst came to worst, she wanted to have a big fire burning brightly all night long, and big fires consumed a great deal of wood. So she forayed farther and farther from the campsite, dragged back downed limbs, dead wood, anything she could find, including bundles of fresh evergreen limbs she could throw on the flames to make a smoke signal should a search plane fly over. At noon she stopped to fix something to eat. Guthrie had been dozing off and on, but he waked when she began to rummage through his saddlebags.

The items she found amazed her. "Green chilis?" she said, holding up a tiny can.

"They're real good sliced into eggs."

"Yes, but you'd actually pack them for the high country?"

"What better place to enjoy scrambled eggs and green chilis?"

She dug deeper. Found a paper canister of oatmeal. Inside, nestled among the whole oats, were his eggs. Unbroken. That they had survived the fall intact was unbelievable. She also found a slab of bacon, two cans of beans, a pound of coffee, several packets of dried soup, a plastic jar of peanut butter and one very squashed loaf of oatmeal bread. "You eat pretty good," she said. "A lot better than me."

"Anyone eats a lot better than you. Half the time I don't think you even eat."

"I eat plenty. What's your pleasure for lunch?"

"Soup."

"Okay." Soup was easy. Soup was hydrating, and Guthrie needed fluids more than anything. She put the billy can over the coals and poured water into it. Both water bottles were almost empty. If the senator had camped close by, he must have had a supply of water. All she had to do was find it. Still, that meant walking right past the dead body and climbing up the rock ledge toward the first kill site.

Where the bear might be...

She fixed the soup for Guthrie and helped him drink it. He was beginning to look as though he might live after all. But she knew he was still far from being out of the woods, both literally and figuratively. If Joe Nash had been coming to pick up the senator, wouldn't he already have done so? Might she be wrong about when the senator had died? Had the senator been killed by the bear while covering up the dead horse? Had Joe seen his body yesterday on his later-afternoon flyby, spooked and run for home? For all anyone knew he was out of the country by now.

Funny she hadn't thought of that possibility before. Now it seemed the only plausible explanation, which meant that no one would be searching for them until Billy made it back to the ranch. And if Billy grazed his way lazily back home, it might not be until tomorrow that anyone began to worry. What if he ducked through a lot of brush and scraped off the note she'd tied to the saddle horn? What if he busted a leg and never made it back at all?

"That man," Guthrie said suddenly. "The Indian."

"Steven Brown," Jessie said. "The lawyer."

"Do you see him much?"

"He acted as McCutcheon's attorney and my friend and adviser. He was at the property closing."

"But other than that, did you see each other?"

Jessie glanced at him and felt the heat coming into her cheeks. "Is jealousy rearing its ugly head?"

"Just curious. The last time I saw him he was acting mighty interested in you and the two of you were sharing a bottle of wine."

"We invited you to join us, if you recall. How does your head feel?"

He reached his hand to touch his fingers to the sutures. "It feels fine. I guess that means you're not going to answer my question," he said. "And you're right, I suppose. It's none of my business."

"A couple of times," Jessie said, dropping her eyes. "We saw each other a couple of times over the summer.

He came by to keep me up-to-date on things, to show me the latest draft of the deed and the different conservation restrictions we were working into it. I relied on him a lot through the whole process. He knew what future I wanted for the land and he made sure it all happened the right way. I owe him a huge debt.''

"I sure hope he's not asking for any kind of payment.''

Jessie shot him a dark glance. "Steven never asked me for anything.'' She paused a moment, reconsidering. "I take that back,'' she said. "He did ask for one thing.''

"A kiss,'' Guthrie predicted gloomily.

Jessie hesitated, noting the despair that clouded Guthrie's eyes, and then shook her head and smiled. "Not exactly,'' she said.

CHAPTER SEVENTEEN

MID AUGUST.

A day so hot, heat waves rippled off the ground, the wind scorched and the shade gave no relief. As the sun swung westerly toward the Gallatin Mountains a green Jeep Wagoneer rolled along the shaded dirt track bordering the creek. She could see the plume of dust rising from a long ways away. Steven had said he'd arrive by noon with the final draft of the deed, and here it was, nearly five o'clock. He parked, climbed out of the Jeep and walked to the foot of the porch steps, looking thoroughly exhausted and for all the world like a motherless calf.

"Bad day?" she said, leaning over the porch railing.

"Bad day. Sorry I'm late. Everything's okay as far as you're concerned. I brought the papers with me. I can leave them here for you to read, but there's no rush. McCutcheon's in Paris right now, visiting his wife. He won't be back until October. We've set up a tentative closing date for the tenth." He stood there, tie loosened and top buttons undone. "Can I ask you something?" he said. "Is there someplace along this creek I could jump in on my way back to Bozeman?"

She took him to the swimming hole, where for a long time he floated on his back in the circular current of the deep pool, letting the cool clear mountain water wash all the heat and the stress of the day from him. Afterward she asked him to stay for supper, and was instantly sorry be-

cause she had no idea what she would fix for him. But the
expression on his face was one of such humble gratitude
that she felt small for regretting her impulsive invitation.
He insisted on driving into town to pick up a bottle of
wine for the occasion, which worked out perfectly, since
it gave her nearly an hour to miraculously create a gastro-
nomic delight out of a larder that was nearly always bare.

She was in luck. There was a frying chicken in the ice-
box. She would cut it up and fry it in the Dutch oven the
way Ramalda used to, though it wouldn't taste quite the
same—Ramalda had been a very good cook. Jessie decided to also fix a salad from the wild greens that grew
along the banks of the creek, pick blackberries for a cobbler—all tasks to be completed within the hour so that by
the time Steven returned with the bottle of wine she would
be decked out in her only bit of feminine finery, a cotton
print sundress, with a pair of leather sandals on her feet.

No jeans and boots for this Montana cowgirl, not tonight! This was her first real date since Guthrie had left
back in May. She was still so angry that the very thought
of him caused her stomach to churn. She cut the chicken
up with a knife that had seen sharper days, dredged the
bird in the mix of milk, flour and herbs that Ramalda had
used and left it on the sideboard while she went outside
to pick the blackberries. In no time she had harvested a
quart, though not without also harvesting some deep and
painful scratches from the wicked brambles. She left the
berries in the shade of the porch steps and carried an old
colander down along the creek, picking sorrel and water-
cress and Miner's lettuce, adding the blossoms of edible
wildflowers, a few stray berries and some wild onion.

Should she make biscuits? No, too hot to run the oven.
Still and all, they'd go nicely with the supper, and she
could use the oven to make a blackberry shortcake instead

of a cobbler. They could eat out on the porch at the little table. It would be cooling off then, and the view of the sunset would be romantic.

Romantic?

Yes. Romantic! She felt like being romantic. She felt like sipping a glass of wine sitting on the porch with a man at her side and admiring the sunset. She wasn't particular about the man, except that it couldn't be Guthrie. And it just so happened that Steven Brown was very, very nice.

Whereas Guthrie… Running off like that! She stomped up the porch steps with the colander of greens and the pail of blackberries, entered the kitchen and slammed both down upon the counter, causing some of the blackberries to bounce out of the pail and Blue to bolt out of the room. Guthrie! Slinking out of Katy Junction like a whipped dog with his tail between his legs. And to Alaska of all places. How dramatic! Perhaps by now he'd found some cute little girl who didn't mind being treated like a brainless idiot.

She mixed up a batch of biscuits, flour flying like a February blizzard and pea-size chunks of shortening hitting the floor like shrapnel. She was going to have a good time tonight. She was going to put on a pretty dress, fix her hair up nice and have a fine time with an extremely nice man.

She rolled out the biscuit dough, and then, before cutting the biscuits, she lit the propane oven, or tried to. Nothing happened. Tried a stove-top burner, with the same results. Of all the times to run out of propane! She ran out the back door and tapped the tank with a wrench. The pitch alone told her it was mighty light. Grabbed hold and gave it a vigorous shake. No doubt about it. Empty!

But there was a cookstove in the kitchen, as well, and where there was wood, there was a way. Thank goodness for the simpler things. She kindled a quick hot fire in the firebox. Beads of sweat prickled on her forehead, stung her eyes. She cut the biscuits, laid them in a rectangular baking pan, fed more wood into the stove. The kitchen heated up. She crushed the blackberries, added sugar to taste, washed the greens in the colander and left them to drain in the sink. That done, she ran down to the creek, stripping off her clothes as she did, and flung herself stark naked into the deliciously cool deep water of the swimming hole. No time to waste. Steven was probably halfway back by now.

In her bedroom she shook out the cotton dress, found dainty cotton underthings in her bureau drawer. She dressed with haste and then unbraided her damp hair and brushed it out before, pinning it into a French twist atop her head. She regarded herself critically in the mirror over the bureau and carefully pulled a few tendrils of hair loose to frame her face. Better. More feminine. She was so thin. Her face, her body. This past year had been so hard…

Quick! She heard a vehicle drawing near. Heard Blue bark. Heard a car door slam. She slipped her bare feet into sandals and walked out to meet him, and the expression that lit his face at the sight of her made the five minutes of dandifying worthwhile.

"Wow," he said, halting at the bottom of the porch steps. "You look beautiful."

"Thanks," she said, suddenly feeling very tongue-tied and awkward. "Did you get the wine?"

He held up the bag. "Not a great selection at that store, but I hope you like it."

"I'm sure I will." She clasped her hands in front of her and then switched them behind, fingers twining nervously. "Well, I thought we could eat out here on the porch."

"That's a fine idea." He climbed the porch steps and

set the bag atop the little table. He removed the bottle. It was a white wine, chilled and covered with beads of moisture. "I figured cool was better. If you have a corkscrew..."

"Follow me, but I warn you, the kitchen's a mess...."

The kitchen was worse than a mess. It had to be at least two hundred degrees inside—Jessie stopped when she entered the room and raised a hand to her mouth, shocked. "Oh, no!" she said.

"What?" Steven stepped around her, eyebrows raised and wine bottle in hand.

"The chicken. It was on the sideboard. Right there." She pointed to the flour-covered surface. "A whole chicken, cut up for frying."

"Gone," he confirmed with great solemnity.

"Blue!" She called the guilty cow dog's name, not really expecting her to put in an appearance after committing such a heinous crime, and she didn't. "I'll get you for this!" she threatened, then turned to Steven with a helpless gesture. "I'm so sorry. There's nothing else."

He shrugged, smiled a calm smile. "We still have the wine."

"And biscuits. I'll make us a nice blackberry shortcake." She popped the pan of biscuits into the hot oven and then rummaged through one of the kitchen drawers for a corkscrew. "I know I have one somewhere."

But it was not to be found. "No problem," Steven said. "I'll use my knife. Do you have any wineglasses?"

"I think so." She went through all the cupboards with an increasing sense of doom. Where could they be? She turned. He had pushed the cork down into the bottle with the tip of his knife. "Sorry," she said. "I'm afraid we'll have to use water glasses."

"They'll work just fine." He took them from her and

she followed him out onto the porch. Even though the heat outside was still oppressive, it felt wonderfully cool after the raging inferno of the kitchen. He half filled two water glasses with white wine and little pieces of cork and handed one to her. "To the sunset," he said, lifting his glass toward the magnificent spectacle of an enormous molten August sun sinking slowly behind the wall of mountains.

They drank a toast to the beauty of the hour and sat in the gathering twilight, sipping wine and talking. He told her about his day, about a court case he had lost—an injunction to stop a road from being built into a proposed wilderness area by a logging company notorious for its large clear-cuts. She listened sympathetically, thinking what a good man he was to become so emotionally involved in what he did.

"No wonder you looked so beat up today," she said. "Sometimes you must feel you're fighting a losing battle."

He sighed. "Sometimes we are," he said. "You have to pick your fights, and it hurts to lose a single one because they're all important. But we win some, too. Those are the sweetest moments of all—standing up to the big corporate giants and triumphing...a bunch of grassroots activists and a two-bit lawyer."

"Don't call yourself that!" Jessie leaned toward him, laying her hand lightly on his forearm. "You're wonderful to do what you do, and you're very good at it How did you get involved in environmental law?"

"I grew up on the Crow Reservation near Fort Smith. Four brothers, two sisters. My eldest brother died when he was thirteen from sniffing gas fumes. My baby sister was killed when the truck she was riding in rolled over one night. The driver was drunk. I couldn't wait to get off the reservation. I had no ambition for college whatsoever, so

I traveled around and tried all sorts of jobs but didn't stick long with any of them.

"I ended up in a little town north of Seattle, pumping gas at a big gas station. All the logging trucks gassed up there. I saw all these redwood logs chained down on the backs of these trucks. Sometimes only one log would fit they were so enormous. I began thinking about how many of them I saw come through there, and then one day I decided to go see the trees while there were still a few left.

"Have you ever stood at the base of one of those giants?" he asked. Jessie shook her head. He sat back and his dark eyes grew thoughtful. "Standing among those ancient trees changed the way I felt about this planet. I saw firsthand what the logging companies were doing and I didn't like it. I joined a local activist group and right away got arrested for handcuffing myself in a human chain around one of the trees to keep it from being cut. Spent a night in jail, and while I was sitting on that bunk in the cell I decided to go back to school and study environmental science. From there I worked my way through law school, and here I am. Still fighting, but with better ammunition than a pair of handcuffs." He paused and sniffed the air. "Do you smell something burning?"

"Ohmigosh! The biscuits!" Jessie leaped to her feet and raced back into the scorchingly hot kitchen. Smoke was pouring from the oven. She jerked open the oven door, grabbed a pair of pot holders, whipped out the pan of biscuits and hurled it out the back door. She stood there for a moment, wavering between laughing and crying, and then reached for the colander of salad greens. She lifted it from the slate sink and stared. In the heat of the kitchen the greens had wilted into a dark soggy mass. Certainly not the stuff of a romantic gourmet meal.

When she returned to the porch she carried the bowl of sweetened blackberries, a big spoon, two little bowls and two smaller spoons. She set this down on the table and dropped into her chair in a gesture of defeat. "About dinner," she said, "how do you feel about blackberries as appetizer, entrée, and dessert?"

"I love blackberries," Steven said. "One of my favorite foods. Shall I dish them out?"

As the cool air poured down from the mountains they sat and ate August blackberries and sipped white wine that was no longer chilled. In spite of the disastrous supper, the evening was really quite enjoyable until the moment he said, "Tell me. Did you ever smooth things out with your friend?"

Jessie felt her stomach twist up. She took another sip of wine. "No," she said. "He's in Alaska right now."

Long silence. Then, "I'm sorry."

"Don't be. Guthrie... He could be very controlling. Overprotective. And we were never going to see eye to eye about the fate of the ranch. Things between us just got uglier and uglier. As far as he was concerned I couldn't do anything right." She thought about what she had just said and felt a twinge of guilt. "Actually, he isn't nearly as black as I paint him. I'm just angry with him."

"Really?" Steven said mildly, causing her to laugh.

"I guess what I really needed was the chance to yell at him one more time. To kick him in the shins and get the final word in. Instead he ran off to Alaska!" She laughed again, ruefully.

Steven gazed at her in quiet contemplation for a long moment. "What would your final word have been?"

Jessie sat in silence for an equally long moment and then she met his eyes. She shook her head. "I can't imagine a final word." She drew a deep, even breath and shifted her gaze to the distant mountain peaks. "That's the whole problem, isn't it?"

He departed before it was fully dark, kissing her gently and with genuine affection on the cheek. "I had a good time tonight. Thanks for asking me to dinner."

"You're welcome." She smiled. "But next time, if you really want something to eat, better bring it with you."

"Can I stop at your swimming hole on my way out?"

"You better. It's a long hot drive to Bozeman."

"SO THERE YOU HAVE IT. He asked if he could use the swimming hole," Jessie said. "Twice. I figured that was a cheap price to pay for all the help he gave me. He should have lifetime rights to that swimming hole. I should've had it written into the deed."

Guthrie shifted his upper body, inching it upward into more of a sitting position. "He kissed you?" he said.

"On the cheek. It was very sweet."

"Sweet. Is that how you would describe my kisses?"

She glanced down at him with a slow smile. "You must be startin' to feel a whole lot better."

COMSTOCK LISTENED to the recorded phone messages in the kitchen while Ellie, humming softly, went into the bedroom to unpack their overnight bag. One night in Bozeman and she glowed like a newlywed. He should take her out more often. She deserved so much better than to be married to an old worn-out game warden.

He played the messages again, wondering. First it was Badger, yesterday morning, sounding on the edge of all-out full-blown importance. Bad things afoot, the senator and the grizzly up on the mountain, Guthrie gone looking for Jessie's mares, Jessie going after Guthrie on a hunch that something was wrong. Dark happenings afoot, yessiree!

A second message hard on its heels from Bernie. Tentative, worried, wondering about both Jessie and her brother's possible whereabouts. Finally, a third message from Bernie at 5:00 p.m. last night, in a much more cheerful voice, saying that all was well, not to worry, that she had just talked to McCutcheon, who'd been flying with Joe Nash, and he'd seen them from the air; Jessie and Guthrie had found the mares and were bringing them back down into the valley.

He sat at the kitchen counter and pondered for a few silent moments, then picked up the phone and dialed Joe Nash's number. No answer. Phoned the senator at his hunting lodge. His aide answered but would give no satisfying information except to say that the senator could not come to the phone and could Comstock please leave a message? He dialed up the airstrip and got Joe's boss. Got the scoop about McCutcheon—how good a pitcher he'd been for the White Sox, how rich he was, how good an account this could turn out to be, etcetera, etcetera. Hung up and leaned his elbows on the counter and pondered.

He stood, reached his gun belt from its peg by the door and strapped it on. Took his wool Filson jacket from the peg beside it and walked into the bedroom to kiss his wife goodbye. "Ellie, I'm sorry," he said. "I have to go to work."

Young Bear.

Steven wrote the name above the scratched-out name Brown on his business card. He sat at his desk, staring at the card but remembering a dream he'd had the night before. A powerful dream. He tapped his pen on the desktop, pushed back in his chair and glanced out the office

window. Traffic, people, noise. Had he expected anything else?

He sighed.

Remembered.

A grizzly had walked through his dreams. The grizzly
was being hunted, driven from its wilderness haunts by
white men with guns. There was danger all around, and
death was near. Bulldozers pushed down the big trees and
the grizzly ran. The white men fired shots after it, and the
grizzly ran. He was running, too, not sure at first if he was
running after the grizzly or with it. When the grizzly was
brought to bay by the end of the wild spaces on Jessie's
mountain, it spun around and faced him.

He felt no fear. He turned to face the white men behind
him, lifting his arms in a gesture to protect the bear, and
in that one motion he became the bear. As they raised their
rifles to shoot him he stared them down and waited calmly
to die.

He had woken in the darkness and lain in silence, his
heart beating a rapid cadence in the early-morning quiet,
as he thought about the power and meaning of that dream.

He thought about it now, sitting at his desk. "I am like
the bear." He spoke the words from a forgotten time and
heard in his voice the voice of his grandfather's father. "I
hold up my hands, waiting for the sun to rise."

Young Bear.

Jessie had given him back his name, and the bear had
come to him in his dream and given him back his inner
self, reconnected him to his wild side. Steven loosened his
tie, pushed out of his chair and walked to the window. He
remembered the dream and thought about Jessie's mountain. There had been death all around him, and terrible
danger.

It had only been a dream, and yet he heard a voice inside

himself telling him to listen, listen.... He gazed out the window, listening. It was a fine day for late October. It would be beautiful in Jessie's valley, in the shadow of Jessie's mountains. He could drive over with the insurance papers McCutcheon had inquired about.

Maybe Jessie would be there.

It would be good to see her.

COMSTOCK STOPPED by the Longhorn first, hoping to run into Badger there, but Bernie hadn't seen him since the day before, when he had departed with Charlie to ride up into the mountains. "My guess is both of them stayed out at the ranch," she said. "They didn't get the mares back until fairly late. McCutcheon said they were still quite a ways out when he spotted them, and it was close to midnight when they finally trailed in."

"Did McCutcheon mention seeing Jessie or Guthrie?"

"He couldn't make out who the rider was from the chopper, but when he called me late last night he said Badger and Charlie had taken the mares from Jessie, and she'd gone back up on the mountain to wait for Guthrie."

"Maybe I'll head out to the ranch and check on them," Comstock said, finishing his coffee.

"Do you think anything's wrong?" Bernie's voice was suddenly terse.

"No. I just think Badger and Charlie are a little old to be trailing a bunch of mares up in the mountains. And I'd kind of like to know where Jessie and your brother are. When I find them this time, I might just lock the two of 'em up in a jail cell, so's to give myself a little vacation."

At the ranch he greeted the bleary-eyed pair of old cowboys sunning themselves on the porch and working on cups of coffee liberally laced with some of McCutcheon's brandy. "Good stuff." Badger nodded, holding up the bottle of brandy and his mug of coffee, offering the same to Comstock, who politely declined. "Good for whatever ails you, especially lameness after a long ride."

"I believe it's called old age and arthritis," Charlie said.

Comstock verified that it was Jessie who had brought the mares down to Badger and Charlie. "She said Guthrie was behind her?"

Badger nodded again. "Said she was going to wait for him. I think they just wanted to camp somewheres together, just the two of 'em. Kind of romantic, if you ask me."

"So she had seen him?"

"Hell, I guess! Why else would she be waiting for him? I knew that boy'd find the mares. That Guthrie could track a whisper in a big wind."

Comstock tugged at an earlobe and canted his head to one side questioningly. "You figure the senator's still up there?"

"Yessir, I do," Badger nodded. "Maybe we called it wrong, but we all of us had the same hunch. Startin' with Jessie. She was so sure Guthrie was in trouble that you couldn't 'a stopped her with a forty-foot rope and a snubbin' post."

"Where's McCutcheon? Down at the old cabin?"

Badger exchanged a sly glance with old Charlie. "Well, now, here's what's shakin'," he said, and told the warden about McCutcheon's early-morning flight with Joe Nash. "So you see," he concluded, "we was thinkin' that if we could somehow keep Joe Nash tied up, you'd have time to catch the senator red-handed tryin' to shoot Jessie's bear."

"Huh." Comstock turned and gazed out toward the mountains. He stood like that, squinting out thoughtfully across the distance, until Badger and Charlie rose laboriously to their feet.

"I can't guarantee the fare, but you're welcome to join us for lunch," Badger said.

"Thanks. You boys go on in. I have to make a call."

While Charlie and Badger hobbled inside, Comstock radioed the airstrip from his vehicle and asked Joe's boss to tell him that he had another lost-person emergency and needed him to rendezvous at the Weaver ranch as soon as he could. Boss was not pleased, because Joe Nash was squiring around a very important client, but he agreed to pass the information on as soon as he could reach him.

After that, it was just a matter of waiting, and Comstock was not a very patient man.

CHAPTER EIGHTEEN

"WHAT'RE YOU DOING?" Guthrie watched while Jessie unraveled the spool of twine and cut off several long lengths.

"I'm going to make us a shelter. Something to turn the weather if it should get bad."

Guthrie hitched himself a little higher. "Why bother? I thought you said Joe Nash was on his way."

"Well, the thing is," Jessie said as she wielded her knife on the twine, "Joe should've been here a long time ago. I'm beginning to wonder if he's even coming."

"Good thing I brought that can of green chilis," he said.

"Good thing." She glanced up at him and flashed a grudging smile. "And the beans and the eggs and the oatmeal and the bacon and the coffee and the salt and honestly, Guthrie, a pepper grinder?"

"I like the taste of fresh ground pepper."

"Well, the way I figure it, it might be a day or so before reinforcements get here. I'm going to make sure we're comfortable, that's all."

"A day or two. Do you think in a day or two we might make amends?"

Jessie wrapped the cut lengths of twine into separate balls and stuffed them in her pocket. She closed her knife, packed the spool of twine in the saddlebag and glanced in his general direction. "I don't know," she said. "But at least we'll be warm and well fed while we hash things out.'' She stood. "I'm leaving my rifle with you. The senator's gun is lying right beside him. I'll take that with me and find his campsite. Bound to be a whole lot of comfortable stuff there that we could use.''

"Jess, we don't need much. Stay here. As long as we have each other, we'll be okay.''

"We'd be a lot more okay if we had more water and a tarp. He probably has at least that much, and enough gourmet senator food to feed us for a month. I'll be back as soon as I can. There's plenty of wood. Keep the home fires burning.''

"Jess?''

She turned back. He was looking at her with an expression she had never seen and she felt a pang. She nodded. "I'll be careful,'' she promised.

HE HAD KISSED HER. Steven Brown, the Indian lawyer. The man who shared her passion for protecting the environment, who shared her vision of the future for the land she loved and who had led her safely through the hottest of fires while he himself had run to Alaska and hidden from the memory of her cruel words.

Steven Brown had kissed her, and she had described his kiss as sweet. Sweet! How did one quantify such a description? It didn't sound all that dangerous, but nonetheless he had kissed her and she had allowed him to kiss her, and such a thing was very threatening from his own perspective.

Guthrie lay with his shoulders propped against the fallen log and let his thoughts wander. He felt all right, really, much stronger than he had. The soup had helped, and she had given him something for the pain, something strong enough to put a dull, fuzzy spin on things and push back the feeling that things were hopeless and dark. He felt that he might live after all, and if he and Jess were stranded out here for a couple more days, maybe it would make a difference. Maybe it would change things between them, soften the hard edges, weaken the barriers they had both built to protect themselves from hurt.

Or maybe not. Maybe she closed her eyes and dreamed of a different man. Could he really blame her? He had been wrong to doubt her, to question her decisions at a time when she so desperately needed emotional support. She had every right to seek out the company of another, for he had offered her nothing but arguments and unasked-for advice.

Steven Brown. Guthrie felt a twist of pain deep inside himself and he wasn't sure if it was because a horse had rolled over on top of him or because he feared losing Jessie to another man.

THE SECONDS, the minutes, the hours passed with such agonizing slowness that Joe Nash was sure he was going to have a nervous breakdown before this day was through. McCutcheon wanted to eat lunch in the prettiest spot on the ranch. And where might that be?

"Near the line camp on Piney Creek. It's up in a high valley, the mountains ring it and it's one of the prettiest spots in all of Montana," he responded.

So he flew McCutcheon to that pretty valley that he now owned and he set the JetRanger down gently in deference to its previous insult. They ate lunch sitting on the banks of Piney Creek, or at least McCutcheon did. Joe had no appetite. He was dwelling on bears and bodies and brush piles and was so obsessed with feelings of impending doom that he could hardly swallow two bites of the ham sandwich that McCutcheon handed him.

"What a day," McCutcheon rhapsodized. He raised a

bottle of iced tea to wash his sandwich down. "What's wrong? Don't like ham?"

"It's fine. I'm just not hungry."

"You've been kind of quiet today," McCutcheon observed.

"Guess I'm not feeling up to snuff." Joe wished the inquisition would end. There was something unnerving about McCutcheon's questions. A sudden inspiration struck him. "And neither is the chopper."

"Huh?" McCutcheon lowered his sandwich and raised his eyebrows. "What do you mean?"

"Haven't you felt those funny rotations during landing?"

"No."

"There's something not quite right with the tail rotor."

"Really?"

"See, the tail rotor keeps the chopper from spinning in circles due to the torque of the main prop. It's pretty important when you're flying."

"And you think it might be malfunctioning?"

Joe nodded. "It happens, sometimes with catastrophic results."

"Huh." McCutcheon lifted his bottle of iced tea. "Maybe tomorrow you should have your mechanic look into it."

Joe glanced at the older man, perplexed. His feeling of uneasiness grew. He held the thick ham sandwich in a hand that came perilously close to shaking and stared out at a heart-clenching beauty he did not see. McCutcheon knew! He was sure of it! Somehow he knew about the senator. About the illegal hunt. About what Joe had seen. The brush pile. That big goddam pile of brush! Something inside him snapped. He had to tell what he knew. He couldn't keep it bottled up a moment longer.

"Look!" he blurted, and at the same time there was a loud burst of static behind them where the chopper sat. The radio crackled to life and a man's gruff voice droned unintelligibly. Joe leaped up and brushed off his trousers with one hand, still holding the ham sandwich in the other. His entire body thrummed with tension. "That's my boss. I better go see what he wants."

He trotted to the chopper, weak with relief at his reprieve until he heard what Boss was saying. He listened to another full transmission before putting on his headset and responding. He keyed the mike. "Ah, yeah, I copy that."

McCutcheon was approaching, but he couldn't have heard what Boss had just said, what had just passed between them. Joe sat in absolute stillness for a few moments, immobilized by utter despair.

"What is it?" McCutcheon asked, looking as cool and calm as a frigid nun on a Monday morning.

Joe shrugged. "He's wondering why I haven't called in. He's a little pissed off. I guess Comstock's waiting back at the Weaver ranch for me to pick him up. Seems there's another missing person to search for."

"No kidding. Did he say who?"

Joe shook his head. He flung the ham sandwich as far as he could and then fumbled in his pocket for another stick of gum. "No," he said, unwrapping it. "No, he didn't. But I have a pretty good idea. Get in, and I'll tell you about it."

FINDING THE SENATOR'S camping place wasn't hard, and Jessie had been right. There was enough food and comfort to keep a man in good shape for a long time. She bundled most of it into a tarp, then twisted the tarp up and slung the heavy load over her shoulder. Going back would be slower, especially down that steep stretch of rock. Harder, too, because she would have to grip the tarp in her good hand and carry the senator's rifle in her weak hand. If the bear showed up, she'd be at a distinct disadvantage.

She had passed very near the kill site on her way to the senator's camp, and she nodded when she saw that it was the black mare, Coaly, or what was left of her. Just as she had thought. So she had lost two good horses to this bear, though she could hardly blame the bear for either loss. The bear was just being a bear. Perhaps the senator was just being a man. Perhaps it was in all men to kill, not just to eat, but for sheer pleasure of it. For the ultimate and egotistical domination of another living creature.

No, that couldn't be. Guthrie wasn't like that. He'd kill a bear if he had to, and he'd shoot to put meat on the table, but he would never set out to do what the senator had. Not all men killed for the blood sport of it. There were some who understood how the pieces of the puzzle fit together, how nature worked.

Jessie paused to rest. She laid the bundle down and flexed her shoulders. Already the sun was westering. How had the day passed so quickly? And where was Joe Nash? Had Billy made it back to the ranch? He liked his oats awfully well, and knew that they were dished out about this time of an afternoon.

She didn't rest long. The shadows were lengthening; the daylight hours were growing short. She hefted the awkward bundle and carefully negotiated the downward slope of rock, slipping once and landing painfully on her behind but not losing her grip on either the precious bundle or the senator's heavy rifle.

Past the dead senator again, her eyes carefully averted; a painful glance at Kestrel, that beautiful mare; then back into the woods, the darkness closing around her like a cloak. She caught the tang of wood smoke in the cooling air, then spotted the flickering fire, and Guthrie lying beside it, waiting for her.

She let her burdens fall to the ground near the fire and dropped beside them with a weary moan, easing a cramp in the small of her back.

"How'd you make out?" Guthrie said.

"Good." Jessie flexed her bad hand. Her arm ached abysmally. "Got a tarp, two blankets, lots of food and a gallon or so of water."

"So what did the senator eat?"

Jessie glanced at him. "Strange stuff, if you ask me. Vienna sausage, franks-and-beans in tomato sauce, SpaghettiOs, Spam, canned brown bread and, thank the Lord, Colombian coffee."

"He must have had a cooler. Meat. Beer. Stuff like that."

"I didn't see one."

"Did you find the tree stand?"

"No."

"That's where all the good stuff would be stashed. Up in the tree stand, where the bear couldn't get at it," Guthrie said.

Jessie cradled her aching arm on her raised knee and glared at him. "Well, I didn't find the tree stand! And you want to know something else? I didn't look for it. If you think you could've done better you should've gone yourself. Lord knows you're a whole lot smarter than me!"

Guthrie gazed at her for a long moment and then he shook his head in defeat. "If I were the least bit smart I wouldn't be lying here thinking about all the things I did wrong that hurt you. I wouldn't be regretting all the stupid things I've said. If I were the least bit smart I wouldn't have done or said any of them." He shook his head again, wearily. "I'm not smart, Jess. I'm so dumb I keep doing the same old things over and over that get your dander up, and that just makes me not only dumb but crazy, because all I want is for us to be on good terms again, and it just seems so plain damn hopeless."

Jessie pushed slowly to her feet, gathered an armload of wood and laid it near the fire. She untied the tarp, unloaded its contents and then dropped it over a long pole lashed at shoulder height between two spruce. With the lengths of twine in her pocket she tied it off to form a lean-to over their campsite. She opened a tin of franks-and-beans and set it on the coals at the edge of the fire to heat, filled the billy can with water for a pot of coffee, tucked another blanket around Guthrie and then stretched next to him. "I'm tired," she said, staring up through the spruce branches at the darkening sky and feeling as if she were floating. "I'm so tired I can't think."

Guthrie shifted onto one elbow, took the blanket she'd laid over him and adjusted it as best he could over her. "Sleep, then," he said. "I'll let you know when the beans start to burn."

"Guthrie?" She pulled the wool blanket up to her chin and drew a long breath. She reached out and took his hand in hers. "I guess if you're dumb and crazy, so am I. Because in spite of all the dumb, crazy things that have happened between us, the thing is... What I mean to say is, I still feel... I mean, I still think..." She felt him squeeze her hand reassuringly in his big grip and she squeezed back, her eyes stinging. She drew his hand to her cheek and pressed it there. "What I'm trying to say is, I guess hell will be a glacier before I ever quit you."

COMSTOCK WONDERED what was taking Joe Nash so long. He imagined all sorts of dark scenarios while he waited, for he hated to wait on anything, anywhere, anyhow, and time stretched itself out in a mean way when people's lives hung in the balance. When he finally heard the chopper he was sure he'd aged another five years, and had given long and sober considerations to Ellie's recent and compelling argument that he retire.

He stood on the ranch-house porch and watched the chopper approach. Badger and Charlie came out to join him, along with McCutcheon's lawyer, Steven Brown, who had arrived at the ranch shortly after lunchtime with some insurance papers for McCutcheon to review. Jessie's cow dog whined deep in her throat as the big whirling machine set down between the pole barn and the house.

McCutcheon levered himself awkwardly out of the JetRanger and hobbled stiffly to the base of the porch steps as Comstock descended them. "Joe told me everything about the senator and the grizzly," he said. "The senator's still up there. Any sign of Jessie and Guthrie?"

"Jessie's horse came back here an hour or so ago," Comstock replied. "There was a note wrapped around the saddle horn. Said that Guthrie had been hurt pretty bad and that Joe would know right where they were."

McCutcheon leaned on his crutch, visibly shocked. "Is Jessie all right? Did she mention seeing the senator anywhere?" he said as Comstock headed for the chopper. The warden paused and glanced back over his shoulder. "The note said that the senator was dead. I've radioed for the state police."

McCutcheon's lawyer followed on his heels and as he reached the chopper he spoke loud enough to be heard over the idling rotors. "Like some help?" he said. Comstock regarded him for a brief moment, appreciating the man's powerful build and calm demeanor. He nodded curtly.

"Never refused it when it was offered," he said.

Comstock climbed in beside Joe. "Joe Nash, Steven Brown."

"Young Bear," the lawyer corrected, settling himself in the back seat. "Steven Young Bear." Comstock glanced over his shoulder at the Indian, one eyebrow raised questioningly. "My tribal name," he said, his dark eyes revealing nothing. Comstock nodded and faced front again.

"Seems that lately we've been doing an awful lot flying together, Joe," he said, buckling himself in.

Joe's mirrored sunglasses hid his eyes but couldn't hide the haggard lines on his face. "Yeah," he said. "We sure have."

"The senator's dead, Joe. Take me to where you left him," Comstock said. "I guess we'll find Jessie and Guthrie right close by."

Joe sat for a few moments and then shifted in his seat. He drew a deep breath, let it out slowly, nodded and throttled up the chopper. "Yeah," he said. "I guess we will."

GUTHRIE THOUGHT that he could stay like this forever, watching Jessie sleep. She looked so peaceful, so beautiful lying next to him. So close he could hear her soft breathing. Close enough that he could reach out and brush a stray lock of hair from her forehead, adjust the blanket that covered her. They were nearer now than they'd been in many months…and yet just as far apart. She'd said she'd never quit him, but what exactly did that mean? Friends never quit each other, either, so she hadn't been promising undying love, just the steady loyalty of a good friend. Perhaps that was all they could ever have together. Friendship. A chance meeting in the Longhorn every now and then—painful encounters that wrenched both of them and left them feeling bereft and miserable and unbearably lonely.

Perhaps that was all the future held.

Or maybe… Maybe she'd meant something more. Maybe she'd finally forgiven him for quitting her when she needed him the most.

"Jess," he said, his voice a mere whisper, scarcely louder than the crackle of the wood fire, the wind through the trees. He smoothed the hair from her forehead. Her eyelids fluttered and she moaned in denial. "Jess!" he said again.

"No, please, I'm so tired," she murmured, not opening her eyes. "Let me sleep."

"The beans are burning. And I hear something. Sounds like a helicopter."

Her eyes shot open and she sat up so suddenly that she lost her balance and reached out for him impulsively. His hand gripped hers. "Oh, God!" she said, staring at him wide-eyed. "I hear it, too!" She pushed the blanket back, loosed his hand and scrambled to her feet. She grabbed a big handful of evergreen boughs from the stack she'd made and tossed them on the fire. Thick smoke billowed upward. "It's Joe!" She glanced around wildly, spotted her rifle and snatched it up. "I've got to make sure he doesn't leave us here!" she said. "I have to stop him!"

"Jess," he said, "what the hell are you talkin' about?"

"What if he sees the senator is dead and takes off without us!"

"Of course he's goin' to see the senator's dead. Joe Nash is about as far from blind as a man can be. What are you plannin' to do—gun him down on general principles? Joe'll see the smoke from our fire and he'll come lookin' for the senator. You stay right here with me."

"But what if he spooks and flies away!"

"He won't leave us. What the hell, Jess. He may have

poor judgment in clients and lousy hunting ethics, but he won't abandon us here. Put the rifle up.''

Jessie turned away from him and listened to the approaching chopper. Guthrie was right. Joe Nash might be in the senator's pocket, but when he found the senator dead and realized how badly Guthrie was hurt, he'd help them out. There was nothing else he could do.

''C'mere, Jess. Come sit beside me. It'll take Joe a while to park that chopper and climb down over the ledge.''

Jessie looked back at Guthrie and felt all the adrenaline ooze out of her, leaving her weak and shaky. She stood the rifle against the trunk of a tree and went to where he lay propped against the fallen log. She sat down beside him and felt his arm encircle her shoulders and draw her against him. She rested her head on his shoulder and closed her eyes on the burn of exhaustion. Her body melted instinctively into his, absorbing the very essence of him. She needed Guthrie the way a ship needed a safe harbor in a hurricane, and she always would. He was to her very existence the way the wild places were to the soul of Montana.

''What if he doesn't find us?'' she murmured, eyes closing.

''What if the sun doesn't rise tomorrow?''

''But what if…''

''Then we'll just camp out here until someone comes. We have enough food to patch hell forty miles, and we have each other—''

''Jessie!'' The deep powerful shout carried easily over the sough of wind through the spruce and fir. ''Jessie Weaver!''

Jessie stiffened in shock. ''That's not Joe!'' she said, pushing to her feet. ''That's Steven!'' And then she shouted back from the depths of her own lungs. ''Down here! We're down here!'' She whirled to look at Guthrie, relief surging through her, erasing the fatigue and the worry and the stress of the past few days. "It's Steven! He found us!''

"The Indian lawyer,'' Guthrie said. He tipped his head back and groaned. "My lucky day.''

She ignored his wry comment and raced out of their camp, approached the brush pile and dodged around it, ran past the dead senator, began scrabbling up the steep rounded ledge toward a man who was already descending it. They met somewhere in the middle, his arm reaching to steady her on the steep rock face as she struggled to catch her breath. She tried to speak but couldn't. She looked up into his calm strong face, caught his dark gaze, and her throat tightened up. "It's all right,'' he said, his hand squeezing her shoulder reassuringly. "Comstock's here, too. Are you okay?''

"The senator's dead and Guthrie's hurt bad,'' she managed past the lump in her throat.

"We know. We got your note. We brought medical supplies. Joe Nash has an elk carrier stashed in the chopper. He and Comstock are bringing it down. We'll use it as a litter to carry Guthrie.''

"Oh, Steven. Thank you for coming!''

"You can thank your bear for that,'' he said. "Last night he ran through my dreams, so today I came to your mountain.''

"Last night that same bear ran through our camp,'' Jessie said, "and killed the senator.''

CHAPTER NINETEEN

TWO WEEKS SPENT in a hospital bed was two weeks longer than any cowboy born Montana tough should ever have to tolerate. The first week was just a dull fog, hardly remembered. There'd been several surgeries, and the medications they'd administered had looped him. But the second week, time dug in hard and dragged its heels.

His sister, Bernie, arrived without fail at 10:00 a.m. each morning, between breakfast and lunch hours at the café. McCutcheon visited daily in the early afternoon. But it was Jessie who was there when he opened his eyes upon the day, and when they gave him the nighttime meds that knocked him out after supper it was Jessie who was sitting beside his bed. She came in the morning before breakfast, left when Bernie arrived, and returned after doing evening chores.

She sat beside his bed and read aloud to him from different books she borrowed from the hospital library. She told him stories about what was going on at the ranch and how McCutcheon was settling in. "His wife is flying out to visit," she announced one evening. "He told me when he bought the place that she never would, but curiosity must be getting the best of her."

"She's probably jealous as hell, knowing that you're living at the ranch with him," Guthrie said.

Jessie shook her head. "Doubtful. From what McCutcheon says, they see each other three or four times a year and are comfortable with that.''

"Mighty peculiar behavior for a married couple, if you ask me."

"I think all those wild stories she's been hearin' about senators and grizzly bears and wild horses have her all stirred up. She probably just wants to see what really goes on in the last great place."

Guthrie grinned. "Maybe she's afraid he's gone over the edge, spinnin' such tall tales as that."

"Maybe he has. He's been a little distracted lately. We take our supper together up at the main ranch house, and of late he seems…''

"You're eating together?" Guthrie said.

"Yes. It only makes sense. I cooked the first few times, and then he kind of stepped in and took over, in his own self-defense. He's a good cook, lots better than me. Almost as good as you. But lately…''

Guthrie stared, his heart plummeting. "Okay, Jess. Break it to me gently. Does the Indian lawyer eat with you, too?''

Jessie scowled. "I wish you'd quit about that!" She jumped up out of the plastic chair and paced the hospital room, still holding the book she'd been reading aloud from. "There's nothing between Steven and me but friendship, and if he hadn't been there to help get you to the chopper…''

"Lord A'mighty, I'll be hearin' about how grateful I should be to that man till the day I die."

"Well, if he hadn't…''

"If he hadn't, I'd have had to work a little harder, that's all.''

Jessie's eyes sparked with anger. "What a ridiculous thing to say! If Steven hadn't been there, you might be dead. You were unconscious for most of the trip. You barely made it to the hospital, Guthrie. It's only been one week. One week! Are you so quick to forget how those three men helped save your life?''

"Hell, no. I don't guess I'll forget that humiliation as long as I live.''

"Humiliation? What are you talking about? We owe that man a great debt!''

"Did you call your professor, Jess?''

"Yes, I called my professor,'' she retorted. "He said I'd get notification in the mail about when I would be returning to school. He thought it would probably be spring semester.''

Guthrie tried to study her face, tried to read the truth in her eyes, but he felt himself drifting away. It was like that. One moment things were crystal clear, rock hard and real and the next, he felt as if a thick bank of fog had rolled in and dulled the very thoughts in his head, numbed every nerve center in his body. The fog was bad, but the pain was worse. And so they medicated him to keep the pain at bay, and he drifted in and out of the fog and gave up trying to fight it because he never won.

That was day eight.

JESSIE HATED this hospital. She despised the smells, the sounds that echoed within its halls, the fluorescent lights, the frighteningly high-tech equipment that reduced mere mortals to the cellular level. She hated how her father had died here. She hated her feeling of helplessness when she sat at Guthrie's side, watching the nurses come in, the doctors, different shifts, different faces, everything shifting all the time, until the only constants were seeing Bernie at 10:00 a.m. and knowing that she could leave to go do her chores at the ranch because Bernie would be sitting with him, watching over him, making sure the hospital staff knew that this man was loved, cared for, wanted, needed and very important to a whole bunch of people.

Making sure that Guthrie didn't die.

Day twelve.

Bernie arrived at 10:00 a.m. sharp. Guthrie was asleep. Had been for an hour. "He's feeling a whole lot better," Jessie said as she gathered her things. "The doctor told me this morning that Guthrie might be able to come home this weekend."

Bernie's face lit up. "That's great news. Terrific news! He must be pretty excited. I've got the spare bedroom all ready...."

Jessie shook his head. "He wants to go home, Bernie. I offered to take him to the ranch, but he just wants to go home."

Bernie gazed for a long silent moment at her brother, who for the past four days had been blessedly free of the monitors and the oxygen and the surgical drainage tubes, and reluctantly nodded. "Okay. If that's what he wants, but..."

"Bernie..." Jessie looked at Guthrie's sister and her eyes blurred with tears. "I don't know if we can work it out, Guthrie and me. But whatever happens between us, whatever the future holds for us, I love you like a sister and I always will."

They hugged fiercely, clinging to each other in their anguish. "Me, too," Bernie whispered. "No matter what."

Jessie walked down the hospital corridor in a fog not unlike the ones Guthrie got lost in. She hardly remembered how she came to be standing in the frigid air outside the hospital entrance. She had no idea how long she had been standing there. She heard her name spoken but couldn't respond. A hand touched her shoulder. "Jessie?" She shook her head to clear it.

"Steven," she said.

He looked at her for a brief moment and then said, "Come with me."

With his hand firm upon her arm, he led her to his Jeep Wagoneer and settled her securely in the passenger seat. She was shivering, though the vehicle was warm. He drove through the Bozeman traffic, took her away from the hospital, away from Guthrie; took her to a place she'd never been before, a little cedar-clad post-and-beam house at the end of a long winding driveway near Gallatin Gateway. He led her inside the warm dwelling and guided her to the sofa. "I thought you were going to faint on me back there," he said. "When was the last time you ate anything?"

And then he repaired immediately to the kitchen, making noises, domestic sounds. If she craned her neck she would probably see him, for the house had an open floor plan, but she was too exhausted to move. She focused on the immediate surroundings. The brick fireplace, where embers from the previous night's blaze still glowed; the bookcases flanking both sides of it, filled with leather-bound legal volumes, timeless classics and environmental treatises. The simple western furniture, the hardwood floor covered with beautifully woven wool rugs, the Ansel Adams prints on the whitewashed walls, the big wooden beams spanning the ceiling. The feeling of simplicity, of safety, of peace.

Steven returned, carrying two mugs of something hot. "To hold you over," he said, handing her one.

She took a sip. Swallowed. Her eyes watered and a comforting heat settled in her stomach. "What is it?"

"Guaranteed jump starter," he said. "Coffee. Really

strong. Mixed with hot cocoa mix. Really strong. Big dollop of real vanilla extract. Really strong." He took a taste from his own mug. "Strong stuff, huh?" he said.

"Strong stuff," Jessie agreed, taking another swallow.

"It's got all the makings," he said, dropping onto the couch. "Caffeine, sugar, a little alcohol in the vanilla extract...."

"Give me a few more minutes," Jessie said, "and I'll be dancing."

"If you just stop looking like you're about to faint, I'll be happy," Steven said. "I'm heating up some leftovers."

"I'm not hungry."

"After you eat, you should have a nap." He stood up and went back into the kitchen. More domestic noises were forthcoming. Jessie relaxed on the sofa, cradling the mug of hot elixir, breathing the steam, taking a small sip, then another. Already her head felt clearer.

At length Steven reappeared, carrying a deep earthenware bowl with a spoon in it. He set it in front of her. "Beef stew. Last night's supper." He returned to the kitchen and in a few moments Jessie heard him speaking on the phone. She drank more of the hot liquid that seemed to be infusing her with strength. Five more minutes passed.

Steven came back into the living room carrying a thick slab of warm corn bread on a plate. "I called the Longhorn," he said, setting the corn bread in front of her. "Badger and Charlie will do your chores tonight. Badger says he still remembers how to feed a bunch of worthless old hay burners. So you eat, and then you take a nap. You've been living on the edge for too long."

She obediently picked up the spoon. "Tell me about your dream," she said. "The dream you had about the bear. The dream that brought you to the mountain."

While she ate, Steven told her about the bear that had

run through his dreams. "When I woke, I thought for a long time about the dream and then I went to your ranch and met the game warden there, and the rest you know.

"My grandfather once said that when an animal runs through your dreams, it is a powerful vision. He said we must pay attention to what the animal is trying to teach us. He said that we walk in the shadow of our dreams, and that our dreams guide us and help make us who we are. That bear brought you and Guthrie back together, and it brought me to your valley, to your mountains, and reconnected me to my roots. It has a powerful spirit, that bear."

"Maybe it's a bear walker," Jessie said. "My grandmother told me about them. Their spirits walk around the edges of the camp, just outside the light of the fire."

Steven nodded. "A bear walker. Maybe."

"I have to go to the courthouse the first Tuesday in December, to give my statement in a closed hearing. I don't know why. I've already answered all the questions they could possibly ask, and so has Guthrie. What else do they want to know?"

"When an investigation involves a senator, they make a bigger fuss. What time?"

"At 2:00 p.m."

Steven nodded. He rose, picking up the empty bowl and plate. "The guest room is through that door," he said. "In two hours, I'll drive you back to the hospital."

Jessie couldn't remember the last time she'd had a nap, but she knew that she would never forget Steven's kindness.

FRIDAY. Day fourteen. Any one of them would have driven Guthrie home after the hospital's discharge papers were signed, but McCutcheon did the honors. Guthrie planned it that way. He told Jessie and Bernie that he was being released on Saturday, then asked McCutcheon if he could pick him up at 1:00 p.m. Friday. McCutcheon agreed, though his confusion was evident when he arrived.

"Why all the secrecy?" he asked when they were headed back toward Katy Junction.

"I hate fuss," Guthrie said. "Bernie would fuss. She'd want me to come home with her. Jessie would feel she had to be nice to me even if she didn't want to be. Hell, she's been behaving like that for the past two weeks, and she's still workin' on a big mad."

"She's not mad. Maybe if the senator were still alive she would be, but there's no satisfaction in being pissed off at a dead man."

"Oh, she's mad—make no mistake. Got every right to be. I killed her best horse. Kestrel was the finest Spanish mustang she ever raised."

"Like hell you killed that mare!"

"And then there's that Indian lawyer."

"Steven Brown's not even in the picture."

Guthrie slumped in the soft leather seat of the silver Mercedes. "Oh, hell, every time I open my eyes, he's in the picture." He gazed out at the wall of rugged mountains. "Anyhow, I don't want to bother her. She needs a break from sittin' at my bedside. She needs about a week of bed rest. She's nothin' but skin and bones and permanent scowl, and that girl's way too young to have a permanent scowl. I feel I'm the cause of it. I don't guess I'll ever figure it out."

"What's that?"

"What it will take to make her smile again. Speaking of which, she told me your wife was coming to visit."

McCutcheon drove silently for a few beats, then drew a deep breath and let it out slowly. "She's come and gone. Only spent the one night."

"Too rustic," Guthrie guessed, sympathizing.

"She asked me for a divorce. Said it was something she couldn't do over the phone or through the mail after twenty years of marriage. Told me she had to do it face-to-face."

Guthrie stared out the side window. "I'm sorry."

"Nothing to be sorry about. I guess it's been coming for a long time. She's a great lady and no doubt she'll be a whole lot better off without an aging has-been baseball pitcher trying to play cowboy. But for some reason that doesn't make me feel any better right now."

McCutcheon drove his low-slung Mercedes cautiously up the old dirt road that led to Guthrie's cabin on the banks of Bear Creek. He was the first to spot the familiar truck parked in the cabin yard, though Guthrie's soft curse followed close behind his own.

Jessie was standing on the cabin porch, broom in hand, watching their approach. Blue was there, too, and while the little cow dog trotted down the steps to greet the two men with much enthusiasm, Jessie remained on the porch, as Guthrie struggled to extricate himself from the deep bucket seat and McCutcheon awkwardly hobbled around the vehicle on his walking cast to assist him. She said nothing at all and made no move to help. Just leaned on the broom, her expression ominously blank.

By the time he made it to the bottom of the porch steps Guthrie was weak in the knees and sweating from the effort of it, but he shrugged off McCutcheon's assistance and stood in what he hoped was a strong and reasonably upright position. "Hello, Jess," he said.

She straightened, holding the broom in both hands as if it were a rifle resting with its butt between her feet. "You told me just this morning that you were being discharged tomorrow," she said in a calm, even voice, "so I came over here this afternoon to tidy things up and get the woodstove going. Takes a long time to heat up cabin logs, and this place has been dead cold for two weeks.'' She laid the broom against the cabin wall to the right of the door. ''Won't warm up proper until tomorrow, I don't doubt,'' she said, ducking back inside briefly to grab her parka.

''Thanks,'' Guthrie said when she reappeared. ''I appreciate you coming over here. I didn't want to trouble you.''

She descended the porch steps and paused in front of him, her face impassive but her dark eyes conveying all the hurt she felt. ''It was no trouble,'' she said, then marched past McCutcheon without so much as a sidelong glance, chin high and eyes straight ahead, whistled Blue into her truck and departed for the ranch.

Guthrie climbed the porch steps one at a time, using the pain to drive away the image of Jessie's eyes, and the dark emotions he had read in them. Using the pain to punish himself for his own shortsighted stupidity. He had thought to spare Jessie the trouble of driving him home. The bother of fussing over him. He had thought she'd be relieved to be rid of the bedside vigil, but once again he'd been wrong, and in his supreme ignorance he had only made things much, much worse. When he reached the top step he turned and looked back at McCutcheon. ''Thanks for the ride home,'' he said.

The older man regarded him skeptically. ''You all right?''

''Yeah. I'm fine.''

''Well,'' McCutcheon said, raising his shoulders around a helpless shrug. ''I guess maybe women like to fuss and worry.''

''I guess maybe.''

''I'll come by tomorrow.''

''No need.''

McCutcheon limped back to the Mercedes and climbed in. "Tomorrow morning," he said before closing the car door. "First thing."

After he had gone, Guthrie lowered himself onto the wooden bench that flanked the cabin door. He breathed carefully around the cracks of pain that radiated from so many places within and without and waited for the light-headedness to pass, for the sound of the creek to replace the sound of his ragged breathing, for his rapid heartbeat to slow and steady, for the ice-cold sweat to dry on his forehead—and for the anguish he'd seen in Jessie's eyes to fade from his memory.

But he knew it never would.

CHAPTER TWENTY

STEVEN YOUNG BEAR walked down the gleaming corridor in soft-soled leather shoes that squeaked beneath him. He changed his pace to silence the noise, searched the waiting area outside the courtroom for a familiar face, and when he finally spotted it he halted and felt that familiar surge of gladness.

"Hello, Jessie," he said as she came toward him. She was dressed conservatively, in a woolen gray skirt and blazer with a pale-pink blouse that brought out the color in her cheeks. Her long glossy black hair was swept up into a French twist. She looked slender, sophisticated and heart-wrenchingly beautiful. He took her hands in his and kissed her gently on the cheek. "Have they called you yet?"

"Yes," she said. "I told them everything I know about everything I know, and then some."

"Have you had lunch?"

"I ate at the Longhorn while Bernie fixed my hair. She said if I was going into that fancy courthouse, dressed in these fancy clothes, my hair ought to be fancy, too." Jessie smiled.

"You look beautiful," Steven said. "The folks who took your deposition are probably still trying to remember what it was you said. I see your arm is back to normal."

"Not exactly, but almost. They removed the pins yesterday. I was supposed to have therapy to restore the strength, but since I never really stopped using it, they nixed that idea." She laughed, lifting the offending arm and working her fingers. "Feels a little weak, but it's nice to have it back again."

"I bet. How's Guthrie doing?"

"All right. He was released from the hospital two weeks ago. Bernie tried to get him to stay with her family for a while, but he wanted to go home. He's at his cabin, making do and getting by. The doctor told him he'd always have a limp, and he probably shouldn't ever ride again because of the injury to his hip. But the doctor doesn't know Guthrie. Montana cowboys are tough. If they weren't, he wouldn't have survived that ruptured spleen or the fractured skull."

"Are the two of you...?"

Jessie's cheeks warmed with color and she dropped her eyes. "We're doing okay." She shifted her gaze to the wall and then lifted it again to his calm eyes. "I'm going back to school in January, Steven. They've accepted me back. I'll be repeating the last half of my third year of vet school, but I guess that's fair. It's been a while, and I'll be playing catch-up."

He smiled. "That's the best thing you could do for yourself right now."

"What about Joe Nash, Steven? What do you think will happen to him?"

"Oh, he'll probably get a big fine. But they'll go easy on him. In the end he did the right thing, and he was remorseful about all the wrongs he'd done at the senator's bequest. I suppose if the senator himself were still alive, he'd be in a lot of hot water. Perhaps your bear walker did him a favor."

"Perhaps that bear did all of us a favor," Jessie said.

Steven took her hand and squeezed it gently. "Study

hard. When you are a veterinarian, maybe you would doctor our *bi'shee*.''

"I'd be honored." Jessie smiled. "You hold 'em—I'll vet 'em. Can't be much worse than trying to doctor a wild longhorn steer."

"Well, the buffalo are a little bigger, but it's a deal." Steven nodded. "I wish you all the best," he said. "And if you ever need legal advice or anything at all, call me. I'm in the phone book." He paused a few steps down the corridor and looked back. "Young Bear," he said.

He walked back down the gleaming courthouse corridor with the sad certainty that, knowing Jessie, she never would call.

BY THE TIME Jessie returned to the Longhorn it was nearly dark, for dark closed in early around December afternoons. She went inside to say hello to Bernie and have a bowl of soup before heading back to the ranch. Charlie and Badger were there, as always, and she listened to their banter, answered Bernie's questions about her adventures in court and slowly ate the bowl of hearty minestrone Bernie set before her.

"So, what about Joe? Will Comstock have to find another chopper pilot to squire him around?" Bernie asked, refilling Jessie's coffee mug.

Jessie laughed. "Joe might be grounded for a while and they've smacked him with a big fine, but he'll live to fly again."

"He just got caught up in his own loop, that's all," Badger said philosophically. "I expect he'll straighten out right smart after this."

Jessie pushed off the counter stool and stood. "Thanks for the soup, Bern. It really hit the spot."

"Oh, Jessie!" As if suddenly remembering something,

Bernie gestured for her to wait. She returned carrying a cardboard box. "I haven't had a chance to drive out to Guthrie's place today—it's been so infernally busy. I thought maybe you could drop this by on your way home. That is, if you don't mind. It would save me a lot of time. Little Aaron's sick and I really need to get home early tonight…"

Jessie took the box reluctantly and then shook her head with a sigh. "You never give up, do you?" she said.

Outside, the cold wind made her wish she had dressed more sensibly. She climbed into her truck, incongruously clad in her courtroom clothes, and began the drive to Guthrie's place. It wasn't very far out of her way, after all, and she hadn't been out to the cabin since the day McCutcheon had brought him home from the hospital.

It was nearly dark, but she could still see the frozen white edges of Bear Creek where it tumbled through the jumble of boulders just shy of the cabin. She drove into the yard and cut the engine, then sat for a while in the stillness. Such a pretty cabin it was, everything about it straight and square, sturdy and pleasing to the eye. Smoke rose from the chimney; lamplight glowed from the windows. She saw the shadow of a man cross in front of the window nearest the door, and then the cabin door opened and he was standing in the doorway, waiting, a tall broadshouldered figure leaning on a crutch.

She pushed open the truck's door and climbed out. "Hi," she said. "Bernie sent me over with some food." She lifted the cardboard box off the seat and nudged the truck's door shut with her hip. She climbed the steps onto the porch, entered into the cabin's warmth and heard the door close behind her. Without pausing, she crossed to the kitchen and set the box atop the counter.

She turned and looked at him, and at the little cow dog

who stood beside him, wagging her tail and immensely happy.

"It's good to see you," he said.

"What's Blue doing here?"

"McCutcheon came over around noon for a visit. He left her with me. Said she was a good baby-sitter and that you'd probably be by to pick her up later."

"I see," Jessie said. Bernie and McCutcheon were obviously in on this little matchmaking scheme. Guthrie was wearing an old comfortable pair of Levi's and a thick chamois shirt with the sleeves rolled back. His hair was tousled and he had a pair of thick wool socks on his feet.

"You sure are dressed pretty," he said.

"I had to testify in court this afternoon."

"You should testify in court more often."

"You look like you just woke up."

"I did," he admitted. "Just before you drove in. Seems all I do is sleep. I wake up, eat breakfast, lie down and sleep. Get up, fix lunch, lie down and have a nap. I guess it must be suppertime now, huh?" He grinned at her.

Jessie felt herself beginning to melt. To be so near him and not feel that old, familiar chemistry kick in was hard. "Close enough. Let's see what she sent."

"Hell, I can see what she sent without opening that box," Guthrie said, limping across the room toward her. "She sent you."

"Yes. That's a very clever sister you have. Come to think of it, McCutcheon's no slouch, either."

"If I'd known my askin' McCutcheon to drive me home from the hospital was going to fash you that way, I'd never have done it," he said, leaning against the counter and laying the crutch aside. "I was tryin' to save you the trouble. And truth, I wasn't sure I'd be able to climb the cabin steps. I didn't want you to watch me fall on my face.

You've seen enough of that to last you a lifetime.'' He reached for her hand and she stepped back, putting a safe distance between them.

"Dammit, Jess, I know you're still mad, and I don't blame you. I'm sorry about Kestrel. Somehow I'll make it up to you. I swear it.''

"I don't hold that against you. You didn't kill her—the senator did. I'm not mad about that, Guthrie.''

He lifted his hand, ran his fingers through his hair, ducked his glance away from her. "The doctor told me I'd probably never ride a horse again because of my hip.''

"And you laughed at him, I trust.''

"McCutcheon's hired your Indian lawyer's friend, Pete Two Shirts, to take care of things while I'm laid up.'' Spoken like another hangdog admission of his worthlessness.

"Pete will take his directions from you. You're the ranch foreman, Guthrie. You're the boss.''

"I'm not much of anything right now, Jess, but I'll make it back.'' He caught her eye, and the intensity of his gaze wrenched her. "I swear I will.''

"I know that.'' She tried to smile, but the effort fell short. "I suppose you've heard that Ramalda's been hired back on. She'll take care of the place, and cook for all of you.''

"Ramalda?'' He shook his head. "That's good to hear. She must be in her late sixties by now. What about Drew?''

"Drew's dead. He died the night I spent up on the mountain with Blue. That's why Dr. Cooper was drunk the next morning. He and Drew were good friends, if you recall.''

"Drew? You should've told me, Jess. Drew…!'' Guthrie's face mirrored his shock at this unexpected news.

"I'm sorry I didn't, but by the time I found out, you were nearly dead yourself. I didn't think you needed to hear it right then."

"Where are you going?"

Jessie paused in the act of turning toward the door. "It's getting late, and you need your rest."

"Stay."

She shook her head, unable to meet his eyes. "I can't." She hesitated and then raised her hands in despair. "I'm so mixed up! I love you, Guthrie, but I'm not sure that's enough. I don't know what to think. About you and me. About all the stuff that's happened between us, all the things we've said and done, all the words we can't take back. I'm talking about how you are, and how I am, and how I don't know if there can ever be another 'us' the way there used to be. I'm talking about..."

She stopped, staring at him in speechless anguish, arms still raised in a gesture that encompassed every moment since that day so many years ago when they'd first set eyes upon each other. She held them out for a moment and then let them drop to her sides. "Oh, hell and damn, I don't know what I'm talking about! I don't know how to put what I'm feeling into words."

"I found the note you'd started to write me. The day I came home from the hospital."

The heat came into Jessie's cheeks. "I was writing it when you drove up in McCutcheon's car, and I forgot and left it behind, I was that mad. I don't understand you, Guthrie. Just when I think that maybe I'm starting to, you go and do something stupid like that. Why didn't you let me bring you home? Why did it have to be McCutcheon!"

"You hungry?"

"What?" She stared at him, not sure if she should laugh, cry or kick him in the shins.

"No sense letting Bernie's great cookin' go to waste. Why don't we have something to eat. We can talk over supper."

Jessie struggled to subdue her anger. "Bernie fed me before I came. I'll leave now, so's you can eat, and then you can go to bed and sleep. How's that suit you?"

Guthrie quartered away from her, struggling with something inside himself. "In your note you spoke about dreams," he said, gazing at someplace she couldn't see. "About how we walk in the shadow of them. About how maybe the two of us were standing in the shadow of the same dream and didn't know it. I've been thinkin' about that."

"That's just an old Indian belief," Jessie said. "I must have been crazy when I wrote that note."

"I've been designing a new barn." Guthrie limped to the counter and picked up a notebook that lay there, studying the page it was folded open to. "It'll hold more hay, more horses."

"That's real nice, Guthrie. Goodbye." Jessie tried again for the door, and again he stopped her.

"It's for you," he said, holding the notebook out like a peace offering.

She swung around, her color still high. "I'm perfectly comfortable where I am, thanks."

"For your horses. For the mares when they get tired of roughing it. For Billy, who's too old and too honorable to be putting his rump into the wind in dirty weather."

"My horses are fine right where they are. McCutcheon's agreed to keep them for me while I'm away. And there's a perfectly adequate barn at the ranch, in case you've forgotten."

"He doesn't know horses the way I do."

Jessie shook her head. "He doesn't have to. He has a

ranch manager by the name of Guthrie Sloane, so I'm told.''

"If he still wants a gimpy wrangler."

"He didn't mention otherwise," she said, and her voice gentled. "You're on the payroll. You have been since the morning of the accident, thanks to McCutcheon's quick thinking. Workmen's comp is going to cover most all your medical bills."

Guthrie dropped his gaze to the floor for a long moment, then lifted his eyes to hers and nodded. "He's a good man."

"He's a great man." She turned toward the door.

"Jess?" he began. "Did you mean what you said to me back on the mountain—about hell being a glacier before you'll ever quit me?"

Hand on the doorknob, she paused again. "Yes," she said. "I meant it."

"Then don't quit me now. I know you're still working on a big mad, but I love you, Jess. I have since the moment we first met, and you were just as thorny then as you can be now. I know we've had hard times, and I'm not making any promises that I've changed into a man you'll be tickled pink with till the end of your days, but something happened to me up on Montana Mountain."

Jessie stood flat-footed at the cabin's door, caught off guard by Guthrie's words. "You nearly died. That's what happened to you."

"Maybe. I only know that experience changed how I felt about things. It made me realize that the important things are the small things I took for granted day by day and just didn't pay much attention to. The color of the sky at sunrise, the smell of fresh coffee just coming to a boil, the feel of sunlight on my face, the beauty of your eyes in the firelight, the sound of your laughter.

"Those are some of the most important things, Jess, and lying there I thought if I could just see you one more time, hear your voice, I'd give anything. Anything at all. And then you came, and told me the story about the bear."

"Guthrie, I never told you a story about a bear up on that mountain."

He shook his head. "You told me that story, that old legend, and then the bear came. I know it sounds crazy, Jess. I know I was hurt, and maybe I imagined it. But that bear was real. I talked to it when it uncovered me and it told me the way of things. But it didn't speak, didn't make words. I can't explain how we communicated, but we did. And then I was falling and you reached out and caught me in your arms. What happened up there changed me somehow. Made me see things differently."

"Those were just dreams," Jessie said, unsettled by his revelations. "Hallucinations."

"Maybe," he said. "Or maybe that bear helped us in ways we don't understand." He tossed the notebook onto the countertop and limped toward her. "Jess, please, I'm begging you. Don't quit me now. I love you. You said you were afraid love might not be enough, but it's what came of us being best friends. Best friends, Jess! That should count for a lot. Give me another chance. Let me build you that barn, take care of your horses and Blue while you're away at school. And maybe when you return…"

"What if I don't?" Jessie challenged, her throat tightening around the words, her chin lifting in brave defiance and tears sparkling in her eyes.

"I know you, Jessie Weaver. You'll be back. And I'll be right here, waiting for you, because you were wrong when you said we didn't have anything in common. We do. We have each other. We have years of shared memories, good ones, great ones, a whole lifetime's worth! And oh, yes, don't forget that play by Shakespeare and that immortal moment when I looked at you and said...'But soft! what light through yonder window breaks? It is the east, and Jessie is the sun!'''

''Guthrie Sloane, you said no such thing!'' Jessie wavered, wiping her cheeks impatiently with the palms of her hands. ''Those weren't your lines!''

''Maybe not, but they're best in the play and I can't help but think of them when I look at you, when I want to kiss you the way you used to let me. The way you used to want me to.'' He held her gaze for a long, emotional moment. ''You're my sunshine, Jess,'' he said. ''You always will be.''

''I leave here in less than a month.''

''I know that.''

Jessie's chin trembled. ''I'll be gone for a long time.''

''I expect you'll visit us once in a while. There's summers...''

''More than a year.''

''More than a year,'' he agreed.

''We'll both be different. We'll change.''

''I'll certainly be older and wiser and handsomer, and maybe I'll have walked my way right out of this limp,'' he said.

Her eyes stung. She blinked hard, bit her lower lip and tried to push back the emotions that threatened to dissolve her, but suddenly it seemed foolish to hide how she really felt from the man who knew her better than anyone on the face of the earth.

''I don't want to leave this place,'' she said in a voice barely above a whisper.

''I know that. But you won't be gone forever. And when you come back, you'll have so much to give to this community.''

"What if you find somebody else while I'm gone?"

Guthrie was shaken to his soul. He reached for her, and this time she didn't move away. He gripped her shoulders and stared into her dark tear-filled eyes. "When hell freezes over," he said. "I won't ever quit you, Jess. Not ever again." He drew her into his arms and she allowed him to hold her close, and her arms slipped around him and it was the sweetest thing he'd felt in a long, long time. He bent his head over hers and breathed the sweet essence of her, felt the strength and the vulnerability and the courage in her slender, trembling body. "Would you mind too awful much coming back home for holidays and school breaks?" he murmured.

"I will," she said, her voice muffled against his shoulder and choked with tears. "And would you mind coming to visit me any chance you get?"

"I'm sure something can be arranged. Colorado. That's someplace south of here, isn't it? Downhill and easygoin' all the way...."

She pushed away, gently disentangling herself from his embrace. "I have to go," she said, wiping the tears from her face with her palms. He watched with confusion and concern as she turned and fumbled for the door. "I have to go," she repeated, looking over her shoulder at him as if he would surely understand why she did. But he didn't. He shook his head, moving as if to stop her. "I'll be back," she said, and whirled away, fleeing everything she wanted and needed, and everything she feared.

"Life is short, Jess," he called after her, his guts twisting in his anguish at her leaving. "Don't be too long!"

He stood in the doorway while she ran to her truck and climbed into the cab. The truck's engine caught, headlights blazed on, and she backed out, turned, and then he was watching the truck's taillights dwindle into the darkness.

He stood there with the door open long enough to chill the cabin down, while Blue leaned her shoulder against his leg and thrust her cold nose against his hand, and he stood there still, filled with a kind of pathos and melancholy that he thought might make him cry. Stood and listened to the tumbling waters of Bear Creek, to the tug of the night wind through the spruce near the cabin. Stood and listened to the stillness of a big and lonely land.

And then he heard something else. The sound of the truck coming back. Headlights swept across the cabin's porch. The truck pulled to a stop and the engine cut out. Silence stretched out for a long moment, while he waited with bated breath and dared not hope. Then the door wrenched open and a slender figure emerged, to walk swift and sure to the foot of the porch steps and climb them one by one. She stood before him and looked at him with those fine, steady eyes that spoke to him in a way that made his heart jump.

"You came back for Blue?" he said.

She shook her head. "For you," she said. "I came back for you."

He took her hand and drew her from the cold, lonely darkness into the warmth and light within.

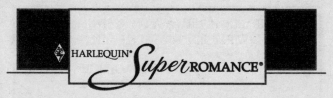

HARLEQUIN *Super*ROMANCE®

One of our most popular story themes ever...

**Pregnancy is an important event in a woman's life—
and in a man's. It should be a shared experience,
a time of anticipation and excitement.
But what happens when a woman is
pregnant and on her own?**

**Watch for these books in our
9 Months Later series:**

What the Heart Wants by Jean Brashear (July)

Her Baby's Father by Anne Haven (August)

A Baby of Her Own by Brenda Novak
(September)

The Baby Plan by Susan Gable (December)

Wherever Harlequin books are sold.

HARLEQUIN®
Makes any time special®

Visit us at www.eHarlequin.com

HSRNM

Princes...Princesses...
London Castles...New York Mansions...
To live the life of a royal!

In 2002, Harlequin Books lets you escape to a world of royalty with these royally themed titles:

 Celebrate a year of royalty with Harlequin Books!

Available at your favorite retail outlet.

HARLEQUIN®
Makes any time special®

Visit us at www.eHarlequin.com

HSROY02